From the Rhine
To Penn's Woods

For Anne and Millie

From the Rhine To Penn's Woods

A Pennsylvania German Family
in the
American Revolution

~~

An Historical Novel

Carl Frey Constein

Green Button, Inc.

Copyright © 2008 by Carl Frey Constein
ISBN 978-0-9656842-4-8

All rights reserved. No part of this book may be reproduced, restored in a retreviel system, or transmitted by any means, electronic, mechanical, photocopying, recording, or otherwise, without written consent of the author.

This book is a work of fiction. Except for historical characters, places, and incidents, all names, characters, places, and incidents are either products of the author's imagination or are used fictiously. Any similarity to real persons, living or dead, is coincidental and not intended by the author.

Dr. Carl Frey Constein
9 Reading Drive, Apt. 227
Wernersville, PA 19565
ConsteinHPA@aol.com. 610-927-8753

Preface

From my apartment in Wernersville in southeast Pennsylvania I look north to the spire of Hain's United Church of Christ. German Palatinate immigrants built a log church on this site in 1735, among the earliest Reformed churches in America. Accepting William Penn's invitation, they landed in Philadelphia and trudged here to the Cacusi region of the Tulpehocken Settlement, the Lenape Indians' Land of Turtles stretching westward on today's U.S. 422 from Reading on the Schuylkill River. A second group of Germans had been recruited earlier by Queen Anne to work the pine forests of the Hudson Valley for naval stores. Deceived and mistreated, they left Schoharie, New York, canoed down the Susquehanna and joined their countrymen here.

Thirty years later they built a larger, grander stone church. I live a half-mile from the church on land they first farmed 275 years ago. I travel roads once their cart paths. A native of Berks County, I understand their culture and the German dialect they spoke. During Sunday worship in the sanctuary enlarged from their 1766 structure, I visualize the wineglass pulpit and I gaze at the three-foot-thick walls of the original structure. I marvel at how they survived on the harsh frontier, ultimately fighting a glorious revolution. Graves of fifty-two Revolutionary War veterans in Hain's Cemetery attest to their sacrifice.

The Tulpehocken settlers were among tens of thousands of lower class and middling Palatines who played a major role in the 18th century experiment called "America." Leaving their homeland forever, they braved an horrendous two-month ocean voyage below deck, survived in the dense wilderness, raised families, became active in colonial politics, and fought a war to free America from British rule. With a third of the colonists favoring separation and a third opposed, the conflict had the aura of a civil war, pitting neighbor against neighbor, brother against brother. After the war, holding strongly to the new Constitution's right to oppose laws of their own government, they vehemently opposed a tax levied on their land and houses.

What resulted was the Fries Rebellion. A war hero from Bucks County, John Fries led 500 protestors from the Pennsylvania frontier counties of Bucks, Montgomery, Lebanon, and Berks on a march to Bethlehem to free nineteen Northampton men held prisoner in the Sun Tavern for protesting the tax. Fries and two others were sentenced to death for treason! President John Adams' eleventh-hour pardon brought havoc to the Federalist Party and contributed to his defeat in his bid for a second term. The novel ends just before the tumultuous election of 1800.

Germans who emigrated from the Palatinate and neighboring principalities brought with them their Palatine dialect. We know it as Pennsylvania German. I have included in the novel a scattering of dialectal words and phrases, depending for spelling on four Pennsylvania German dictionaries, two based on German orthography, two on equivalent English sounds. Where the dictionaries differ, I chose the spelling that mimics speech sounds I recall from my youth. For the reader's comprehension I have included a glossary of Pennsylvania German words and phrases. For readers interested in further reading, I have also included a select topical bibliography.

Dr. Carl Frey Constein

Also by Carl Frey Constein

Born to Fly the Hump

Orchestra Left, Row T

Sadie's Place

Tales of the Himalayas

War Memories and Civilian Musings

Missing in the Himalayas

Manuscript Missing

ONE
Frankenthal, Rhenish Palatinate
1752

ADAM STAUDT INKED THE PRINT PLATE AND with weary arms pulled down the platen. Not yet apprenticed, he was the shop's part-time printer's devil, busy setting type and pressing broadsides that extolled the wonders of William Penn's land of promise across the sea. He hung the last sheet on the drying line, took off his leather apron, and said goodbye to Jacob Schmidt, the shop owner.

Adam plodded homeward, his thoughts jumbled. He was happy his first full week's pay in months would put more food on the table, but his face twitched when he thought of the promise he'd made himself.

He picked up the pace as he passed the open farmland encircling Frankenthal and glanced toward his strip. He couldn't recall exactly when he'd resolved to leave the homeland and make a new start in America, but just as he was about to share his dream with Catherine, her father died and her mother came to live with them. But now he was determined to face up to the hopelessness and despair that tormented him.

As he walked on, he mused about how Catherine and he met. She lived in the village of Rheinstein, a few miles away. From the time she was twelve, she spent summers visiting her widowed Aunt Esther in Frankenthal. She and Adam liked each other from the start. Winters were long, especially for him as he dreamed of next summer's first glimpse at her dimples and, probably, her new curves. They were married in 1740. All eyes were on the bride, blond and blue-eyed, comely and fair. Then, as now, Catherine and Adam were very much in love.

His thoughts turned to a recent conversation he'd had with *Herr* Schmidt. At the end of the day, Schmidt had said, "Adam, you are *umgerennt*. You neglect your farm strip because you work for me, *gell*?"

Adam leaned on the worktable and shook his head slowly. "*Nay, nay*, not that." Adam turned and faced him. "I make a big decision. I go to America."

"Ah, Penn's woods. *Ya*, things get no better here. If I am young like you, I go tomorrow. You have this idea a long time?"

"*Verleicht* a year," Adam said. "Then *die Mudder* Christman moves in." He looked down and shook his head. "We must wait. Catherine never leaves her mother."

"*Ach*, can't one of Clara's sons take their mother?" *Herr* Schmidt said. Adam had asked himself that question many times.

As he continued his weary walk home on this calm April evening, Adam crossed the town square. What mattered, he told himself, was not *when* he decided to go to America, what mattered now was sharing his dream with Catherine. The broadsides he printed for William Penn all week were a reminder of his promise to tell her soon.

Adam's thoughts turned to his father. Dietrich Staudt was born near the close of the seventeenth century in a region once the garden spot of Germany, now left barren by thirty years of ferocious war. In all of Europe, the Palatinate had been the favorite stomping ground for armies of feuding dukes and margraves who sacked the cities and towns and farms, decimating the population, destroying the economy, imposing their own religions. Then in the last decade of the century, in a war that surpassed earlier horrors, Louis XIV of France reduced the Palatines to utter poverty and hopelessness.

Cessation of warfare brought the end of serfdom. For the first time, common people felt a sense of ownership, even if communal. They held dear their assigned strips of open land.

Adam recalled questioning his father about that. "*Daadi*, most have one strip. Why have we three?"

"*Ya, die Mamm* and I work hard." He stopped, looked down and said softly. "I think of her often, *abaddich* when I go to concerts in Mannheim. We loved the new music of Bach and Handel, and the young Haydn."

"*Ya*, I never forget the first concert you took me to." Adam smiled. "*Un* I remember how she read to me when I was little. I remember how you taught me English."

Adam's reveries ended as he turned the corner onto Ludwigshafen Street and arrived home.

"*Wie gayt's, Liebschdi?* How is Sarah?"

"*Besser.*" Catherine looked at him tenderly. "You look exhausted."

"*Ya, awwer*, I work only to noon *mariye.*"

"*Hock dich hie* and rest a while."

After dinner Catherine knitted as Adam read. He looked up. The time may have been right to share his dream with his wife, he reflected, but his eyes were heavy. Besides, he planned to ask his father's advice. They went to bed. Perhaps tomorrow night they'd enjoy more than snuggling.

At noon the next day, the workweek over, Adam lumbered to his father's house. He knocked on the door and entered.

"*Wie bischt, Daadi?*"

"*Guud. Wie gayt's bei dir?*"

"*So zimmlich.* I need your advice."

"*Huck dich hie.*" Dietrich paused. "You think of joining cousin Peter in Pennsylvania, *gell*? Why do you wait so long?"

Adam's eyebrows shot up and he stared at his father. "*Ach*, then you think it is *allrecht*?"

"*Ya wohl.* There is *gaar nix* to keep you here."

"*Nay, Daadi*, leaving will be the hardest thing I do."

He looked down and put a hand to his eyes. He waited then sat back. "But we can't go now. Catherine never leaves her mother."

"*Ya, ich verschteh.*" Dietrich waited. "Why not take her with?"

Adam jumped up. "*Ai, ai, ai!* I never even thought. I think she is too old."

"*Gaar net.* She is a strong *Weibsmensch.* She helps with Sarah, *net?*"

Adam sighed. "*Ya, verleicht* you have right." He paused "But we do not want her to suffer like those poor *Leit* forty years ago."

Dietrich sat back and puffed on his pipe. "*Ya*, that was terrible. I tell you a little. They go down the Rhine to Amsterdam. Newlander agents cheat them on tickets on Dutch ships. After they cross the channel, they are kept in warehouses and tents." He paused and shook his head. "The London *Leit* go out on weekends and gawk at 'the poor Germans.'"

"Did the people have enough *Geld*?"

"Not all. Some sign to work as servants in America for their passage." Dietrich paused. "*Ennichau* it was a half year before they sail for New York."

"How many were there, *Daadi*?"

"Ten ships, two thousand souls. Peter is one of them. The people settle in Schoharie and work the pine forests of the Hudson Valley. Peter gets married there. When they are abused and cheated, the people leave and go to the Tulpehocken settlement in Pennsylvania."

"*Ya*, remember I show you the letter Peter sent. He said he helps us get started. I go now. I must tell Catherine."

Adam started to leave then stopped abruptly. "*Daadi, sei guud* and go with us. You are only a little older than Clara. *Sei so guud.*"

"*Nay, sohn.* I stay here with the others."

Adam embraced him, turned and left, his head down.

Catherine was waiting for him. "Where is *die*

Mudder?"

"She goes to market."

"I go out to our strip, but first we sit a minute."

She put a hand to her face when she heard his plan. "Oh my. I . . . I don't know . . . I don't know what to say." Tears came to her eyes.

He embraced her. After several minutes he rose. "I hope *die Mudder* will want to go," he said.

They sat silent for a long minute. "I leave now. If you want to wait, we talk with her together when I come back."

It was dark when Adam returned. All three of his females were waiting, smiling.

"*Ya*, Adam," *die Grossmudder* blurted out, "I am not afraid. I go with to America."

"*Wunnerbaar!*" Adam said. He shocked her when he gave her a first-time peck on the cheek.

"Oh Adam, Adam," Catherine said. She smiled broadly and hugged him. "*Liebschdi*, we all want to go." She whispered into his ear, "We go to bed early tonight and celebrate."

―――

The next weeks were filled with excitement, questions popping into their heads daily. Adam visited his father often. How much money will we need? How do we buy land? What should we take with us in the trunk? How long will the passage take? Peter will help us, but how will we eat and take care of ourselves the first months? In his letter Peter wrote about countrymen in Germantown who take in newcomers before they move on. How do we do that? How can we send a letter to Peter? How do we sign up for passage?

"Hold your horses, Adam," his father said, holding up a hand when he heard the recital. "One question at a time."

"We have little money. We must be indentured."

"*Nay Sohn*, I put aside money for you children. You take your share now."

Dieter shook his head slowly. "Oh *gross Dank, Daadi. Danke schay vielmols.*"

"*Gaar nix.*" Dietrich paused. "I know people in Worms to answer your questions. First you write to Peter. We pay a sailor bound for Philadelphia to deliver the letter. In time it reaches him."

"*Ya, awwer* I do not do much writing."

"Write it and I look it over."

Every day brought new questions, new doubts. To leave Frankenthal and never return! To leave family, neighbors, friends, companions in the fields! To leave the familiar town, the old church and cemetery with the graves of ancestors! And the greatest sorrow — he will never see his dear *Daadi* again! He visited him every day.

One day Adam noticed Catherine was not herself. "*Was iss letz, Liebschdi?*" He sat beside her and took her hand.

"*Ich wayss net.* Sometimes I think it is better to stay right here."

"*Nay, nay.* The voyage will be dangerous, *ya*, and the first year is hard. But then we have a better life. Nearly 100 leave every week."

"I know," she said. "We put our trust in God."

"And we think of our children." He paused and smiled. "Sarah, and maybe a few to come."

"You have right." She put an arm around him. "*Gross Dank,* Adam. I am better now."

Adam put off writing to Cousin Peter, fearing the irrevocable commitment he was making. Finally he took up the quill. After he finished, he hurried over to his father's house and handed him the letter.

November 14, 1752

Liewer Cousin Peter,

Thank you for your kind letter. We received it in October and read it with great interest. Tulpehocken settlement sounds like a wonderful platz to live, although I believe in your letter you spare us the hardships you encounter. The thought of owning and farming my own land inspires me and brings me joy and excitement.

As you know, it is hard to make ends meet in the Palatinate. It gets no better. It gives times we do not have enough to eat. There is no future. I talked with Daadi, Catherine, un Jacob Schmidt, the printer where I sometimes work. They all say go.

So we decide to come to America. We are four — Catherine and her mother, Clara, our daughter, Sarah, and me. Catherine is very religious and she believes America will be a place of freedom and prosperity. She will pray often.

We plan to sail down the Rhine to Rotterdam in February and set sail for Philadelphia in March. That gets us to Philadelphia in May or June. We have one trunk.

I can't tell you how good it feels to know you will help us when we get to Tulpehocken. I worry about how we get there from Philadelphia, but I was glad to hear that Mennonites in Germantown feel it their Christian duty to look out for German newcomers for a few days. I do not understand how this works without knowing our names. Do you know anyone there? Can you tell them our plans?

I think Uncle Walter and der Daadi were blessed to have good parents. They taught them to read and write, even got them started learning English. And our fathers passed on their love of learning, books, and music to us so we and our families are also blessed. I'm sure it is hard to get along in Pennsylvania without English.

Both Uncle Walter and der Daadi are well at this time. We owe them much for urging us to go to a new land, not to hold us back as some have done. I pray they will be in good health for many years to come.

If I learn the name of our ship, I will write before we sail. God bless you and your family. I believe we met only once as children. I eagerly look forward to seeing you. I remain,

                                                Respectfully yours,

                                                Cousin Adam

"*Guud*," Adam said. "I take it over to Erstein and get it down the Rhine."

On one of Adam's visits, Dietrich said to his son, "I learn something about land companies. One is the Pennsylvania Population Company. Another is the North America Company. I don't know how they work, but it gives help on it in Germantown and from Peter." He paused. "Don't worry, son. You have the money, you get the land."

"Thanks to you, *Daadi*." He sighed deeply. "I will be a landowner!"

"*Ya*, more than I can say," Dietrich said softly. "But it won't be easy. The English make you take an oath of loyalty to their king." Dietrich chuckled. "They will laugh at you for the funny way we talk."

"Catherine and I wonder about the best time to leave," Adam said. "Winter is bad for storms on the ocean so if we sail in March we miss them. The trip down the Rhine is slow, so I guess we allow six weeks to get to Rotterdam. Maybe we leave about three weeks after Christmas."

"*Ya*, everyone will want to have a party for you."

"*Nay*, it will be better if we see people alone."

———

A frigid west wind struck hard. Catherine mused about this last Christmas in the homeland. She hoped for snow for Sarah's sake, even though it would mean hard travel for the start of their journey. She would do all she could to make it their best Christmas ever. They would have the finest *Grischtdaagsbaam* in Frankenthal.

Christmas Day broke bright and clear. Sarah was up early, excited, chattering like a magpie. She rushed to the window. "*Gucke mol do, Mamma*, it snowed! It snowed!" When she spotted her present her jaw dropped and her eyes grew as large as coins. She ripped off the wrapping and gaped at a pretty wooden doll with a bisque head and hands. "*Oh gross Dank, Belznickel*." She grabbed the doll and hugged her. Smiling broadly, she said, "Her name is Lizzie. I take her with to church."

As she left her precious church, Catherine wiped away a tear. She took one last long look then stepped out into the snow. At home, she finished preparing Christmas dinner.

Guests began to arrive after noon. There'd be ten — Adam's brothers and sisters, his father, and Catherine's family. The children played happily. But the others stepped carefully on this last day together.

Catherine spoke up. "This is no way to be on our Lord's birthday. We love you and we feel your love. Put away your long faces and make this a joyous day for all to remember. It is what we want to do. Now let's all be happy on this holy day."

It was 9 o'clock when the company stirred to leave. Catherine said, "I already give one prayer today, but it gives one more short one. Take hands.

"Dear Lord God, on this day of your Son's birth, we thank you for all your mercies. We thank you for our dear families and friends. They will be with us in our hearts and our prayers always. We pray that we meet again someday in a better world. Amen."

The bittersweet day ended tearfully, poignantly. There would be no second day of Christmas this year. Heard was only the soft, awkward *Glichlich Nei Yaahr*.

TWO

IN THE DAYS FOLLOWING CHRISTMAS, ADAM AND Catherine moved with strain and heaviness. Adam's dear father visited every day, helping wherever he could, gently holding them up. On his advice, they signed for passage on a Dutch ship.

The only other Frankenthalers planning to make the voyage were the Werners. The Staudts strolled across the village to visit them. "We see each other sometimes," Catherine said, "but we should talk."

"*Ya, ya, kumm rei,*" Emma Werner said. "Hannah and Sarah are about the same age," Catherine said. "They are good playmates on the long journey."

"How long is it?" David Werner asked.

"Eight to ten weeks, *der Daadi* told me," Adam said, "depending on the weather."

"*Ei, ei, ei.* That is a long time," Emma said. "I hope it don't give sickness."

The families spent an hour together, sharing their fears and their hopes. As the Staudts left, Catherine embraced Emma. "We pray for the best."

―

Finally the day came. Up early, Catherine bustled to Sarah's bed. "Time for you and Lizzie to get up. It's the big day, *Liebschdi*," she said softly. Silence pervaded the house.

After a hushed breakfast, the Staudts turned and quietly left their past behind.

Dietrich hired a gig for Sarah and Clara; he, Adam, and Catherine walked. When they arrived at the pier in Erstein, they saw passengers already boarding the Rhine barge from Basel. Adam and his father lugged the family chest on board.

Dietrich waited with them until the last minute. He hugged them, Adam last. "Good luck, son. *Ich hab dich gaern.*" It was the first time Adam heard open words of love from his father, the first time he'd seen tears in his eyes. Dietrich stepped back and waved a slow farewell. Motionless, he remained on the pier until the sail of the barge became a tiny dot on the broad Rhine.

The voyage down the river was filled with more excitement than the Staudts expected. Without cover or awning, they were rained on some days, baked in the sun on other days. They gazed in wonder as the river flowed through gaps in the mountains and between lush farms and vineyards. From time to time, they were slowed down when boats and rafts collided in the Rhine's swift waters. They were happy to reach Cologne, about halfway, and to catch sight of pretty stone houses in the narrow streets, and above them, a huge unfinished cathedral.

The river barge got to Rotterdam six weeks after leaving Erstein, tolls at three dozen border crossings causing long delays. Hugging the city's clean outer limits as they walked, the travelers caught glimpses of old Rotterdam's city hall and museum.

The port was crowded with emigrants and their families and a jumble of burly sailors and stevedores. Itinerants, ship company agents, and hangers-on waited for their chance to latch onto something. Adam spotted the *Neptune*. He was shocked by the brig's condition—paint peeling, sails dirty and needing patching, the hull reeking of pine oil.

"We stay together," Adam cautioned. They trod up the gangplank unsteadily and Adam handed his tickets to the wily Newlander, the Dutch shipowner close by watching every move.

The passengers were herded along like cattle. A gruff bo's'n screamed, "Move down to your berths. Quick." As Adam passed him at the hatch he smelled rum. It mixed with foul air rising from the deck below.

"Something smells funny," Sarah said, holding her nose.

Adam rushed his family down the hatchway. As he had suspected, "Move down to your berths" was a cruel joke: there were no berths. They'd have to use extra clothes for beds. The air was putrid from bilge water, filth from the last sailing, and lingering odors from the triangular trade—cargoes of sugar, molasses, fish, work animals, and unwashed bodies of African slaves.

Adam looked around. Passengers were gray-skinned, disheveled, some men filthy, most in ticklenberg shirts and hair-cloth breeches. Adam suspected some owned little more than the clothes they wore and were indentured to work off their passage. Some carried Bibles, some food, some tools.

A mate came below and yelled, "Grab a slop pail." He guffawed. "It'll be your best friend. And no one goes topside till we tell you."

"Oh Adam, I knew there'd be little privacy, but this is even worse than I thought," Catherine said. "This is a *schmutzich* pig sty!"

"Empty the chest. I'll stand it on end to mark our space." At least, he thought, our chest is with us, not like sailings he'd heard of when chests were loaded on a different ship.

Catherine took charge as Clara and Sarah removed clothing from the chest, folding some, hanging some on the line Adam had stretched from the chest to a bulkhead. She rearranged what remained in the chest—*Ebbel Schnitz*, medicine, heirlooms, clothing, writing paper, a few books.

Suddenly, earlier than he'd expected, Adam heard a creaking of the hull and felt a surge. He grinned. "*Guud*, the tide's going out. We sail." As the *Neptune* picked up a favorable wind, they heard the flogging of sails and the rhythmic thud of halyards hitting the deck.

A bearded devil appeared at the hatchway. "If you want a last glimpse of land, go topside. But stay out of our way." Most of the men went up. The wind was brisk. Adam and David Werner watched the bustle of the sailors as they worked the sails.

The *Neptune* drifted out into the Markemeer with the tide then stopped abruptly. The wind became still.

David sheepishly put a hand on Adam's shoulder. "I don't want to be a nosy *Wunnernaas*, but how much were your tickets?"

"One hundred fifty guilders for each of us, half for Sarah." Earlier Adam noticed David's tickets were different. He felt certain the Werners were bound out as redemptioners.

David shook his head slowly. "Ours were higher—one hundred ninety for us, ninety-five for Hannah. We didn't even have half that. We handed over our savings then signed a paper promising not to leave the ship without the captain's permission." He shook his head again. "I could not believe it when they told us if anyone dies farther than halfway, the family must pay full fare."

"*Dunnerwedder!* Adam said. "But your condition may turn out all right. After you work off your debt, you will have the same chances as the rest of us, *net*?"

"I hope it gives a good man to work for," David said." He paused and looked down. "I worry we get sold to different buyers."

Adam's head jerked back. How sad to contemplate. He quickly recovered and said, "When the time comes, maybe you come to Pennsylvania."

David was silent. Would his dream ever come true—to be a free man, to be owner of fertile land with good crops, animals to hunt, fruit to pick, and clear streams with fish to catch?

Daylight was failing fast. "I was too hopeful," Adam said, "when I said we were on our way. It doesn't give a breath of wind, and I doubt it does tonight." They went below and joined their families.

"We force ourselves to think only of our new home,

our new life," he said to Catherine. "We must be brave for Sarah and *die Grossmudder*."

"*Ya*, and we pray together more than at home," she said.

After an hour, a galley hand rushed down and barked, "Heads of families line up for mess." Adam returned with salted bacon, flour, rice, peas, and water.

Sarah turned up her nose. "I don't like this."

Night was soon upon them. It suddenly came to Adam—if the hatch is closed they will be in pitch darkness till sunrise! "*Heilich Dunnerwedder!* How can we stand it?"

"Don't swear, Adam." Catherine paused. "We start every night in prayer. *Alliebber* take hands. 'Dear God, we are in your hands. Be with us every minute of our long voyage. We pray for strength and courage and for your hand to guide this ship. Lord, look after us and the families and friends we leave behind. Now we pray the prayer Our Lord taught us. '*Unser vater, der Du bischt im Himmel, Geheilich sei Die Naame. Dei Reich soll kumme. Dei Wille soll geduh ware, uff die Erd wie im Himmel. Geb uns heit unser daiglich Brot. Vergeb uns unser Schulde, wie mir annre ihre Schulde vergewwe. Fiehr uns net in Verschung, awwer mach uns frei vum Schlechdes, fer Dein is es Reich, un die Graft, un die Herr lichkeit im Ewichkeit. Aamen.*' "

The Staudts were tired and weary but too excited to sleep. They sat silent. After awhile Catherine said, "We lie down now and close our eyes. Good night and God watch over us all."

After a short time Sarah sat up abruptly. "What's that noise?"

Catherine hugged her. "*Liebschdi*, this ship is old and croaks and groans like an old woman."

"*Nay, nay*, not that. It sounds like something chewing."

Catherine saw rats earlier. "It's your imagination, *Liebschdi*. Go to sleep now."

Snores and grunts mixed with the ship's clatter. Adam's brain was racing. He determined to do something about bringing light to their deck.

The next morning Adam waited on the deck for the captain to come out of his quarters. He was clean, tall and trim, and had a full beard. Unlike his motley crew, he spoke courteously. Adam followed him down the companionway.

"I am Captain Vandergut," he announced in a firm voice. "I hope we will have a good sailing. The wind should pick up this afternoon. Now open your luggage. There must be no guns or food or drink."

Adam watched as Captain Vandergut and the first mate made their inspection. When they finished, Adam stepped up and said, "Sir, the nights will be long without light. Can we have five or six lanterns?"

"It would require crew time to light the lamps. We will see."

Shortly after noon the passengers heard a sharp crack of the sails and felt a strong surge as the ship hit its stride. The sun out brightly, nearly everyone came up to rejoice in the start of the long voyage. They lined the bulwark, gazing back to old Rotterdam then ahead to the broad horizon. Somewhere out there was their future. Most stayed topside until the huge red ball directly ahead disappeared in a brilliant sunset.

At dusk, two crewmen came below, each carrying two lanterns. They hung them on nails on bulkheads. Before they went topside, the surly-looking mate said to Adam, "Making requests of the captain, are you? This ain't first-class, you know."

The weather turned cold and blustery. Women and children put on as much clothing as they could and stayed below, shivering. Adam, David, and a handful of other men ventured topside on sunny days, checking the height of the waves, watching the crew reefing the sails. Occasionally, a young crew member made conversation. Probably homesick, Adam thought. Probably impressed into service.

There was much talk among the men about the mysteries of sailing. "How do they know where they are?" one asked.

"*Der Daadi* read something about that," Adam said. "They tell latitude with a sextant. A few ships have a new thing *der Daadi* called a *chronometer* to measure longitude. I wonder if it gives one on the *Neptune*."

"I hope so," one man said with a chuckle.

Nights were more tolerable with the lanterns. Strange, Catherine mused, but it was the total darkness after the lanterns were extinguished that she and Adam looked forward to. In the blackness they lay close and comforted each other, feeling secure.

Every day at noon Adam lined up for the same awful food. The portions were meager and the taste flat. The water had a bitter flavor.

Boredom set in. Adam had put into his chest only one thing for pleasure, the copy of *Gulliver's Travels* his father gave him as a parting gift. He read daily, slowly, savoring every word of Gulliver's visits to strange lands. Catherine passed the time reading her Bible, knitting, and visiting with Emma Werner. *Die Grossmudder* made friends with everyone, jabbering especially with other grandmothers. Sarah and Hannah Werner were together constantly, Sarah sharing her doll.

Lack of privacy brought terrible shame. Adam hung a sheet on the line. Several times a day he trudged topside with the waste pail.

"There is a *Weibsmensch* I haven't seen for a few days," Catherine said one day. "She looked sick."

"I know the woman you mean. If she died, people won't go near the family." Adam paused. "I guess they slid her into the ocean."

"Oh, how sad—to die and not have a Christian burial," Catherine said. "In all my fears, that's something that never came to mind."

Several days later Adam said, "I noticed Hannah doesn't play with Sarah yesterday. "I wonder if Hannah is sick."

"Oh my. I go see."

When she returned, Catherine asked, "Where is Sarah?"

"*Die Mudder* takes her for a walk. It's nice and warm today."

"I'm worried, Adam. I can't believe how bad Hannah looks. She is so hot and thirsty. Oh dear God, this comes so fast."

Hannah died the next day, the inside of her mouth black. Catherine and Adam went to the Werners as soon as they heard. Fear of contagion kept everyone else away. Alone, pitiful, David and Emma sat still, staring straight ahead. A piece of old sail cloth covered Hannah's body. As Catherine embraced her, Emma burst into tears.

"Oh, this is so sad," Catherine said. "Take hands, *alliebber*."

After Catherine's soothing prayer, they remained silent for a long time. Finally Adam said, "We know what must be done when this happens. We are your friends. We go with you."

"If you like," Catherine added, "We have a Christian service."

David nodded. He said only, "*Ya*, tonight."

The next morning Sarah asked, "Is Hannah still sick? I miss her."

Taking her hand, her mother said, "*Liebschdi*, this is hard. Last night Hannah went to Heaven."

Sarah sat still, eyebrows slightly raised.

"She was so sick. Now she's in heaven," Catherine said.

Sarah rose suddenly and screamed. Grabbing her doll, she dashed to the hatch and ran topside. Adam ran and caught her.

"Leave me alone! Leave me alone!" she shouted. "Where is she? I don't want her to go to heaven. I want her here." Tears gushed from her eyes.

Adam carried her down the steps to the comfort of *die Grossmudder's* arms. Sarah's loud cries slowly turned to sobs.

In the next days everyone except the Staudts ignored the Werners. Emma looked weak and pale. The *Neptune* continued its journey west, tacking at times, and life on the lower deck went on. The weather was fair, the wind steady in the sails. Passengers prayed that no calms or contrary winds delay them. The weather was almost too fair for too long, Adam feared.

Sarah was sullen. She put her doll away and talked little. Thank God, Adam mused, for the strong faith of his wife—and the imagination of his mother-in-law. Every morning she read to Sarah from a children's book no one knew she had packed.

It was the twenty-ninth day, about halfway through the voyage, Adam figured. *The Neptune*, 180 tons, 80 feet stem to stern, square-rigged with a high superstructure, was slow, vulnerable to gales and storms. Suddenly, the passengers below heard deafening claps of thunder. A huge wave struck out of nowhere. The wind picked up, its shrieks terrifying. The crew struggled to reef the sails. In an instant, the *Neptune* was a toy boat lost in mountainous waves, helpless in the tempest.

The ship pitched and rolled in twenty-foot seas, sending chests, clothing, tools, and everything not tied down flying across the deck. Foul-smelling waste from the pails was everywhere. Violent, vicious, deafening sheets of rain and hail struck the sails. Passengers were sea-sick, retching and groaning, vomiting, adding to the unbearable mess and stench. Many cried, covering their faces with handkerchiefs. Adam saw a scene from hell.

Mercifully, the storm ended that night. Early in the morning, Adam knew, all hands would be busy repairing masts, spars, and sails. But we can't live with this mess, he told himself. We will all be sick.

He pushed open the hatch and walked topside to the captain's quarters. "Sir," he said, "I know the crew is busy making repairs, but we can't stand the mess below. If you give us mops and pails, we get the deck cleaned up."

"I will have them brought down right away."

Women and children and older men went topside while the ablest men took the mops. They worked half-hour shifts, half the team going topside to get fresh air. Finally they finished the job and Adam joined his family, dead tired. He slept well.

In the morning Sarah spotted the sun through a crack in the hatch. "Papa, Papa, Lizzie and I like to see the sun. We want to go up."

"*Wunnerbaar*," Adam said. "I'm glad you both feel good. *Verleicht* tomorrow is even warmer."

Adam, Catherine and *die Grossmudder* took Sarah topside. Catherine turned toward the stern. "Oh, look!" she cried. "Are those birds? *Ya ya*, they are seagulls come to greet us. Look Sarah, look at the birds."

Adam spotted the captain's mate walking toward them. "Does this mean we are near land?"

The mate chuckled. "It means we are more than halfway, close enough for the birds to fly out and trail us for what we throw overboard."

"*Awwer* it is a good sign," Adam said.

The *Neptune* sailed on. Passengers grew weaker and thinner. Clara, always plump, lost many pounds and was not her cheerful self. But she was still Sarah's best friend. There were no signs of contagion, but there was sickness. And more deaths, so many the captain let it be known he would no longer be able to spare sail cloth for covering the dead.

Catherine was devoted to her Reformed religious faith. For all families who asked, she conducted a funeral service. She smiled when she recalled her childhood pride in being first in her class to memorize the Heidelberg Catechism and the Apostles and Nicene Creeds. Through the years she had come to love them as much as the Psalms and Scriptures she treasured. She read from the Bible and composed prayers for the soul of the deceased and comfort for their families. Each service ended with the Lord's Prayer. Then she stepped back as the body was given to the deep.

The Staudts and the Werners were the only families who joined grieving families on the main deck. But fellow Palatines below expressed sympathy in another way. A short time after one funeral group returned, a clear baritone voice lined out "*A mighty fortress is our God. . . .*" Soon the whole deck joined in. Most Palatines were Lutheran or Reformed and knew their hymns. Some were leaving their homeland seeking freedom to practice their faith freely, but most, Adam believed, were like him—simply seeking a better life.

Late one night in a whispered embrace, Adam said, "Catherine, destiny brought you on this voyage. Of the hundred souls on this ship, you are the only one who brings comfort. We can not do without you."

She smiled. "*Verleicht* John Calvin's predestination."

"You are strong. You never show regret about our decision. You must have feelings of sorrow about home."

"*Ya*, but they fade when I think of how happy we will be in a free land. I feel blessed that everyone I love is here with me." She paused, awkwardly. "I believe you think of your dear *Daadi* often."

Adam sighed. "Every day, many times every day."

She embraced him. "I know, I know." She waited. "But this is what he wants for you."

Adam sighed. "I hope I am half the man he is."

Catherine wiped a tear from his eye. "I love you, Adam."

Boredom aboard the *Neptune* brought unbearable ennui, competing with ever-present hardships—filth, rats, lice, barely edible food, gnawing hunger, dirty water, the stench of human waste, sneers of the crew, homesickness, fear of illness, turbulent seas, doubts about the future.

Hardest of all for Catherine and Adam to bear were the laments of their daughter. Sarah mentioned Hannah's name every day. Her mantra was, "Will we ever see land again?"

Adam was first to notice. On the main deck one morning he said to David, "Do you sense something different in the crew today?"

"What do you mean?"

"I can't say but I detect spring in their walk and more chatter. Does it mean we're close to land? Do they know something we don't know?"

When a stream of daylight filtered through the hatch the next morning, Adam immediately got up and went topside. His arms on the bulwark, he waited anxiously for the sun to rise. Convinced his premonition was accurate, he kept his glance toward the stern. Slowly, nearly imperceptibly, rays of light from the rising sun struck the deck, and he turned toward the bow.

Adam couldn't make out what he was seeing in this first glimpse of the New World. But it was something. It wasn't just a cloud, he was sure. His heart quickened. Oh, my God, *gross Dank!* Resisting the urge to cry out "*Land! Land!*" he opened his eyes wide and strained to make out more. What was he seeing? Was it a structure? A stand of tall trees?

Sailors, some who had never been to America, lined the rail and talked excitedly. Land was a promise for them too. Soon passengers streamed up the hatchway and shouted for joy.

Adam's family joined him. He picked Sarah up. "There it is, Sweetheart, what you wait for. We are soon on land!"

All but the sick and fragile came topside and remained all day chattering, praying. They watched as the ship sailed into the bay, land on both sides now. They oohed and aahed with delight as they took in the landscape, an amazing variety of greens in a panoply of shrubs and bramble against the tall dark trees of the forest beyond.

Dusk was approaching. All but Adam and David and a few other men went below. On the main deck they suddenly heard streaming through the hatch the familiar lines of *Old Rinkart: "Now thank we all our God . . ."* louder and louder, joy in their voices. At last, Adam said to himself in prayer, the long brutal journey is ending. *Dank Gott!*

The next morning the passengers were up early, packing, straightening out, chattering. At about 9 o'clock, Captain Vandergut and his mate stepped down the hatchway.

"Good morning," he said with a smile. "We are in

the Delaware Bay. Depending on the tide and breeze, we will dock tomorrow or the next day. At that time, those of you who have paid for your passage in full must line up and show your receipt to the purser. The rest will debark later. The nice weather is a good omen for you. After you finish packing, come topside and enjoy the views of your new land. I wish you Godspeed."

Ships and boats of every size graced the harbor; the newcomers waved as they passed. "Oh look at the pretty houses," Clara said. "It must give a thousand. I can't wait to step on land."

Suddenly there was a clang as the anchor was dropped. Night came on and the passengers, soon to be immigrants, went below for what they hoped would be their last night aboard the *Neptune*. Tomorrow would be a new day in a new land.

Just before daybreak, the clank of the anchor chain awakened anyone below deck able to sleep. The tide was coming in, the land coming closer and closer, houses and buildings bigger and bigger. The *Neptune* was soon docked, the bowsprit extending into Front Street. A sailor jumped off and secured the ship with a line and two seamen dropped the plank.

A small boat pulled up and a stiff-legged surgeon carrying a medical satchel came aboard and immediately went below. Passengers he suspected of carrying a disease were taken aside.

After the surgeon left, fully-paid passengers were called topside. Adam and David shook hands and parted with, "*Mach's guud.*" Emma said goodbye to Catherine and Clara in a tearful embrace. As they were about to step onto the hatchway, Sarah ran back to Emma and threw her arms around her waist, crying uncontrollably.

Catherine asked the family and the Werners to join hands for one last prayer of thanks. She ended, "And Heavenly Father, keep safe our friends Emma and David and look over them until we see them again. Amen."

Paid-in-full passengers were ordered on deck. A broadside printed in English was shoved at each one. Thanks to his father, Adam understood it, cringing as he read "...promise to be faithful and bear true allegiance to his present majesty King George the Second and his successors ... and strictly observe and conform to the laws of England." He shook his head slowly and sighed.

He looked to the pier and saw in the brilliant sunlight an amazing array of people—well-dressed merchants, families there for excitement, longshoremen and sailors, and a person the Staudts had never before seen—a black man. They heard fading drums and fifes as they watched a squad of British Red Coats disappearing into the distance.

Nervous, anxious, the Staudts rushed down the gangplank and took their first steps in a new land. Adam looked up and down the wharf, his eyes darting, desperately hoping someone from Germantown would be there to meet them. What if Cousin Peter was wrong? Where would they go? What would they do?

Catherine took over. "We get on our knees and fold our hands. 'Lord, this is the day we have been dreaming of. *Grosss Dank, Gutt in Himmel,* for delivering us safely across the angry sea. May we never forget this glorious day. Make us worthy of your trust. And may we always remember our families and friends in the old country.' "

Some newcomers were on their knees, solemn. Some seemed too tired and weak to do anything but stare. But most were excited, hugging, raising their arms in praise, pouring out their joy. A few shamelessly kissed the ground. A new world! A new start!

THREE

T HE STAUDTS ROSE FROM THEIR KNEES AND looked around in wonder, refreshed by a clean, crisp breeze. Catherine and Adam, their hands still joined, silently prayed for someone from Germantown to appear. "We must have faith," she said. "If no one comes, we ask. If we must, we stay tonight in the city."

Suddenly they heard *"Hallo! Deitscher! Deitscher!"* and spotted two people with arms high, waving. The couple rushed to them, the man with a full beard and long hair, dressed in black and wearing a straw hat, the woman wearing a patterned loose dress and a white prayer cap. "We are the Grosses. We take you to our house in Germantown. *Was iss eier Naame?"*

"We are called Staudt," Adam said.

"Guud. That is who we look for. Come, we have horse and buggy. Have you luggage?"

"One trunk. How do you find us?"

"Your cousin said you are young with *ein* Grossmudder *un ein glay Maedel."*

As the men climbed aboard the *Neptune* for the trunk, *Hausfraa* Gross said to Catherine, "The little one is pretty. *Was iss ihr Naame?"*

"Sarah."

"She and my Nellie they play together. *Die mudder.* What is her name?"

"Clara."

"What is the name of your town?"

"Frankenthal."

"*Schay Schteddel,*" *Hausfraa* Gross said.

Herr Gross and Adam carried the trunk from the ship. "When we get to our house," *Herr* Gross said, "you take out what you need, then I store it in my shop. When you are set on the frontier, you come for it."

"We are so dirty and smelly," Catherine said. "I am ashamed."

Herr Gross said, "We have welcomed many to America. *Mir verschteh.*"

After the men lifted the trunk onto the carriage, Adam helped Clara, Catherine, and Sarah climb up. *Hausfraa* Gross took the reins. Reaching up and taking Catherine's hand, Adam hoped for one last glimpse of the Werners. There were only sailors on the deck.

The trip north took them through the streets of Philadelphia. Walking, Adam and *Herr* Gross had much to talk about. As they left the city, the landscape suddenly became rural.

After two hours, *Herr* Gross said, "We are nearly there. South of the town you see small farms and log houses. Our farmers do not live in towns like in the old country. Tradesmen have shops in the town. Mine is next to our house. But we are glad for the farmers. It gives fruits and vegetables from them."

When he spotted the first farm, Adam rushed over and dug his heels into the dark loam. "*Ei, ei, ei.* I hope my soil is rich like this."

"Ya, *un* it gives more farms north of *es Schteddel,*" *Herr* Gross said. "They are maybe three acres."

As they continued on, they came to log houses and shops lining the streets of Germantown. Standing out were a few large stone homes. The wagon turned onto Wissahickon Street and came to the Gross' log house.

"Your house is nice," Clara said, as the females were helped down off the wagon.

"*Ya*, we have flowers, like in the old country. *Kumm rei.*"

Herr Gross led them through the narrow kitchen into a second room. "This is the *Schtubb* where we eat and spend our time." Adam noticed a ladder leaning against the wall. "You sleep up there," *Herr* Gross said, motioning with his head. "We have tick pads."

"Take turns washing and I make supper," *Hausfraa* Gross said. "Do you like *Schnitz un Gnepp?*"

"*Schnitz un Gnepp! Ya gewiss!*" Clara exclaimed.

Catherine and Sarah joined the others after their baths. "We feel clean and fresh, *gell Liebschdi?*"

"You stay with us till you are strong for walking to the frontier. *Grossmudder*, it is your turn," *Hausfraa* Gross said. "I get water and towels."

Adam and *Herr* Gross sat in the main room. "We are followers of Menno Simons," *Herr* Gross said. "When we cannot practice our religion in Krefeld, we accept William Penn's invitation. Thirty-three come first, led by Dr. Pastorius. He helps them survive the first winter in cellars and caves."

"*Ya*, a cave might be our first home too," Adam said.

"But your cousin and *deitsch* farmers help, *net?*" *Herr* Gross said.

"*Ya*, we look first for Peter. I sent him a letter." Adam looked down. "I hope he gets it."

"The Germans are not liked by the Philadelphia *leit*," *Herr* Gross said. "They think we dress funny and talk and act funny. Some call us the Dumb Dutch." He chuckled. "But they change their minds on Wednesdays and Saturdays when our farmers fetch fruits and vegetables and apple butter and grapes and woven goods to Market Street."

They continued talking until Adam's turn came to bathe. When he returned, he smelled the dinner cooking. "*Wunnerbaar*. Our first dinner in *es nei Land!*"

Nellie and Sarah sat on the floor in a corner, chattering. Catherine was pleased to see how quickly they became friends.

"*Herr* Gross, you say most are tradesmen. What is

From the Rhine To Penn's Woods

your trade?"

"*Schuhmacher. Mei Daadi* taught me."

"It wonders me if it gives tradesmen in the Tulpehocken settlement," Adam said.

"*Verleicht* at Weisertown. Some tradesmen go out to the farms and make tools for the farmers."

Hausfraa Gross came in carrying a steaming pot. "*Kumm esse,*" she announced with a big smile.

After they sat down at the long plank table, *Herr* Gross said, "Bow your heads. 'Our Heavenly Father, we thank you for today. We thank you that you brought these four *Deitsclhenner* across the sea. We are grateful we can help them. Be with them in the days ahead. Keep them safe. Watch over them as they go north to live in the wilderness. We pray for all travelers, for all oppressed people wherever they are. Now we ask your blessing on this food. In Jesus' name we pray. Amen.' "

As *Hausfraa* Gross got up and went for other dishes, Catherine said to *Herr* Gross, "*Der Gott* bless you."

After one taste Clara said, "*Schmacks guud!* This is the best *Schnitz un Gnepp* I ever eat." The Staudts nodded. On the side were bread, apple butter, and dandelion.

The pot seemed bottomless. After second and third helpings, *Hausfraa* Gross said, "Now comes dessert." Sarah's face lit up when she saw a plate of *Lepkuchen* and a pitcher of milk.

After dinner the women fussed with clean-up. "*Hausfraa* Gross, does it give a *Reformiert Karich* yet where we go?" Catherine asked.

"We hear of two." *Hausfraa* Gross paused. "I am glad to hear the question. You are Christian people."

The men took chairs in the far corner. *Herr* Gross pulled his clay pipe off the fireplace shelf and lit it with a pine knot. "You people sleep late. You need rest. When you get up, come next door and I show you my shop. Maybe you want to look at the farms too. The farmers will talk with another German *Bauer* any day."

"*Guud*. Was it hard to buy land?"

"*Nein*, Dr. Pastorius arranges it with William Penn. The farmers have three-acre plots, but the house lots are small. Up in the Tulpehocken wilderness you get maybe fifty acres. Your cousin helps you, *gell*?"

"*Ya,* I don't worry." He paused. "The only thing I worry about is *mei Daadi* in the old country." Adam shook his head slowly. "I think of him all the time." He paused. "Do you have writing paper and ink? I let him know we are here."

The evening passed pleasantly, the children playing, the women chatting, Adam struggling with his letter, *Herr* Gross reading his Bible. *Hausfraa* Gross left and brought in a tray. "Before bed, we have a bite to eat. Do you like *Bretzels*? I make them with winter wheat."

"My oh my," Catherine said, "we haven't had *Bretzels* for a long time."

It was 9 o'clock. Sarah said, "*Mamma,* I'm tired."

"*Ya, Bobbel,* it's time for bed." Catherine turned to the Grosses. "A wonderful day. *Dank.* God bless you."

Sarah was first to climb the ladder. "Look at me, *Mamma,*" when she stepped cautiously on the planked floor and glanced down.

Catherine was next. "Duck your head when you get up," Sarah said, laughing.

Then came Clara. She lost many pounds on the voyage, but she was still plump. "Will this ladder hold me?" she asked, chuckling. Halfway up she said, "I can't go any higher."

"*Grossmudder,*" Adam said with a hearty laugh, "I get you up if I have to push you by the *Hinnerdale.*" The Grosses roared in laughter. "Going down will be easier," Adam told *die Grossmudder,* chortling.

"Sleep well," *Hausfraa* Gross said. "*Gut Nacht.*"

Taking Sarah's hand, *Grossmudder* pulled one of the mattresses across the floor. "We are used to being bed partners, *gell? Was iss sell?*" she said. "I smell pine needles." She felt the bedtick. "What else does it give? I believe corn husks. *Ya well, besser wie nix.*"

Soon Adam heard Clara's loud snoring. He reached for Catherine's breasts. "Do you think . . . do you think we can do it tonight? I'm so anxious," he whispered.

"*Ach, liewer Adam,* I'm afraid the corn husks will be too loud."

"*Dunnerwedder!* That's a new one."

"Ssshhh." She giggled. "Settle down, Adam."

"So you say no?"

"*Liebschdi,* I am as anxious as you, but we wait a little longer. Hold me close. *Ich hab dich gaern.*" She waited. "The Grosses are good people, but how long do you think we stay?"

"We go the day after tomorrow."

Catherine's mouth dropped. "*Nay, nay.* You and I are ready, but Sarah and *die Grossmudder* need rest."

"*Nay!* We go! We find Peter. I must build shelter before it gives winter."

"But our young one and our old one are worn out. What does it make if they get sick?"

"Enough of this," he said, raising his voice. He rose and sought his own space. "*Donnerwetter nochemol,*" he cried as he hit his head on the low ceiling.

Catherine giggled. "Adam, don't be stubborn. Come back here."

He answered with silence.

Dawn came and a beam of sunshine broke through a crack between logs and the roof. Adam went down the ladder quietly. "*Guuder Mariye,*" he said to *Hausfraa* Gross.

"*Guten Tag.* Did you sleep well?"

"*So zimmlich.* Did *Herr* Gross go to his shop already yet?"

"*Ya,* he comes for breakfast when everyone is ready. He says for you to come over."

"*Kumm* rei," *Herr* Gross said when he saw Adam at the door. "These are shoes I make for customers. Here, I show you." After the demonstration, he and Adam returned to the house and joined the *Weibsleit* for a breakfast of mush and blueberry pie.

After breakfast Adam said, "Is it all right if I go out and walk around on a farm?"

"*Ya,* go to the north plots. The farmer on the first one is Jacob Schlegel."

Jacob dropped his hoe when he saw Adam plodding through the field. He called, "*Hallo.* Are you lost?"

They shook hands and Jacob motioned for Adam to walk with him. He was a tall, rugged man, about fifty, Adam judged. They sat beneath a tree at the edge of the field and for a half-hour Jacob talked about how he cleared the land, where he bought his horse and wagon, what kind of fruit trees and vegetables do well.

"First I build a log house," Adam said.

"*Ya,* clearing land and building with the logs is first. If you get help, it goes up before winter. If not, you make a hillside cave, like our early settlers." Jacob paused. "*Ya well,* I must get back to hoeing. Make yourself at home."

Adam was back at the Gross's house at 5 o'clock. He spotted the womenfolk walking from the opposite direction.

Sarah ran up and threw her arms around Adam's waist. "*Daadi, Daadi,* we have fun seeing the houses and shops. Where were you?"

"I was on *Herr* Schlegel's farm. *Bobbel,* you look tired."

"*Nay,* we play with our dolls now."

Hausfraa Gross got to work in the kitchen. "It gives *Seifleesch un Sauergraut* tonight," she said. "Wash up and I call you."

Herr Gross and Adam had just settled when they heard, "*Allrecht,* everyone, supper is ready."

After grace, Clara put her fork into the mashed potatoes and sauerkraut "*Sell is himmlisch!*" she said at the first bite. The Staudts smiled in agreement.

After supper the two men sat and talked. "You have been kind. Some day we repay," Adam said.

"*Nein, nein.* It is our religion. It brings happiness." He paused. "You do not think of leaving yet?"

"I must build shelter for the winter."

"*Ich verstehen.* But your journey to the wilderness is hard. You must rest."

"How many days does it take?"

"*Verleicht* five or six. But a road for carts now runs from Philadelphia to the frontier." Gross chuckled. "First it was buffalo path, then Indian trail, then bridle path. Now they call it Tulpehocken Road. Some call it Reading Road. When you get to the town at the ford, you cross the river then go west to get to the Tulpehocken frontier."

"I am surprised it gives a road."

"*Ya well*, if it doesn't, it takes hours to walk a short distance through forest and bramble. Farmers need the road to haul their things to market in Philadelphia."

"And wheat for shipping to England and Europe, *gell?*" Adam said, dreaming of prosperous days ahead. "Does it give a town farther west?"

"*Ich wayss net. Verleicht* where the Indian negotiator Conrad Weiser lives."

"Does it give settlements from here to Reading Town?" Adam asked.

"*Ya*, you follow the Schuylkill River. You see farms in little settlements like Trappe, Skippack, Goshenhoppen, Stowe, Oley, Exeter Meeting."

Clara, Catherine, and *Hausfraa* Gross were busy jabbering, but Catherine caught every word of the men's conversation.

"*Ya*, if you have the *Geld* you stay at inns." *Herr* Gross said. You see taverns with signs out. You look for *ordinaries*. Some are dirty and you sleep on the floor. They are not marked, but you ask."

"Will people take us in if it gets dark and we can't find a place?"

"*Ya*, if they are Christian—and if they are *deitsch*. If the latchstring is out, you are welcome."

"I think we start out early the day after tomorrow," Adam said.

"Remember what I tell you. You are welcome to stay until you feel strong."

It was bedtime. The Staudt family climbed the ladder, a bit easier than last night. Adam lay down with Catherine until *Grossmudder* and Sarah were asleep. Then he went to his private place.

Catherine followed him. "Adam, what am I going to do with you? Come back to bed and we make up. I heard most of what *Herr* Gross told you. We talk about it."

He said nothing.

"Adam, I am a Christian woman, but I dare take my part." She raised her voice. "You are not the only one who decides things. We have a little one and *die Grossmudder* to look out for. We stay at least three days more. *Du bischt ein Rinskopp.* If you don't get over it, we stay here till you do."

The days passed quickly, the girls playing with their dolls, the women out and around enjoying the good weather, Adam doing chores on Jacob Schlegel's farm. "I never spent an idle day in my life," he told Schlegel, "and I don't start now."

After he returned, Adam said, "*Herr* Gross, if you have plaster I fill in between the logs where some is out."

"I get some."

Adam spent the next day chipping and filling. That night he slept on the mattress with Catherine.

"It was kind to work on the house," she said. "They are our angels. I thank them every day in my prayers."

"And me? Do you pray for me?"

She smiled. "*Gewiss.* Most days more than once."

"*Allrecht,* you win. When do we leave?"

"Maybe two days after tomorrow. She *rutsched* over and kissed him. "*Schloof guud.*"

FOUR

THE NEXT MORNING THE STAUDTS CAME DOWN the ladder as soon as they heard *Fraa* Gross stirring. The sun was not yet up. After a breakfast of samp and milk, *Herr* Gross went to his shop, the women and children left for a walk in the town, and Adam strode to the Schlegel farm. By the time he returned late in the afternoon, the pot of turnips, carrots, and onions had been cooking a couple hours. "*Arig guud,*" Clara said with the first taste.

After a pleasant evening of socializing, it was bedtime. *Herr* Gross left and returned with a large sack. "Here," he said, "you have a long walk. You need these." He pulled out four pairs of shoes.

Catherine and her mother gasped. "*Mei Gott nochemol,*" Catherine said. "Your kindness never ends."

Die Grossmudder scuttled to *Herr* Gross and kissed him lightly on the cheek. "I hope *Fraa* Gross does not mind," she said, chortling.

"We are glad you like the shoes," *Fraa* Gross said.

"Try them on," *Herr* Gross said. "I free them up if they are tight."

"Mine are right," Adam said. "You lose a few days' wages just for us, *net? Gross Dank.*"

The Staudts said goodnight and climbed the ladder

for the last time.

It was dark when they came downstairs the next morning. *Fraa* Gross was preparing a breakfast of mush and waffles with molasses. *Herr* Gross said grace. "Heavenly Father, we thank you for bringing this fine *deitsche Familye* to us. Be with them on their journey into the wilderness and in the days and years ahead. If it is your will, may we meet again. Amen."

It was time to leave. "Here, I pack something for your first day," *Fraa* Gross said. She pulled out of the bag what looked like a big yellow egg. "In the old country," she said, "we never see apples grow in spring. These are good and sweet. Look for May Apple trees at the side of the road. And look for a tree called persimmon, and nut trees, and strawberries, huckleberries, and raspberries bushes." She chuckled. "You won't starve. And I pack some vegetable and flower seeds for a little garden."

"You think of everything, *Fraa* Gross," Catherine said. "*Gross Dank.*" Catherine wiped away a tear. "It feels like we know you all our lives. God bless you."

The Staudts left and walked north through Germantown, Adam squinting to get a good last look at the Schlegel farm as they passed. As they turned onto the Tulpehocken Road, straight ahead the sun peeked through the clouds. Rocks, thick tree branches, and puddles required little detours. They trudged on in silence.

Something caught Catherine's eye at the side of the road. "Look at these pretty flowers. God sometimes plants things where no one sees them. These God plants for us."

Clara made a game of who could spot the tallest tree. "There, *Grossmudder*, that one is the biggest yet," Sarah called out.

At midmorning they crossed a foot-deep creek that cut across the road. "Let's rest here and take a drink," Adam said. "Are you hungry? *Fraa* Gross packed *Bretzels* for us."

After ten minutes they got up and continued, stopping for short rests every hour. The weather was ideal, sunny but cool. "We make good time," Adam said. "If we keep it up, we get to King of Prussia in about two hours.

Maybe we stop to eat. Whoever spots the inn first gets an extra *Bretzel*."

Clara claimed the reward. "I can't read the sign, but this looks like it. I give the *Bretzel* to Sarah."

The innkeeper directed them to a table and served them soup and bread. "I expected better," Adam said to Catherine, "but we had a rest. We see how far we get after noon. I don't think we make Trappe today."

About 5 o'clock Catherine spotted a tavern sign. As they approached, they read "The Golden Goose Inn."

"*Willkumm!* Come have something to drink," the innkeeper said.

Adam smiled when he heard German. "Cider for the little one, rum for the rest," he said. "Have you rooms?"

"*Ya*, I show you."

The rooms were small and had double beds. Adam's spirits rose. Did Catherine have the same thought? he wondered.

"*Wie viel?*" he asked.

The price cheaper than he expected, Adam said, "*Ganz guud*. We take two."

At 6 o'clock the innkeeper called, "Supper is ready." The guests, eleven in all, sat at the long table for rivel *Supp un Lattwarick Brot*. Sarah ate one bowl, everyone else asked for more. Some guests tarried after supper, but the Staudts were ready for bed.

Adam walked to the other room and pulled tight the rope holding the mattress. "Now you two can sleep tight," he said, smiling. "Don't let the bedbugs bite." He left and returned to Catherine.

"Can you believe it, *Liebschdi*," she whispered, "we are alone." They quickly got undressed and crawled into bed. "Not yet," she said as he reached for her. "Wait till *die Mudder* and Sarah are asleep." She chuckled. "This time our mattress won't wake them up."

Early the next morning Adam and Catherine awoke before sunrise. "What *a wunnerbaar* night, *Liebschdi*. I love you," she said.

"I love you too."

Sarah and *die Grossmudder* were still sleeping. Catherine went to them and gently shook them. "You two had a good sleep, *net?*"

"*Ya guud*," they said in unison and giggled.

After breakfast they were on their way, hoping to find a place to stay beyond Trappe.

The day was not as sunny as yesterday. Adam kept an eye out for trees and berries. Sure enough, in a short time he spotted a May Apple tree and later a walnut tree. After they sampled the apples and walnuts, Adam filled his knapsack.

"A *Bretzel* would go good with the nuts," Clara said.

"I'm sorry, *Mudder, the Bretzels* are all," Catherine said.

Adam was pleased with their pace, about a mile and a half an hour, he guessed. His thoughts were on their destination. "It wonders me," he said to Catherine, "how we clear enough forest to build a house before winter."

"We pray for help," she said.

By noon, clouds covered the sky. "I feel a little *Schpritzer*," Clara said.

"We keep going," Adam said. "It soon stops."

Suddenly the sky opened. "Over there," Adam directed, pointing. "We keep dry under the thick trees."

Adam found a good spot. "Sit down and rest," he said. "There is no lightning, so we are safe. It is soon over."

Die Grossmudder, always the spirited one, told stories about growing up in Rheinstein, changing the ending from the last telling.

Suddenly the sun broke through and they went on their way.

Late in the afternoon Adam spotted a farm house. They left the road and walked to the house and found the latch string out. Adam knocked. He knocked again. A *Hausfraa* wearing a smocked dress, a bonnet and a *Schatz* appeared around the side of the house. She smiled. "*Guder Owed*," she said, wiping her hands on her apron. "I was in my garden pulling onions."

"We don't trouble you," Catherine said, "but we

walk to the Tulpehocken settlement and ask if there is an inn where we can stay."

"*Ach*, come in and have something to drink. You must be thirsty."

"*Danke, awwer*, we do not trouble you," Adam said.

"*Nay, nay, kumm rei.*"

The *Hausfraa* was a plump woman with a steady smile. "*Mei Mann* is out plowing. There is no inn. We would keep you but our house is small. It gives an *ordinary* about two miles down the road toward Potts Grove. Many stop there."

"*Gross Dank* for the drink," Catherine said. "We go now before it gives dark."

The *ordinary* was large; other travelers were already there. After a supper of fried pig and coleslaw, topped off by spirited chatting, the weary travelers were ready for sleep. The thirty of them picked out a place on the dirty floor and lay down for the night.

The Staudts were the first up and on their way early the next morning. As she walked, Catherine fell into a pensive mood, happy and thankful for the way things were going. In the nights that followed, the family slept on the floor in two *ordinaries* and in beds in an inn. When Catherine saw how filthy the bed sheets were in the inn, she said to her mother, "I think from now on we sleep on the floor of an *ordinary* rather than in dirty beds in an inn."

At midday of the fifth day, Catherine thought she heard the clippety-clop of a horse behind them. She turned. "Look, look," she cried, "a wagon!"

"*Ya! Ya!!*" Sarah shrieked.

"Whoa, Billy," the driver yelled as he approached. The open wagon was empty. The farmer jumped down and gave Billy his feed pail.

"*Wu gehschdt?*" he asked.

"To the Tulpehocken settlement. Do you know about it?"

"*Ya,* it's on the other side of the river, beyond Reading Town. I live in the Oley Valley on this side."

"Yours is the first wagon we see. Where are you coming from?"

"Philadelphia. I haul my produce to Market Street." He put a hand to his jaw. "Do you want a ride? I believe Billy is willing to pull a few more."

Catherine spoke up. "If Billy is willing to carry *die Grossmudder un Kind,* my *Mann* and I walk."

The farmer smiled. "I ask him."

Catherine said a silent prayer and lifted Sarah up. Adam smiled. "We know *die Grossmudder* will be heavier to load," he teased.

"*Ich hayss* Brumbach," the farmer said. "What is your name?"

"Staudt. Is there someplace to stay?"

"I stay tonight at the Black Horse Tavern. It's not *deier.*"

"*Guud,*" Adam said. "Then we stay there too."

Hearing "giddyap," Billy neighed and shook and they were off. Wherever the road was a bit wider, Adam ran up to talk with *Bauer* Brumbach. "Can we get from the tavern to Tulpehocken tomorrow?"

"*Nay, nay.* It gives no inns in Oley, but you can sleep in my barn." He smiled broadly. "But you better ask *die Weibsleit.* The next night you stay at the Brown Bear Inn or maybe go right into Reading Town. From there it gives only a few miles to Tulpehocken."

"Does it give an inn in Reading?"

"We hear *Herr* Weiser is building something."

Just as the sun sank, *Herr* Brumbach called out, "There's the tavern. We make good time."

The Black Horse Tavern was pleasant, the master serving drinks. Bar business was so good, Adam thought, that dinner would be late. After he saw what was served, it wasn't worth the wait, he mused. About 9 o'clock, guests were ready for bed. "Good night, *alliebber,*" the taverner said. "Remove your boots. *Un,* no more than five in a bed."

After a skimpy breakfast, the Staudts took to the road. The women talked about *Herr* Brumbach's offer of his barn for sleeping. "It will be fun," Catherine said. "We just hold our noses and join the cows and pigs and chickens. *Allrecht?"*

"*Ya, ya.* I want to," Sarah said

They arrived at the farm. *Fraa* Brumbach was as pleasant as her husband. She prepared dinner of sausage and corn and left-over blueberry pie. "*Des iss guud,*" Clara said. "I hope when we settle I cook half as good."

After supper Sarah rolled hoops with the three lively Brumbach children until dark. The Staudts were ready for bed.

Laughing, Catherine and Adam found their own corner of the barn in the hayloft. "What does this smell like?" Adam asked.

"*Ya,* the *Neptune.* But that was worse," Catherine said. She shook her head. "I wonder how we ever survive. Well, good night, everyone. Sleep tight."

At the first crow of the cock, all four Staudts opened their eyes. "Everyone get enough sleep?" Adam asked. "Let's go to the house. *Ich denk* the Brumbachs are up already."

At the breakfast table Catherine said, "What a good family you are and what a wonderful life you have. It makes me glad we risk everything to come here." She waited. "*Verleicht* I pray too much, but I offer a short prayer now. If you don't want, I make it a silent one." She glanced at *Bauer un Fraa* Brumbach. They smiled.

The Saudts bid their hosts farewell and hurried down the lane to the Tulpehocken Road. As they walked, Catherine and Adam shared their happiness, just a couple days away from Tulpehocken.

"*Wunnerbaar, wunnerbaar!*" Catherine said softly.

"For days now I think of only one thing—I hope we find Cousin Peter's farm."

"*Ya* Adam, we will. I do not doubt. This will be *besser* than when we come to Germantown and do not know a soul." She paused. "The Grosses were so kind."

They stopped from time to time to rest, usually when Adam spotted a berry bush at the side of the road, strawberries and blueberries their favorites.

In the middle of the afternoon the road became a

sharp decline. Through the trees they caught a glimpse of a shimmering river down below. "Ah, I believe we come to Reading Town," Adam said with a big sigh.

After trudging a half-hour through dense forest, Catherine said, "Look, I see a building down there."

They approached and found the door open. "Hallo. Anyone home?" Adam called.

"*Ya, kumm rei.*"

"We are in Reading Town, *net*?" Adam said. "Is your name Weiser?"

"*Ya, ya.* How do you know?"

"*Bauer* Brumbach from Oley gives us a ride in his wagon. He says you build an inn in the town."

"*Ya*, it is half finished. It gives an inn or *verleicht* a trading post. *Die Schtadt* needs both." He eyed the Staudts up and down. "*Wu gehschdt?*"

"To the Tulpehocken Valley."

"*Guud, guud.* That is where I live. *Wellkumm!*"

"Are you acquainted with my cousin, Peter Staudt?"

"*Ya*, we come from Schoharie down together. I remember he tells me you come. After you cross the river you walk west and come to the Little Cacusi Creek. It winds around and runs across the road again one mile. His farm is there, on the north."

"*Herr* Weiser, is there an inn where we can stay?"

"You stay right here tonight. I go soon home."

"*Guud. Gross Dank.*"

"When you leave tomorrow, you go straight ahead to the Schuylkill River and cross at Widow Finney's Ford. You see people there. It's about three feet deep. From there it gives only eight miles to your cousin's *platz*."

"*Danke.* I like to visit your farm after we settle."

"*Ya wohl, awwer*, I am sometimes away."

"God bless you for your kindness, *Herr* Weiser," Catherine said.

The Staudts had a spring in their step as they marched to the river the next morning. Secure in the firm grip of her father, Sarah had no fear crossing the waist-high river. "This is fun," she said. Clara held back, a frightened look on her face. She finally plunged in.

They were out of breath when they reached the bank. "We take our first step in the Tulpehocken," Adam said. "Bauer Brumbach called it the land of the turtles."

Luckily, the sun was hot and their clothes dried in an hour. Except for Sarah, the Staudts were silent, pensive. Soon Sarah too became quiet, concentrating on being first to see the creek. Just after noon, she yelled, "I see it! I see it!"

"We cross then we have a mile to go," Adam said.

On the right, he spotted fields planted with corn two feet high. They crossed the little creek again, and Adam spotted a stone house and a huge barn. "This is it. This is Peter's farm."

FIVE

THE CLOSER THE STAUDTS GOT TO THE BIG BARN, the more impressed Adam became. "But it wonders me why they have a stone house."

"*Ya*, that is *wunnerlich*," Catherine said.

Adam hurried to the door of the farmhouse. "Hallo! Is anyone here?" he called.

Two young girls appeared from the side of the house.

"Is your father Peter Staudt?" Adam asked.

"No, our name is Jones," the older girl said. "Father is in the back field. We will get him."

"Jones! Jones!" Adam said after the girls dashed off. "They must be English."

"*Nay*, not English, not Scotch, not Irish," Catherine said. She chuckled. "For sure, they are not *Deitschlenner*."

Jones walked up, hurried along by his daughters' tugs.

"How do you do," he said. "My name is Hugh Jones. What is yours?"

"Our name is Staudt. We come to settle in the Tulpehocken."

"Welcome. You come to a good place. Our neighbors are German." His eyes scanned them slowly. "You had a long walk. Come in and refresh yourselves."

"We look for my cousin Peter Staudt," Adam said.

"Yes, their farm is about a half-mile down the road where the Little Cacusi Creek crosses."

"We stay only a minute," Adam said, as they entered the house. "When did you come to the Tulpehocken?"

"Many years ago. But our story can wait. You are anxious to see your cousin."

"*Ya*," Adam said. "Your house is stone. We thought houses are made of logs."

"In Wales most homes are stone, and we were lucky to find limestone here. I know nothing about log houses, but maybe I can help when you build," Jones said.

"*Danke*. We leave now before it gives dark."

As the Staudts approached Peter's farm, Adam was amazed to see a barn even bigger than the Jones'.

Adam walked past the buildings into the field beyond. He spotted a farmer harrowing. When Peter saw Adam approaching, he unhitched the harrow and led the horse to the barn.

"*Ach*, this must be Cousin Adam," Peter said. "At last we meet again. *Wie gayt's?*" He pumped Adam's hand vigorously. "Nettie, come out. They are here," he yelled. He rushed to the side of the house and put his hands to his mouth. "Girls, come quick. Your cousins from Germany are here."

The girls and their mother hugged them.

"We get word to the boys you are here. You must be tired. *Kumm rei, kumm rei*," Peter said.

The Staudts sat at the plank table in *die Kich* and Peter brought in chairs from *die Schtubb*. The cousins busied themselves serving cider.

"It gives *en Briwwi* outback if anyone needs it," Peter said.

"The girls are going to make good supper," Nettie said. "We sit and get acquainted first." She smiled. "There is much to talk."

"We are seven," Peter said. "The boys and the oldest girl are married and on their own so you sleep upstairs or in the lean-to." He paused. "*Der Deitschlenner* around here know how kind the Mennonites in Germantown are to newcomers. They hold your trunk for you to pick up, *gell*?"

"*Ya*, but we do without for awhile," Adam said.

"I take you later to get it," Peter said. He led Adam to the *Schtubb*. "*Hock dich hie.* How was *die Daadi* when you left?" Peter asked.

"*Ganz Guud.* I think of him all the time."

"I had a letter from *mei Daadi* last month." Peter waited. "I believe he goes back. It is a shame it takes so long for a letter to come."

"From what *der Daadi* told me, our fathers are alike. I am glad *der Daadi* taught me some English."

"*Ya, un mich.* You don't make it good here without."

"We stop at the Jones' house to ask where you are."

"*Ya*, they are good people. They are Baptists and hold services in his house before they built a church up the road near a spring they say sinks a little every year."

"Are there many Welsh?"

"*Net viel*, but enough to support the *Karich ennichau.*"

"They were friendly." Adam waited. His voice strained, he said, "I get something off my mind quick. How do I get land? How do I pay? How do I build before it gives winter?"

"You build then you settle later."

Adam raised his eyebrows. "I build before I own the land?"

"*Ya wohl.* You build and till the land then you have rights." He chuckled. "Don't worry, the land agents come after you soon enough. I mark a good parcel for you, a small Indian field with some oak and walnut and tulip trees. Tomorrow the boys come and we cut them down. You stay with us till the house is finished."

Adam raised his eyebrows. "Is it close?"

Peter chuckled and pointed. "*Ya, gewiss.* Right next."

A warm feeling came over Adam. He stared at Peter. This is more than he could hope for. How would he ever repay him? he asked himself.

"You and I eat breakfast before the sun is up," Peter continued. "Then *der Buwe* come with their axes." He laughed. "They are twice as strong as me."

"We were *verschtaunt* to see the Jones' house is stone," Adam said.

"*Ya* well, it gives a big vein of limestone running through here." Peter paused and smiled. "*Un* it makes the soil rich."

"Before it gives dark, I go out and walk in it."

"*Ya gewiss.* I go with once."

As they plodded to a field of shimmering corn, Peter talked about his crops and animals. Adam heard his voice but became lost in reverie. To have arrived, to walk in the loam, to sense the kindness of his cousin and his family, to look ahead to a life like theirs. And to own his own land! He pulled out his handkerchief and blew his nose.

Peter showed him the lean-to. It had two beds on a flat floor of split logs. The room was small, but Adam pictured how the beds could be rearranged for privacy. "We don't use this room since the *Buwe* moved away," he said, "but the girls move in while you are here so you sleep in the house."

"*Danke vielmols,*" Adam said.

When they sat down to supper, Catherine was happy to hear Cousin Peter say grace. The supper was chicken vegetable *Supp*, pepper cabbage, apple butter bread, and apple pie. "*Ganz guud,*" Clara said. "I don't have *Hinkelfleesch* for a year. *Des iss gunz guud.*"

After they cleared the table, the women chatted like long-lost friends. Catherine had something on her mind. "Does it give a church near here?"

"*Ya wohl,*" Nettie said, motioning with her arm, "*Cacusi Reformiert Karich* right up the hill. "It is *verleicht* twenty years old, built of logs."

Catherine was happy to hear 'Reformed.' "Do you belong?"

"*Ya,* we go every Sunday." Nettie laughed. "We don't miss the gossip. You go with."

"That would be *wunnerbaar, awwer* we don't have

nice clothes."

"We take care of that," Nettie said.

Adam and Peter sat in the *Schtubb*. "*Daadi* gives me money to buy land," Adam said. "He says only landowners vote."

"*Ya*."

"I don't want to be *naasich*, but do you own your plot?"

"*Ya*, we clear as much as we need for the house then it gives a warrant for fifty acres. Then we clear more. You do the same."

The evening passed pleasantly. Adam took Catherine aside to tell her about sleeping in the lean-to. They agreed it would be wrong to have the girls move from their room. "But," Adam said with a grin, "I arrange privacy in the lean-to."

She put a hand on his. "*Guud*," she said, "But maybe we wait, *Liebschdi*," she said, smiling broadly. "We see."

"Well, this is a big day and I am ready for bed," Peter said. He lit a lantern and took the Staudts out to the lean-to. "*Schloof guud*."

Sarah and *die Grossmudder* fell asleep quickly. Adam and Catherine whispered about their good fortune. "It is more than that, Adam. It is God answering our prayers. Before we outen the lantern, I say a little prayer of thanksgiving."

It was not yet light when Adam woke up. When he heard a stirring through the wall, he walked to the front of the house and entered. Nettie was preparing mush for their breakfast. "The boys chop down the big trees close to the cart path," Peter said. "You and me fasten a chain to them so the horse pulls them away. Then we saw off branches and clean up. We need fifty feet of clearing before we start the house. This takes *verleicht* four weeks. Then the boys saw logs eleven feet long."

Finished with breakfast, they walked to the barn. Peter put a leash on the horse, and they went out to Adam's lot, his new home at last.

"Which way do we face the house?" Adam asked as they walked.

"South so it gives the sun's warmth." When they reached the lot, Peter said, "Come, I show you something good."

Peter led him fifty tough yards through the dense woods. It was ten minutes before he said, "We are almost there. Keep your ears open."

Just as Adam heard the babbling, Peter said, "Here it is, the Little Cacusi, the Place of Owls, the Indians call it. It winds around and gives good water."

As they returned to the front, Peter said the cleared area would also provide a kitchen garden. "If it gives time before winter," he added, "we clear a little plot for corn. Hay, alfalfa, wheat—you plant them in spring."

"The Grosses in Germantown talk about girdling trees," Adam said.

"*Nay, nay*, it takes too long for them to die. But we cut down more in the back."

Soon Peter's sons Henry and Casper rode up. Muscular, rugged-looking, they dismounted and took up their axes and mattocks. After shaking hands with Adam, they plodded to the first trees assigned by their father. Their loud blows echoed rhythmically in the woods beyond. Heavy chips covered the ground. After both trees were down, Peter led the horse to them.

"My boys are hard workers," Peter said. "We have *verleicht* a dozen down before dinner."

At noontime, Peter said, "*Allrecht, Buwe*, we eat now."

The *Buwe* ate twice as much as Adam—gigantic helpings of *Schnitz un Gnepp*.

After dinner, they quickly resumed their work, no one talking. By 6 o'clock, Adam was exhausted. When will we quit? he wondered.

"After the next two trees are down, we quit," Peter said. "The boys have their own work tomorrow, but you and I have enough to keep us busy."

"*Ya wohl*," Adam said, nodding.

After three long, hard days, Adam was happy to see Saturday. Catherine would have no problem getting him to church tomorrow.

At 9 o'clock, dressed in their Sunday best, the Staudt cousins and their families walked up the steep hill to the log church. "What a *schayni Daag*," Catherine said. "I am so happy."

Eight Staudts entered the church and sat on the only benches still empty. Nettie and her girls chatted with friends. In ten minutes the church was filled. Late-comers would have to stand for the three-hour service.

"There is talk," Nettie whispered to Catherine, "of a new *Karich*. But that will be a long time."

Reverend Decker rode up, entered and immediately began the service. "In the name of the Father and of the Son and of the Holy Spirit."

Response: "Amen."

Parson: "I will come to the altar of my Lord."

Response: "To God who is my joy and hope."

Parson: "Our help is the word."

Response: "Even the name of God who made all creation."

The litany continued for five minutes. Catherine was overjoyed.

A solemn-looking parishioner rose and faced the congregation. "Now it gives hymns of praise to the Lord. Sing as I line them out."

After the collection plate was passed, Parson Decker rose and faced the congregation. Members knew they were in for a sermon of at least an hour and a half. Catherine held up better than most, she believed, pleased the sermon was not fire and brimstone but, at least in a few places, positive and hopeful. She closed her eyes and thanked God for all his blessings.

The service ended with the Lord's Prayer.

After the benediction, the people were ready to stretch their muscles and chat. They would spend the rest of the Lord's Day at home reading their Bibles, relaxing, doing no work except tending to the farm animals.

The new workweek began before sunrise. While the men resumed clearing Adam's plot, the women spun at the wheel and sewed. Sarah was intrigued by the spinning wheel.

After a month of sweat and muscle, the men had cleared enough land for a house, a kitchen garden, and a small field, and they had cut enough logs for the house. At Peter's house, the women made shirts, pants, and dresses to replace the tattered clothes that had seen the family through months of rugged travel.

"You are ready for a raising," Peter told Adam one morning. "I ride out to the neighbors."

Adam and his family were shocked two days later when they spied scores of men, women, and children arriving on foot, on horseback, and by buggies and carts — singing, shouting greetings as they approached. *Der Daadi* had told Adam about German neighbors helping neighbors put up their houses, but the festive mode was a surprise. The women and children stayed at Peter's house.

As Peter planned it, Adam's cabin would be a story and a half, twenty feet long and twenty feet wide with a puncheon floor, a clapboard roof, a door and one window of oiled paper. No nails would be used. Adam would later daub the space between timbers.

Peter took over. Pointing to Adam, he told the men, "This is my cousin from Frankenthal," he said. "I tell him his German neighbors help, *un do bischt.*" The corner men cut the notches and the other men carried the logs and ran them up on skids. *"Allrecht, Buwe, schlag nei."*

The log foundation pulled into place, by noon the walls were up. "All right," Peter said, "we go now to our place for dinner."

The kitchen table was brought outside loaded with *Supp, Schnitz un Gnepp, Warscht, Sauergraut, Ebbel, Kannbrot, Lattwarrick, Schmierkaes,* and a shocking array of pies and cakes. To drink, there was lemonade, cider and a jug of whiskey. The *Mannsleit* smacked their lips.

After the table was cleared and the food put away, the women and older girls came out to enjoy the sunshine. The young children played games and ran hoops, shrieking and yelling. The women gossiped about the big new stone house being built for Conrad Kershner just down the road. "I hear," Nellie said, "the mason and carpenter came over indentured to Kershner and will go free when the house is finished." The men returned to Adam's plot. By 5 o'clock, the house standing, the frolic ended.

In bed that night, Catherine and Adam whispered about their joy. "It gives a week's work before we move in," he said. "And I make beds and a table."

"Our own bed," she said with a smile. "I can't wait."

"Ya, ya, only one thing. The growing season is over and we depend on Peter's family for our food."

"We tell him we pay back everything."

"*Ya gewiss.*"

"I was just thinking," Catherine said. "Would anyone back in Frankenthal believe it if we tell them about this strange, *wunnerbaar Daag*?"

SIX

AS CATHERINE SAT IN CHURCH MEDITATING before the service on the First Sunday in Advent, she looked forward, as always, to this special time of year. She mused about the sacredness of their last Christmas in Frankenthal. Then her thoughts turned to the secular. Would there be a Christmas dinner this year? Would there be, could there be, gifts, even for Sarah?

After the service, as though reading Catherine's mind, Nettie rushed up. "Catherine, we want you to spend Christmas Day with us."

"You are so kind. Will there be enough room?"

"We make room. When your family joins, it will be special."

The two days of Christmas came and went. The weather turned bitter cold and snowy. The winter seemed endless, but at least the Staudts had a roof over their heads, a house of their own. What troubled Adam more than that was that Peter's family provided their food, Christmas dinner a conspicuous reminder. "But we pay them back," he said to Catherine. "We pay them back."

Hard work was the antidote for their winter malaise. On even the coldest days, Adam was out before dawn chopping down trees and clearing out heavy undergrowth. He worked twelve-hour days. For the arduous labor of dragging and piling the felled trees, he waited for Peter to bring a horse around every week. It would be a year, he figured, before he cleared even one acre. In the spring he'd plant corn on every foot of cleared space. But first things first, he told himself as he went about filling spaces between the logs of the house with lime, clay, and mud.

After supper one or two evenings a week, Adam went fishing. Getting few bites in the partly-frozen Little Cacusi, he strolled a few miles farther to a favorite spot on the broad Tulpehocken Creek, the "Tully." He threw in his line, hoping for sunnies, catfish, perch, or bass. If he caught more than two, he kept the rest in the cool spring for another day. Tramping to the Tully one day, he spotted a huge turkey strutting close to the creek. Back home in the old country, he never even fired a shot, but now he needed a gun for hunting—and for protection against Indians! The thought brought a shiver.

Catherine and her mother and Sarah spent their days making linsey-woolsey dresses, shirts, and pants from cloth that cousin Nettie insisted they accept. Humming as she worked the spinning wheel, Sarah was proud of her newfound skill.

The hours between supper and bedtime were their only leisure time. Clara sewed and knitted, Adam and Catherine read, Sarah played jacks or solitary cards before her nightly half-hour English lessons, her parents alternating as tutors.

Halfway through March the weather softened. "Look, there's a robin redbreast," Sarah cried gleefully one morning. She was delighted to be outdoors helping to prepare the kitchen garden for planting and helping *der Daadi* clean out weeds and light brush. Soon Catherine would plant carrots, turnips, potatoes, and sweet potatoes.

In bed one night, Adam whispered, "Remember where we were a year ago?"

"How do I forget? That ocean voyage was the worst thing we ever go through. Thank God that is behind us.

Now, every day gets better, *gell?"*

Adam felt her stomach. "When do you think the little one comes?"

"*Verleicht* July or August," Catherine said. She kissed him tenderly. "I love you, Adam."

One clear, bright day in April Peter rode out to the field where Adam was erecting a snake rail fence. "Cousin Adam," Peter said, laughing, "the Cacusi neighbors who raised your house want to get rid of the winter cobwebs. It gives a stump-pulling bout at your *platz*."

"*Wunnerbaar!*" Adam said. "This is just what I need."

Early one morning two weeks later, the air rang with rowdy huzzahs accented by the clapping of hoofs as wagon-loads of stump-pullers and their womenfolk and children descended on Adam's farm. The men brought the tools allowed in the competition—picks, mattocks, shovels, froes, and crowbars. Peter teamed the men up by lot. *Allrecht, Buwe,"* he announced, "we begin." Laughing, roughhousing, the stump-pullers marched to their assigned areas.

The party broke up at twilight. Everyone agreed the frolic was even more fun-filled than the house-raising—the food plentiful, the children loud and happy, the jug empty, and the stumps cleared away and piled high ready to be burned. "I guess we showed you," Reuben Klopp bragged about his team's showing. "Better luck next time." Adam knew *he* was the real winner. He stared out at a clearing big enough to provide food for the year.

Catherine delivered her first American child in August. *Die Grossmudder* and Sarah vied for holding and spoiling baby Rebecca. Catherine wrote to her sister back home in Lampertheim to tell her the news. Restricting herself to one sheet was difficult with so much to tell, including the amazing new-world custom of farmers pitching in to clear the land and build houses and barns for their neighbors.

Another year passed and it was spring, for Adam the best season, the ancient time of hope. He borrowed a horse from Peter to plow his first field, then, like a sacred ritual, he again planted maize. Of course he needed a horse of his own, a cow or two, and a wagon and tools and a small barn or a shed. He had the money *der Daadi* gave him, but he wouldn't touch it until he had title to the land.

As the hot days of summer set in, Adam watched anxiously for the first sign of life in the field. By July, the corn was a foot high. He measured every week. "I want it maybe two feet by next week," he told his family at supper one evening, nodding. "Maybe it gives a husking bee this summer."

Catherine was in her glory, the baby now nearly a year old. "On Sunday," she told Adam, "I talk to Pastor Decker about having the little one baptized. Some do this at home, but I want it in church."

"*Ya*, and perhaps that day he answers your questions." Adam chuckled. "That will be a long talk, so Sarah takes Rebecca home after the baptism."

On a bright September Sunday morning, the Staudt family sat proudly in the first row of their log Church on the Hill, their Sunday best hidden beneath bulky coats. At a nod from Parson Decker, Adam and Catherine walked to the altar, Rebecca in her mother's arms. After a prayer, Parson Decker performed the sacred water ritual: "I baptize you Rebecca Baum Staudt, in the name of the Father, and the Son, and the Holy Ghost, Amen."

They remained standing while the congregation sang the baptismal hymn, prompted by a baritone up front who lined out:

"This child we dedicate to thee,
O God of grace and purity.
In Thy great love its life prolong,
Shield it, we pray, from sin and wrong.

Grant that with true and faithful heart
We still may act the Christian's part,
Follow the path the Master trod,
And ever do Thy will, O God."

Parson Decker rose to deliver a sermon based on the cycle of life and death. Anticipating the conversation Catherine had requested, he cut back the homily to one hour. Even so, Adam wished *he*, rather than Sarah, had taken Rebecca home.

Ever since her confirmation in Rheinstein, Catherine was tormented by her Reformed Church's belief that only those God selects can be saved. Lutherans, she believed, could reach God through faith and the Scriptures. Reason told her that good works, as the Mennonite Grosses showed them in Germantown, was part of God's purpose for man. Perhaps, she thought, she'd join the Pietists.

The church emptied and the parson and Catherine sat together in the first row. "Reverend Decker, I am bothered by predestination. Is it true Lutherans believe faith in the Scriptures is all that is needed for salvation?"

It didn't take Catherine long to realize she wouldn't get an answer from this parson. He launched into a dissertation about *Reformiert un Lutteraaner* in America, the "church Germans," and the Pietists—Mennonites, Moravians, Schwenkfelders, Amish, Dunkards and others. He told her more than she wanted to know—union-churches, churches in other settlements, the beginning of the Reformed Church in the New World when Reverend Boehm held Communion at Faulkner Swamp in 1725. He spoke of his predecessors here at the Cacusi Church—the Reverends Schlatter and Goetschi. The four-acre plot on which the log church stands was donated by George Hain, Parson Decker added. The parson finally came to an end—Catherine hoped it was an end—when he spoke of needing a larger church.

How foolish she was, Catherine mused, to expect a short answer to her troubling questions. She left disconsolate, unable to ask about two other mysteries that troubled her—the second coming of Christ, and the salvation of non-Christians. She joined her husband and her mother, determined not to show her disappointment.

The Staudt family was blessed with a third child, this one a boy. "We name him Dieter in honor of your *Daadi*," Catherine said, nodding her head, smiling broadly. Adam was overjoyed. The more boys, he mused, the more land we clear. His love for Catherine grew. He was blessed, he knew, to have a life partner so strong, so complete in her faith. Her mealtime prayers overflowed with compassion and hope.

The wife he loved knew him well. "What ails you, Adam?" she asked one evening. "I know *ebbes iss letz*."

"*Nay, des gayt guud.*"

"You do not fool me. Tell me what it is."

"*Allrecht.*" He paused. "*Ya*, everything is all right but we need things and I don't touch our *geld* till we have title to our land."

"We get along all right."

"*Ya*, but I need a horse and tools and a shed. We need a cow, chickens, pigs. I hope we have a buggy soon."

"How much do these things cost?"

"*Ich wayss net.*"

"Peter knows. And he *verleicht* knows how much the land costs. Why don't you take enough to buy what you want and keep the rest for the land?"

"*Nay, nay, nay, verdammptsi, nay!*"

"We talk later," she said and walked away.

Peter rode up one morning and greeted Adam. "*Wie gayt's heit, cousin?*"

"*So zimmlich. Un du?*"

"*Aa zimmlich.* We raise a barn for *Bauer* Dreibelbiss next Wednesday. You and the family come."

"*Ya gewiss.*"

"You need a *Scheier* for your place so you see what it takes to make a foundation. That keeps you busy in the winter, *net?* But the boys and I help."

The Staudt family, laden with *Supp, Brot, un Peies*, strolled down the road to the Dreibelbiss *Baueri*. They were pleased to give something back after the house-raising and the stump-pulling at their place. The work for the men was heavier and more intricate than previous raisings, but they got it done. For the women and children it was a *wunnerbaar Daag*. Adam marveled at the limestone foundation crafted so neatly. Was he up to doing this? he wondered.

Winter made its appearance with a vengeance—heavy snow in late December, in time for Christmas, their fifth in the New World, again bringing bittersweet memories of Christmases in the old country. Now with babies in the house, *Grischtdaag* was a special joy. They extended their celebration to the traditional second day.

On New Year's Day they walked to their Church on the Hill, celebrating with thankfulness and hope. At the end of the long day, before retiring, they held hands as Catherine offered a final prayer for the *Nei Yaahr*.

Spring came and Adam planted the new clearing. Anticipation was great as Catherine awaited the next baby. A second son arrived in June. They named him Hans.

Their joy was shattered when Peter appeared at their door one morning, pale and downcast. As they feared, Uncle Walter had died. "This is hard to bear," Peter said. He shook his head slowly and wiped away a tear. "I dread this moment from the day I leave home."

"*Ya*, we all face it. Uncle Walter lived a full life. You think of that."

That night Adam took out paper and quill.

Dear Beloved Daadi,   *June 20, 1757*
The letter from Cousin James reaches Cousin Peter today. This is a sad time for you and Uncle Walter's family, and for Peter and us in America. Hiwwe wie driwwe, *it is a time we mourn. Uncle Walter was like you. He put aside his own welfare for Peter's, as you did for me. Both of us are forever grateful and ask God's blessing on you both. I think of you every day.*
It would be disrespectful of Uncle Walter for me to

clutter up this letter with any other news. I will write again next week. But I realize that some letters are never delivered, so I will say here what you may already know — that our family now consists of Sarah, Rebecca, Dieter, and the new boy, Hans. We believe there will be more.

Please convey our prayers to Daniel and Leah and their families.

To you, dear **Daadi**, *deep and eternal love,*
Your loving son,
Adam

The following year a dark cloud hung over the Staudts — Catherine's new baby girl was stillborn. Catherine needed her mother's embrace many times in the perilous lives they lived since they left the homeland, but never more than now. It was many months before she wrote her sister.

But there was good news as well. Sarah and Henry Eckert had been courting. Adam and Catherine took their time learning about him — that he was a Christian, was not lazy, and was not a *Gsoffner*. Friends and neighbors were invited to the house for the wedding, a bountiful roast beef dinner, and then a dance in Cousin Peter's big barn. Long after midnight, the bride and groom mounted their horse and left on their honeymoon.

For Henry's brother and a mischievous friend, the best fun, far better than dancing, was yet to come when the newly-weds returned home. Discovering where they'd be living, they organized a surprise reception. Sneaking up quietly one night, a couple dozen friends and neighbors gathered outside the couple's place and at exactly 10 o'clock let loose a mighty din — drums, tin pans, whistles, the strident zing of a *Bassgeig*, and racy huzzahs. They continued their raucous serenade until the embarrassed bride and groom gave in and showed their faces at the window.

Life continued hard as the years went by. Adam cleared five more acres, enough to provide crops for selling or bartering for tools, animals, and household needs. Every night after supper he looked out with pride over rich fields of corn, wheat, and rye. Life was hard, but it was good. His next priority—a barn to replace the overflowing shed.

Catherine's days too were long. Often she reflected on Adam's *Daadi's* advice to take *die Mudder* with them to America. In her grief, Catherine had counted on her mother more than ever. Clara insisted Catherine and Adam go to church every Sunday while she stayed home with the little ones.

On calm evenings the Staudts went "neighboring," mostly to the Lamms on the next farm. Neither they nor the Staudts knew of this in the old country, where farmers worked their strips outside town but lived in the town and socialized with their neighbors. Here in the wilderness, it was a *wunnerbaar* custom, they thought. The children played games before the *Feierblatz*, the womenfolk chatted and gossiped, the men talked of crops and politics. Then it was time for a treat—gingerbread and cider. As they left for home, *Fraa* Lamm said, "Next time you come, you stay overnight."

"*Danke, owwer* you come to us next," Catherine said. On their way home Adam wondered about sleeping arrangements for such an invitation. "Hettie told me," Catherine said, "everyone sleeps on bedding on the floor, the host husband and wife take the center, the others arrange themselves right and left."

"*Ich wayss net*," Adam said. "We think about it."

Neighbor women socialized and gossiped at one other place—quilting bees. Catherine and her mother accepted every invitation, knowing it would soon be their turn to be hosts and end up with another warm, beautiful bed cover. Clara was proud of the neat stitching she became known for and of the profusion of flowers the quilters enjoyed so much.

Adam's main diversion was reading. On his trips to Philadelphia to deliver fruits and vegetables to market, Peter sometimes went to the Pine Street Bookstore to browse and purchase a new book or two from Europe. He shared them with Adam, and they split the cost. On the last trip Peter splurged and brought home *The History of the Five Indian*

Nations, *The Book of Martyrs*, and *Hamlet*.

"*Ich hab un* idea," Peter told Adam. "Why don't we help each other load up our wagons then take turns going to market in Philadelphia. Then we both get to the bookstores. You look for Benjamin Franklin's Free Library."

The nightly ritual of English lessons for the children continued. One lesson referred to Indians. Dieter asked, "Did Indians live here?"

Adam whispered to Catherine, "I take the boys out to Conrad Weiser's *platz*. They will like that. I ask Peter to go with. And maybe Rebecca to take care of little Hans."

That evening Adam rode over to Peter's. "*Ya*, I go with," Peter said. "I have not seen Weiser since we come down from Schoharie together thirty years ago. It wonders me if he remembers." He waited. "*Ya*, the Weiser family had a sad time when they landed in New York Harbor. Two of young Conrad's brothers were taken off the ship and sold. I don't believe he sees them since."

"*Des iss leedmiedich.* Weiser works with the Indians, *gell?*" Adam said.

"*Ya, ganz recht. Un* he helps the Penns lay out Reading Town, and he helps found Berks County."

Two days later the cousins and Adam and the boys rode a few miles west to the Weiser farm. "When you spot the eagle's peak on South Mountain, we are there," Peter said. As they approached the house, they saw Weiser strolling toward them.

"*Herr* Weiser, do you remember me? *Ich bin* Peter Staudt."

"*Ya, ya*, I remember. We go through hard times together up in the Schoharie Valley, *ya?* I know where your *Baueri* is."

"*Guud.*" Pointing to Adam, Peter said. "And this *Mann*. Do you remember him?"

"He looks familiar."

"*Ich bin* Peter's Cousin Adam. We stay in your house in Reading Town ten years ago, before it gets finished."

"*Ya, ya*, I remember. Widow Finney's *Haus* and my place were the only two." He laughed. "Now it gives more than eight hundred. I work with lot owners."

"*Herr* Weiser, this is my daughter Rebecca and my boys Dieter and Hans. They want to know about Indians."

"*Guud.* Come, we sit under this oak and talk."

The Staudts were intrigued to hear that Weiser had lived with the Mohawks when he was young and learned Indian languages and customs. "Indians are good people," he said, "honest and brave"

"But our people are deathly afraid of them," Peter said. "Why do they scalp their enemies?"

"In wars with other Indian nations they take scalps home to prove their bravery."

Dieter tugged on Rebecca's sleeve and whispered into her ear. "He wants to know why they don't like us."

"They are too little to understand, but maybe you can explain it to them. It was their land and Shikellamy and me work out a treaty between them and the governor. The white men promise not to settle north of the mountains, but they break their promise and the Indians become angry."

Another tug on his sleeve. "He wants to know," Rebecca said, "whether the children have horses and do they shoot arrows."

Weiser motioned for the boys to sit beside him. He put his arms around them and related simple stories about Indian boys learning to ride and shoot. They were fascinated.

"I hear at the tavern one night," Adam said, "that white men broke another promise. Something about a walking agreement."

"*Ya*, that was not right. The Indians accepted the white man's goods in exchange for as much land as a man could walk in a day and a half. Then, instead of walking, the white man ran."

"They burn housed to, *gell?*" Rebecca said.

"*Ya*, when white men settle near the Indians' land north of here, they kill them and burn their houses. Here in Tulpehocken they kill only a few. But people in Reading say they sometimes see the smoke of houses burning out here."

"One night in the tavern," Peter said, "a stranger tells us he meets up with troops from Virginia going west."

"*Ya*, that was the start of the war between the English on one side and the French and the Indians on the other. A few years before, I speak for the Pennsylvania colony in a treaty with Miami Indians that go west to the Ohio Valley. They promise to sell furs to our traders rather than to the French. So the French get ready for war and build forts. Major Washington goes out with 400 Virginia troops. He is forced to surrender. He goes out again, this time as a colonel with British General Braddock and an army of 2,500. The French ambush them, and kill the general and a thousand troops." Weiser chuckled. "They say Washington had two horses shot out from under him."

Dieter's eyes got big as saucers.

"The fighting went on for years, *net*?" Adam said.

"*Ya*, back and forth. Some Indians desert the French. The war ends in Quebec when General Montcalm surrenders."

"The Seven Years War, *net*?" Adam said.

"*Ya*, the same enemies, England and France, but they fight in Europe and India."

"We go now. The little ones are restless and we take too much of your time," Peter said. "*Danke vielmols.*"

"*Danke schay*," Adam said, "for answering the boys' questions. They never forget this day."

"*Gaern shayni*," *Herr* Weiser said. "*Kumm widder*," he said as he shook hands, saving Dieter for last.

Catherine was outside waiting. She hugged her boys. "Did you have a good time?"

Adam smiled as he watched. "The best day in my whole life!" Dieter said, his eyes wide.

That night in bed Adam said, "Dieter wasn't the only one excited to visit Weiser. He is a big man in the colonies. *Un er iss en Deitscher!*"

"Meeting him in Reading before it gave a town was a good omen," Catherine said. "We are so blessed. Good night, *Liebschdi*."

Socializing for men of the settlement picked up when Amos Kurtz put the finishing touches on his tavern on the south side of Tulpehocken Road. Cousins Adam and Peter were among the first to visit and sample the rum. The tavern became the haven for farmers and tradesmen to relax, drink a bit, do a little gambling, and pick up news and rumors. News came slowly, sometimes by post riders, sometimes by travelers who stayed at the tavern, sometimes by letters shared, at times from the *Germantowner Zeitung* or the *Pennsylvania Gazette*, both newspapers Peter picked up in Philadelphia.

Thursday nights, when Minnie, the owner's comely and buxom daughter, was on duty behind the bar, became the big night in the tavern. When Adam and Peter got there, the bar room was already crowded. Loudmouth Bully Lenhardt, fat as a tub, front tooth missing, was in his usual form, downing one whiskey after another, shouting down others.

"I don't care if they were here first," Bully was saying. "I don't like those goddamned red men with their tomahawks. They are savages."

Harvey Gaul took a gambit to calm Lenhardt down. "Talking about Indians, I wish Weiser comes to the tavern. He knows more than anyone."

"I don't care what Weiser says," Bully continued, "I know them bastards rape and scalp farm women north of here — a Moyer family, three members of Jacob Hochstettler's family killed and three others taken captive. And right here in Tulpehocken the daughter of Balser Schmidt was taken prisoner."

"*Ya, un* also up north near Bethel Indians scalp Ann and Michael Cleaver and Lawrence Dieppel and his wife, and take two young children," Sam Fidler said.

"*Ya*," Joe Stiely said, "and Regina and Barbara Hartman near Fort Henry. They say Barbara escaped and Regina returned to her mother after the French and Indian War. The story goes that when her mother sang the first line of a song — *Allein und doch nicht gabz alleine* — Regina quickly sang the second line."

"I hear it gives more than a hundred killed by Indians in the county," George Riegel said.

"Weiser is a colonel," Gaul said. "He orders his troops to protect us when we are reaping."

Adam spoke up. "We meet Weiser when we first come, and in June we take the children to Womelsdorf to talk with him."

"Get out!" Bully said. "Where did you meet him?"

"In Reading Town. We stay overnight in the inn he was building. He seems like a good man."

"A man who likes Indians a good man? Are you *verrickt*?"

"They say up in Schoharie," John Lamm said, "Weiser left home to live with a Mohawk chief and learn their language."

"He is one of the big men in the colony," Leroy Gerhart said, "not only with Indians but he is a justice of the peace and judge too."

"I don't know if he is around right now," Gerhart said. "He often goes off to negotiate treaties."

"*Ya*, or *verleicht* he is in Ephrata. I hear he entered *Herr* Biessel's *Kloster* there on the Cocalico Creek," Gerhart said.

"I like to hear more about those Dunkers," Adam said. "Catherine said she heard it gives an order of sisters there too, something about the Roses of Sharon."

A few of the regulars were there to drink, not talk. But among the talkers, voices grew louder as the debates and the smoke became thicker.

Horse hoofs outside signaled the arrival of a traveling family. After they were given a room, the man of the family came into the barroom. The men greeted him with a silent nod. Finally Bully spoke up. "*Bischt du Deitsch?*"

"*Ya gewiss.* My name is Noecker."

"Where do you come from?"

"From the western territory. We thought we'd try it out there but the wife and children are afraid of the Indians."

"Ah ha!" Bully shouted. "What did I tell you?"

"Do you figure on settling here in Tulpehocken?"

Peter asked.

"*Ya verdolltsei.* We hear land is cheap. In Ohio Territory trouble comes between the English and the French. On the way here we see troops marching west."

"*Ya,*" Peter said, "Weiser tells us Washington goes out to reinforce a British post at the place where two big rivers come together." He took a last draft of his rum. "*Ya well, ich bin mied.* I go home. *Mach's guud, Buwe.*" Adam and a few others also left.

Clara and the children were in bed when Adam got home. Catherine always waited up. "Well, what does it give at the tavern?" she asked.

"Bully Lenhardt hates Indians. I tell him we don't survive without their maize. We had visitors tonight. A Palatine family comes back from out west because they are afraid of Indians. It gives war between the English and the French over the Ohio Territory. The Indians fight for the French."

"I hope they don't fight here in the settlement."

No reason to upset her with the stories he heard, Adam thought. "No, it gives stories of Indians killing settlers and burning their homes at the foot of the mountains north of here. But the fighting is not here. Let's go to bed. I start an hour early tomorrow."

SEVEN

YEARS SLIPPED BY LIKE SNOWFLAKES VANISHING in the Litle Cacusi Creek. The Staudt's small log house barely held *Grossmudder* and Catherine and Adam and the American-born children — Rebecca, Dieter, Hans, and now Tillie, Ruth, and Rachael. Sarah, the oldest child, too was doing well, and everyone eagerly looked forward to Wednesdays, when she and her little girls came visiting.

Half-teasing, Catherine said to Adam one evening, "The animals in the barn have more room and live better than we do."

"Well, *so gayt's*," Adam replied. "The lean-to I built is *allrecht* for the girls, *net* ?"

"*Ya, awwer* not in winter." Catherine paused. "Soon it gives a big new church, and also some big new houses, I hear. When is our turn?"

Adam glared at her. "*Dunnerwedder*," he said. "I hate debt more than I hate the devil. If I tell you once I tell you a hundred times — when I am ready!"

Adam reproached himself about not sharing his plan with Catherine, but he was determined not to build a bigger house until he owned the land. After thirteen years in the New World, they had more than they'd dreamed possible — an ox, two horses, cows, pigs, chickens, a barn and storage building, a fruit orchard, furniture, books, nice clothes, and plenty to eat. And they had a buggy that doubled as a wagon for carrying fruits and vegetables to market and as a carriage for going to church, visiting neighbors, riding into Reading Town to buy flower seed, pots and pans and things needed by the *Weibsleit* – all made possible, Adam reflected, by abundant crops, especially wheat, from the good earth.

As their faith required, Sundays were days of rest for the Staudts. For Adam and the boys there was no planting, plowing, reaping, or weeding. Taking care of the animals was their only chore. For Catherine, Clara, and the girls, there was no spinning, sewing, knitting, or tending the kitchen garden. Their only task was serving three meals. Because there was time, a more leisurely Sunday breakfast was the rule. Eggs and pancakes were treats the children loved, sharing three trenchers.

Adam and Catherine alternated saying grace at meals. His was always the same, "Dear Lord, bless this food and bless us all. For Jesus' sake, Amen." Catherine's were varied and longer, especially on Sunday mornings.

Through all their trials and hardships, Adam and Catherine cherished their intimacy. If they were too tired on weeknights for anything but sleep, they were never too tired on Saturday and Sunday nights.

They seldom argued. But Catherine became annoyed by Adam's demand that meals be served at the same precise time every day, Sunday an exception. On workdays he trudged in from the fields and plopped down at the table for dinner at exactly noon.

"Adam," she said one evening, "how do you tell time out in the field?"

He laughed. "My stomach tells me."

"Would your stomach mind if I feed it ten minutes late?"

"You make fun. Now stop it."

Having provoked the quarrel, she determined to continue. "I hear the *Weibsleit* talk about maybe it gives a bell in the new church to call the farmers in for dinner."

"I don't need it and I don't want it," he snarled.

"*Enncihau*, I don't think it makes nothing out when

we eat," she said. "Ben Franklin says in his Almanac the less we eat the healthier we are."

"He thinks he knows everything. He takes capital letters away from our nouns. And I never forgive him for saying we try to Germanize the people." Dieter stopped and shook his head vigorously. "*Ennichau*, I am a stubborn German. I never change my mind—about capital letters or when I eat."

"*Ya, ich wayss, ich wayss.*" Catherine smiled, walked to him and gave him a peck on the check. "Promise me, *Liebschdi*, if you ever figure this out, you let me know."

After breakfast, Adam and Catherine and the family marched up the steep path to their little church. Greeting and chatting with friends, hoping for news, they sat at their usual place. Dieter looked around anxiously for his friend Michael Ege: the family had missed the last two Sundays. Then he saw them walking proudly to their place in the front row. People in the congregation stopped their chatting and stared at the well-dressed family who lived in the mansion at Charming Forge.

Adam learned that George Ege acquired the forge on the Tulpehocken Creek through his uncle, the well-known Henry Stiegel, when it was known as *der Tulpehocken Eisehammer*. Stiegel had come to America from Cologne to manage the iron furnace of *Herr* Huber in Lancaster County. In addition to the forge, Stiegel owned Elizabeth Furnace at Brickerville and a glass factory in Manheim, a town he founded, and large houses in Mannheim and Philadelphia. "Baron" Stiegel fell deeply into debt and his properties were mortgaged.

Ege moved his family into the large mansion. Eight miles west of the church, the mansion was remote and the Ege sons lacked companions. Noticing how well Michael and Dieter got along, Anna Marie Ege asked Catherine what she thought of having Dieter visit Charming Forge every week or two.

Two weeks later the handsome Ege carriage, driven by a black slave, caught everyone's eye as it sped along Tulpehocken Road on its way to pick up Dieter. Anna Marie Ege was right: their oldest son and Dieter, both bright, developed a close relationship. The Eges became fond of Dieter.

On Catherine's mind these days was the church under construction on the crest of a hill a half-mile north of Tulpehocken Road, just twenty yards from the log church. Catherine was the only woman invited to meetings in the Kershner house to plan for the new church and its ministry. Glares and occasional gibes from deacons and elders kept her in her place, but the head of the consistory valued her involvement. With his support, she felt comfortable attending.

Built of limestone, the new church edifice would be forty feet by fifty feet, thirty feet to the eaves. The three-foot walls were already in place. Above the entrance on the east end would stand a tower seventeen feet high, topped by a weathervane shaped like a rooster, crest of the Hain family. The pews would be crafted of walnut, enhanced on the ends by ornamental wood carvings. Members would be especially proud of the pulpit, a wine glass resting on a single column, and nine carved wall panels depicting Bible scenes. Allegiance of the members would be spelled out in an inscription on the east wall above the door: "All who go in and out here shall be loyal to God and the King."

The church structure wasn't all that would be new. The consistory brought in a new parson, Reverend John Waldschmidt, to replace Reverend Decker.

"*Ya, die Karich iss schay,*" Adam said. He smiled broadly. "Preacher Waldschmidt likes the pulpit so much he preaches a half-hour longer."

Catherine had become influential behind the scene in the church. As a woman, she could not be a deacon or participate in services, not even be a church member. But she was there early every Sunday, greeting members, taking care of the young children as she did in her house every Wednesday, preparing the elements for communion, helping Parson Waldschmidt as he wished.

At spelling bees and neighborings, she watched her turn to bring the conversation around to the new church, subtly urging the women to have their husbands contribute generously. "People had to stand again last Sunday in the old church," was a line she used. Her own Adam got the message. "*Ya*, we must be generous for God's blessing in the new world," she said, smiling.

Fall 1766, and the Hains *Karichleit* were excited. Their new Church on the Hill was finished and ready to be dedicated.

Dedication Sunday dawned beautiful. Hundreds of townspeople from Reading, Lebanon, Saucony and other settlements, even Pietist groups from Bethlehem and Lancaster, came in their carriages to see the new edifice. As they entered they noticed above the door the inscription pledging loyalty to God and the king.

Grossmudder Christman and the eight Staudts—Adam, Catherine, Rebecca, Dieter, Hans, Tilly, Ruth, even baby Rachael—filled a pew of their own. Behind them were Sarah and Henry and their children. The front pew was left open for the family everyone knew was the church's biggest benefactor, the Ege family. Heads turned as they entered, Anna Marie elegant in satin, Michael and the other children in new clothes. Michael gave a quick wave to Dieter as they passed. Conversation buzzed through the pews when members spotted eccentric, handsomely-dressed Baron Stiegel.

The service dragged on for three hours, each visiting clergyman having his say. The babies and young children were long since taken home. Finally came the beloved benediction, slowly, emotionally pronounced by Parson Waldschmidt. "May the Lord bless you and keep you . . . . May the Lord make his face to shine upon you and be gracious unto you . . . . May the Lord lift up his countenance upon you and give you peace."

Adam and Peter looked forward to Thursday nights when the farmers gathered at Kurtz Tavern. After a rum or two at the bar, they moseyed to barroom tables. "I see you plant wheat in your new field, *net*?" George Reber said to Adam.

"*Ya, ya.* I hope it works good," Adam said.

"They talk in Lancaster about forty or fifty bushels an acre." Reber chuckled. "But maybe they lie."

"I hope your new wheat don't get sick," Rolf Ludwig said. "They say it comes when trees make too much shade on the field."

"Did you wash your seed first?" Samuel Fiddler asked. "Some say if you don't it gives an ugly weed."

"*Ya* and you heard of blast, *net?*" Joseph Hain said. "I had it once. It comes from lightning."

"*Nay, nay,*" Reber said. "It comes when the moon is not right for planting."

Peter had his pipe in his mouth, a smile on his face. "One thing sure," he said. "Wheat is our best crop for market." Turning to Adam he said, "You have wheat and corn and oats but you want rye too. It's good for straw for thatching roofs, tying fodder, and baskets. When you clear more land you put it in."

"*Ya,* and it is good for one more thing—to drink," Joe Zerbe said, licking his lips.

"It wonders me what news it gives in the other colonies," Sam Fidler said. "Peter, did you pick up Franklin's *Gazette* in Philadelphia this week?"

"*Ya,* here it is," Sam said. "I hear Franklin hates Germans."

"You have right, Sam," Werner said. "He says we get our V's and W's mixed up. *Ennichau,* he has a good paper."

"*Ya,*" Peter said, "you can read the *Germantowner Zeitung* in German, but Christopher Sauer favors the British. "*Ennichau,* about the news. The *Gazette* says Massachusetts and the northern colonies are upset by the Sugar Tax. Sam Adams says if we pay taxes without anyone representing us in Parliament we are slaves."

"*Recht.* I think this tax comes because the British spend so much on the war against France," John Lamm said.

The noisy arrival of Bully Lenhardt and his gang interrupted the talk. As soon as he heard the subject, Bully jumped right in, "The Stamp Act is the worst yet."

"Is anything in the paper about it, Peter?" Reber

asked.

"*Ya*," Peter said, "these stamps must be pasted on legal papers, newspapers, even sermons, playing cards, and dice."

"I hear the British expect to raise 60,000 pounds from it," Lamm said.

"*Ya* and do you know what they use it for?" Bully said. "To support them damn lobsterbacks in Boston."

"The *Gazette* has articles pleading with everyone — farmers, Sons of Liberty, merchants, shopkeepers — to force the stamp masters to resign," Peter said.

"*Ya*, and if we keep it up *verleicht* those bastards in London will repeal it. I do my part," Bully said.

EIGHT

THE YEARS FOLLOWING THE DEDICATION OF THE new church were busy and happy ones for the *Karichleit* of Hain's Church. Membership grew steadily. The men got togther on Saturdays to clear land behind the sanctuary for parking buggies and for socializing after services when the weather was suitable. There was talk of a grove in the future for summer picnics and frolics.

Tables filled with fruit and pies surprised the parishioners one warm spring day after services. Dieter and Michael found a spot to sit. "Baron Stiegel tutors you for college, *gell*?" Dieter asked.

"*Ya*, I go next month but I'll miss you."

Inside the church George Ege caught Adam at the door. "I want to speak with you about an idea Anna Marie and I have." He paused. "Michael begins his studies at the College of New Jersey at Prince Town soon. He and Dieter are close friends. We want to send them both."

"You mean Dieter rides over there with Michael and you."

"*Nay*, we enroll them both as students."

His eyebrows arched, Adam turned, his face flushed. He took a few steps toward the door and stopped abruptly. "We... we don't do this." He shook his head vehemently. "I need Dieter for the harvest."

"But *we* pay. If you want to pay it back, all right."

"*Nay, nay.* We don't do this. *Danke,* but we don't do this." Adam walked to the clearing to find Catherine.

She was behind the table, serving cider. "Adam, what is it? Your face is all red."

"We go home."

She had seldom seen her husband upset. "I first get someone to take my place," she said. He stomped through the clearing and waited at the edge of the woods.

On the ride home, he was silent. At home, the horse and carriage in the barn, he said gruffly, "We go to the orchard and talk."

She knew what was coming. "Whatever is on your mind, Adam, we don't want to spoil this *schayni Daag.*"

"You know what Ege said, *net*? Don't lie."

"Lower your voice." She waited. "Did I ever lie to you?"

"You know what goes on, *net*?"

"Anna Maria hinted George talks to you."

"Is that all you have to say about this terrible thing?"

"You think it is terrible for someone to be kind to our son? I am *iwwerfalle!*"

"And I am surprised at you. You want Dieter out in another colony when we need him here to work?"

"Oh Adam. It gives a future for him in this new world if he is educated." She started to walk away but stopped abruptly. "Do you forget who our first son is named for? Do you forget how your dear *Daadi* sacrificed for you?" Tears steaming down her face, she dashed into the house.

On Thursday night Adam had more rum than usual at the tavern. Catherine was waiting when he returned. "Adam, in two weeks Michael Ege leaves for college. Did you speak to *Herr* Ege about Dieter?"

"He knows how I feel."

"But does he know how *I* feel?"

"You think because *verleicht* I had too much rum you can win me over, *gell?*"

"In all our years together, I make no requests of

you. Now I do. I want you to accept Ege's kind offer." She paused. "If you need extra hands in the harvest, the girls and I help."

"*Ya*, that part is all right. But how do we repay? I must keep *geld* for the patent."

"Ege is a good man. He will never press. Adam, we have a special son."

"I am sleepy. I let you know tomorrow."

The freeze lasted a week. On Saturday evening Adam broke the ice after supper. "I think about our boys. Dieter works like a man."

"*Ya*, he is a good worker."

"*Awwer* why can't Hans do his share? We have our hands full with that one, *ich denk*."

"Now Adam, don't be too hard on him. He is *mei Mudder's* pet, *wayscht*. You told me once you are opposite of your brother Jacob."

"*Ya*, I picture you trying to get Jacob to church." He paused and sighed. "Yesterday Dieter and I clear brambles in the orchard. I tell Hans to pull out weeds along the fence." Adam shook his head. "He sits down to do it and quits in five minutes."

But Dieter! Adam and Catherine were keenly aware early that their son was exceptionally bright. He began walking and talking much earlier than Sarah. His curiosity around the house, and especially outside, astounded them.

Catherine walked over to Adam and put a hand on his shoulder. "It's early but I missed you this week. Let's go to bed."

———

Two weeks later, early on a Monday morning, Adam, Catherine, and Dieter waited outside the house. They heard horse hoofs and saw the handsome Ege carriage, George seated beside James, the black driver. Adam and Catherine said goodbye to Dieter. His eyes down, holding back, Adam said nothing. Catherine hugged her son. "*Liewer* Dieter, this is God's will. God go with you."

His eyes moist, Adam extended his hand. Smiling

confidently, Dieter took it firmly, kissed his mother, turned and walked to the carriage.

As Adam and Catherine lumbered back to the house, the three oldest girls ran to them. *Grossmudder* Christman waited in the doorway.

The carriage began its journey east on the Tulpehocken Road, safely fording the Schuylkill in Reading. The road to Philadelphia a thin ribbon in an endless forest, Dieter and Michael saw nothing but huge trees. Anxious about starting college, they had plenty to talk about.

Herr Ege's plan was to stay overnight in Philadelphia in the City Tavern. Ferries there and at Trenton carried passengers and carriages across the Delaware River, but Ege was uncertain about an inland road to Prince Town. He would inquire at the Tavern. If necessary, he would rent three riding horses, keep his horse and carriage at the livery stable, and have the boys' trunks delivered the next day.

It was dark when they arrived at City Tavern. The liveryman said the inland road to Prince Town was very narrow. He recommended traveling north and crossing the Delaware at Trenton. There was a livery stable in Trenton, he said.

Michael had traveled with his father on business trips and visited City Tavern before. The farthest Dieter had ever been from home was to Bethlehem to attend a concert with his parents. In the tavern he was fascinated by ornately dressed couples having dinner, the men with powdered wigs, silk hose with garters, pumps with large silver buckles. The ladies were resplendent in silks and satins, wide skirts, and towering hairdos. Adam had never seen such splendor. He heard string music wafting in from another room. Haydn, he thought. He was nearly beside himself with excitement.

"*Herr* Ege, that was the most delicious meal I ever ate," he said after he finished dessert. "*Danke vielmols.* And the wine. Do you call it Madeira?"

"*Ya.* I am glad you like it."

It was time for bed. When Dieter's head hit the pillow, the excitement was too much; he was wide awake. Am I really in the famous city of Philadelphia? he asked himself.

The next morning, after a full breakfast the Ege party started out for Prince Town. The liveryman's description was accurate, the road so narrow at places everyone but the driver got off the carriage to avoid being struck by branches. After two hours, Ege said, "All right, *Buwe,* be on the lookout for Nassau Hall. It's the largest building in the colonies. Your new home."

And what a home, Dieter thought at his first glimpse—three stories high, Georgian architecture. They were assigned rooms and James brought in their trunks. After *Herr* Ege and James left for home, the boys settled in then explored the building. They walked into recitation halls and the chapel. When they entered the library, Dieter's eyes grew wide. "There must be thousands of books," he said breathlessly, reverently, "and all on open stacks." He picked out a few and paged through them. Some, he noted, were new, written on contemporary affairs.

Michael and Dieter soon learned the routine. Dressed in their caps and gowns, they attended lectures and chapel and spent the nights studying in their rooms, forbidden to leave for more than ten minutes at a time. They recited in geography, mathematics, and history every day and composed and memorized an oration every week. Fortunately, Dieter mused, students chose their own subjects, and current subjects were encouraged. Lectures they heard were on Latin and English exercises; decimal arithmetic, algebra, fractions; and Homer, Pindar, Cicero, Euripides. Private-hour study readings Dieter especially enjoyed were *The Spectator, The Rambler,* and John Locke's *Essay Concerning Human Understanding.*

George Ege had warned his son he and Dieter might be the only Germans in the college. He chuckled. "You make names for yourselves because of the funny way we talk."

Dieter and Michael met every day for meals. Of the two clubs on campus, they decided on the American Whig Society over the Clios for debating and socializing. Among the Whig members was one who stood out for his brilliant arguments. He seemed like everybody's younger baby-faced brother. "He's small and skinny and has the hands of a girl," Michael said to Dieter.

Aaron Burr was thirteen when he was admitted as a sophomore. "I feel sorry for him," Michael said. "Everyone shuns him. His only friend seems to be Jemmy Madison, but he's a senior."

"That is not right," Dieter said. "We make friends with this little Burr."

Dieter and Michael had fun with Aaron, teasing him at times by talking in Palatine German. They learned he was born in Newark and his parents died before he was three. His parents had been eminent, his father a former president of this college, and his mother the daughter of New England theologian Jonathan Edwards. Aaron was fun to be with, occasionally caught up in boyish pranks. Although Aaron denied it, Dieter and Michael believed he was involved in the stunt of parading prostitutes across the campus to shock the faculty. He talked often about girls.

Dieter wrote a letter home after he was set in his study routine. His parents were pleased that he wrote in English. He described his studies, his professors, the Whig Club, and their new friend Aaron.

"Adam, this is *wunnerbaar*. Our son is *uffgschafft* about college. *Un* he lifts my heart when he offers to teach English to my Wednesday church children in the summer."

"*Ya*, you had right about allowing him to go."

"*Ich saage Dank, Liebschdi*," Catherine said, smiling.

———

Early in May, *Herr* Ege sent James to Prince Town to bring the boys home for the summer. The Staudt girls came running when they saw the carriage. Dieter hugged them all.

For homecoming supper, Catherine prepared *Schnitz un Gnepp*, Dieter's favorite. So much to talk about, it was late before they went to bed.

The next morning, Dieter was up early, ready for work. "Where is Hans?" Dieter asked.

"He gets home late. He is still in bed," Adam said.

"He does not work well for you, *gell?*"

"I don't understand him." Adam shook his head. "One day last week he left after supper and didn't come home till the next morning. *Die Grossmudder iss umgerennt.*"

"*Ya*, we are brothers, but he doesn't like me." Dieter paused. "Maybe I drop out of college to help you on the farm."

"Nay, nay. We don't do that. If he don't work, I hire a man. Come, we eat breakfast."

"*Yawohl.*" Dieter chuckled. "We don't have breakfasts like this at Prince Town." He waited. "In one letter, *Daadi*, you tell me about the Kurtz Tavern. May I go with?"

"*Ya gewiss.* We go Thursday night."

Cousin Peter and *Bauere* Reber, Ludwig, Riegel, Stiely, Lamm, Zerbe and Kintzer were at their tables when Adam and Dieter arrived. In a rite of passage, Adam ordered rum for his son. Minnie threw Dieter a big wink when she plopped his mug on the bar.

"I think you have seen my son Dieter before," Adam said. "He likes politics, so I bring him."

After the usual preliminaries about crops and planting, Joseph Zerbe said, "It wonders me about the letters from this Pennsylvania farmer named Dickinson. Is he a real *Bauer*?"

"Henry Ludwig piped up. "He is a lawyer, not a farmer, if you ask me."

"*Verleicht, awwer* his letters are printed in every colony," Zerbe said.

"I bet he never gets *mischt* on *his* shoes," Ludwig said, guffawing.

"We wait for Bully Lenhardt. He tells us what to think," Zerbe said with a big smile.

Dieter read the Dickinson letters at college and looked forward to the discussion.

"I read a few of them," Paul Stiely said. "Dickinson says England depends on us for trade. I like when he says the cause of one colony is the cause of all."

"I read letter eight," Joseph Lamm said. "He says something I never think of. Why do we have to pay to defend England's colonies like Florida, Canada, and Nova Scotia?"

"*Ya, du bischt recht*," Riegel said.

Bully entered the tavern with a flourish. "*Was*

gebt's?"

"We talk about John Dickinson," Peter said.

Bully put his lips together and emitted a loud whish. *"Seller Mann* is not *en Bauer. Un* he is from Delaware, not Pennsylvania."

"Have you read the letters?" Werner asked.

"Ya, all ten."

Dieter smiled. He knew there were fourteen.

"You better watch him. He speaks out of both sides of his mouth." Bully snickered as he said, "He calls George the Third 'our most excellent prince.' He says we should behave like dutiful children. Wait till I get another drink and I answer more questions."

Riegel changed the subject. "I guess you men saw the "Boston Port Bill" notice outside when you came in. I went to a meeting of freeholders in Reading last week."

"Guud, guud," Werner said. "What happened?"

"Lawyer Biddle runs a good meeting. He was speaker of the Assembly, *wayscht. Ennichau,* we ended up with a motion to support the people of Boston. A committee of Dr. Potts, Mark Bird, and Christopher Witman was appointed to write to other counties."

At the bar Bully listened carefully. He returned to the discussion. "I bet they said they were loyal to the King."

"Ya, but it doesn't mean anything," Riegel said.

"Doesn't mean anything to say you are loyal to the king? Get out."

Always the calm voice, Lamm said, "I'm glad these Reading men are active. I hear there gives a Provincial Convention at Carpenters Hall in Philadelphia. *Verleicht* it soon gives a convention of all the colonies."

"Ya," Dieter said, *"ganz guud. "*

"Awwer, I get sleepy," Adam said. "Come, *Sohn,* we go home to *Mamm."*

NINE

YEARS SLIPPED BY, YEARS OF FULFILLMENT FOR Adam. He finally expunged two hobgoblins buzzing around his head. To get title to his land, he rode to the courthouse in Lancaster. The Pennsylvania Population Company sent out a surveyor, and two months later he returned to Lancaster, made settlement, and rode home at a lively pace with the title in his saddle bag, proud, elated, a freeman. And eligible to vote!

He faced up to his second bogy, building a second log house large enough for his big family. He asked Peter, "Will the Cacusi neighbors raise one more house for me, *denkscht*?"

Three weeks later the neighbors—*Mannsleit, Weibsleit, un Kinner*—were there in force. The wonderful day of festivities and abundance of food that went with the hard work were talked about as the best ever.

Catherine was overjoyed. The new two-story log house gave more elbow room for cooking and spinning and for having the family together in the evenings. With a second floor, the children gave up their small lean-to sleeping quarters. Catherine was shocked when they said they wanted to continue sleeping where they were. As manager of the household, she decided who would sleep where--the two youngest girls upstairs in the new house, the two oldest in the first house, the boys in the lean-to.

Catherine's other joy was the Wednesday Bible class she started for neighborhood children. Careful not to interfere with the school at the church, she conducted her class from 4 to 5 o'clock. What began with three children plus her own grew to eleven. Sarah, who brought her children with her every week, was her mother's assistant. They could hardly wait for Dieter to return from college for the summer to add spark to the class by translating German words from the lessons into English.

"How is your English, Sis?" Dieter would ask.

"*Net zu guud,*" Sarah would reply, laughing.

"No, no, Sis. English, English," he said, chuckling.

After the new church was built, Catherine and a few neighbors pestered their men to stop clearing land and build a school instead. Two years later a log schoolhouse proudly welcomed pupils for five months each winter for instruction in reading, writing, arithmetic, spelling, and singing. Peter Bartram, the teacher, lived in a part of the school partitioned off for him. On some Sundays he substituted in the pulpit for Parson Waldschmidt. All instruction in school was in German. Even the modest price of several cents a day for each pupil was a burden, but the Staudts sent their girls.

Grossmudder Christman was doing well. At 75 she seemed ageless — always smiling, always positive. Her daily routine was making breakfast and helping with the meals, tending to the youngest children, sewing and knitting, working in the garden. Never a burden, always a help. "My legs don't always make" was her only complaint.

Rebecca, the first-born American child, was a joy to have around. Twenty-one, she was hoping to get married soon. She was pretty enough and pleasant enough but had not yet hooked up with the right boy. Other girls too discovered there was a shortage of young men ready to marry because they were unable to leave home and start their own farms. Meanwhile, while she waited, life with her sisters — Tillie, Ruth, and Rachael — was anything but boring.

From early childhood Rachael was sickly with a

chronic cough. Her parents tried home remedies and herbs and Indian remedies they heard of. Sarah urged them to take her to a *Braucher*.

"*Nay*," Catherine said, "we don't do that. Powwowing ain't Christian. We take her to Reading Town. Hettie Lamm says it gives a good doctor on Penn Square by the name of Bodo Otto."

The only other worry Catherine and Adam had was the son they didn't understand. "I guess," Catherine said, "we should be glad he talks and jokes with his sisters. *Die Grossmudder* understands him best. He always goes to her."

"He hates farm work," Adam said, shaking his head. "I look around for a hired man."

"*Ya*, and the girls help."

"Yesterday was the second time Hans did not come home to sleep. Where does he go?" Adam said. "Maybe I follow him and find out."

"*Nay, nay*, we don't do that." Catherine paused. "Maybe I shouldn't say . . . but . . . I smell drink on his breath this morning."

"*Ei, ei, ei!* What are we going to do with that boy?"

"*Ich wayss net.* He is jealous of Dieter. We can't do nothing about that, but maybe we find a trade for him. Maybe a printer." Catherine smiled. "Like you in Frankenthal, *gell?*"

"*Ya, verleicht.* I hear it gives a printer in Reading. I check."

Son Dieter was a complete joy to his parents. Every couple weeks Adam picked up a letter from him delivered to the Kurtz Tavern, withdrew to a corner and read eagerly. He is now teaching *us* English, Adam reflected.

Dieter and Michael, now in their junior year, continued with courses in Latin, Greek, rhetoric, geography, mathematics, and first principles of philosophy. They had fewer lectures in classical languages but more in mathematics and natural and moral philosophy.

But it wasn't all study. Although they didn't have him as a lecturer, Dieter and Michael saw German Professor Heinrich Schneider on campus. After several chance meetings at lunch, he invited them to Sunday dinner at his house. *Fraa* Schneider's *Schnitz un Gnepp* was a treat.

An even better treat was meeting the Schneider's two teen-age daughters. "You may have Edith," Dieter whispered discretely to Michael. "I'll take Mary." Conversation around the dinner table was a delightful mix of German and English, and the afternoon flew by.

The boys left, congratulating themselves on their good manners. "Perhaps we get invited back," Michael said. Not only were they invited again, they were asked to chaperone the Schneider girls at the spring social on campus.

It was April 20, 1775, the final day of the college term. George Ege's driver James was to be in Prince Town in a day or two to pick up the boys. In class, Dieter suddenly sensed an excitement in the hallway. The college provost stuck his head in the lecture hall and motioned for the professor to come out into the hall. What's going on? the students wondered. What could be so important on this last day?

The professor and the provost soon returned. The provost raised his arm. "Students," he said, "please take your seats. A post rider has just visited the president to bring news. It appears there has been a battle between British soldiers and minutemen in Lexington, Massachusetts. Under the circumstances, we will dismiss immediately. I hope to see you next fall."

Even though they had discussed the growing political crisis in Massachusetts in their classes, students were shocked to hear this news. They rose as one and rushed into the hall, shouting to their friends as they met them hurrying down the stairs. "Where shall we go?" Dieter asked.

"Let's go to the club," Michael said. "Or maybe we can learn more on the campus."

They spotted and joined a group of students who had encircled Dr. Cedric Forry, college president, and two professors. "We are all aware of the growing animosity between the British troops and the people of Boston," the president was saying. "The post rider had to rush to continue his ride. He gave me only a few facts."

More and more students gathered. The president conferred with the professors. "Why don't we move to the chapel," he said. "We will meet you there in ten minutes."

The chapel was soon fiilled. The president stood at the lectern. "We are fortunate to have on the faculty Dr. James Eaton, eminent professor of contemporary history. He will lead a discussion. Let me first give you the facts as the rider gave them to me.

"British General Gage led a column of troops to capture military supplies stored in Concord. Minutemen heard about this and waited for them in Lexington. Someone fired a shot. Shots were exchanged and a few Americans were killed. The colonials withdrew and the British continued on to Concord. Now I ask Dr. Eaton to take over."

Several students rose. Dr. Eaton nodded to one. "Did the British capture the supplies in Concord?" the student asked.

"We do not yet know that."

Another asked, "Was there a skirmish in Concord as well as in Lexington?"

"Again, we have to wait to learn that," Professor Eaton said. "I correspond with a colleague at Harvard, Dr. John Freyberg, authority on colonial warfare. He keeps me apprised of the precarious situation in Boston. From what I learned from him, I would speculate that just as minutemen were alerted in Lexington, even more would be alerted late that night and into the morning around Concord. In fact, militias might have been called out."

"If they were," a student asked, "wouldn't they be defeated by the trained British troops?"

Dr. Eaton smiled. "One would think so, but according to my Harvard colleague, it might be an even fight. He would probably say the British superiority would be offset by the Americans' tactics of firing from hidden positions rather than in the open in the old style of fighting. He would also point to the superiority of American rifles."

"Professor Eaton," Dieter asked, "As a historian, do you believe this is the start of a war between Great Britain and the colonies?"

"It could be. If it is, some of you may postpone your

degrees. We may not see you all here next fall. Wherever you are, whatever you do, the college wishes you well."

Dieter and Michael left the chapel and walked to their rooms. "Did you expect this so soon?" Dieter asked. "I didn't."

"No, but Boston is a hotbed of dissent. Sam Adams is a troublemaker for the British."

"What will you do, Michael?"

"What do you mean?"

"Will you will sign up with the militia?"

"It never occurred to me. I always thought I'd work with *der Daadi* at the forge after college. Are you thinking you may not return in the fall?"

"I'm not sure."

More news came the next day. Dieter and Michael joined students gathered around the post rider on the campus. No one knew, the rider told them, who fired the first shot on Lexington Green. Major Pitcairn, commander of the British troops, ordered the rebels to lay down their arms and disperse. Captain Parker ordered the minutemen not to fire unless they were fired upon. More shots were fired. Eight militiamen, including the captain, were killed. A single British soldier was wounded.

The British continued their march to Concord, the rider continued. Word about the Lexington battle reached Concord and 400 militiamen assembled on a ridge overlooking the town. At the bridge, three British soldiers were killed and nine wounded. Lt. Col. Smith ordered a retreat to Boston. Militiamen from every farm and village between Concord and Boston crouched behind walls and trees and picked off the British. Seventy-three redcoats were killed, twenty-six missing, and one hundred seventy-four wounded. Americans suffered forty-nine dead, five missing, forty-one wounded.

The rider sped off and the crowd of students dispersed. Dieter and Michael returned to their room.

Early the next morning James arrived with the Ege coach. Dieter and Michael had little to say on the long ride home.

Catherine and the girls were waiting in front of the house. When they spotted the carriage on the road, they ran to meet it. Dieter hugged them all. He asked, "Has the news reached here yet?"

"*Ya*," Catherine said, "Isn't it terrible. Does it give war?"

"*Verleicht*. We must hear more. Where is *der Daadi*?"

"We go in now," Catherine said, ominously. She held her son back as the girls went ahead. "Dieter *liewer*, a letter came from Uncle Jacob in Frankenthal. *Der Grossdaadi* Staudt died."

Dieter looked down.

After a minute Catherine said, "*Derr Daadi fiehle schlimm*. He sits in his chair and doesn't talk. Let's go in. Maybe you comfort him."

Tears came to Adam Staudt as they hugged. "*Sohn*, he would be proud of you." He paused. "He gave himself up for me. Now I see him in you."

Dieter smiled but said nothing.

After a long silence Adam said, "Peter told me it would be hard, even though we knew it had to come." He wiped his eyes and rose. "I am *allrecht* now."

Dieter knew *der Daadi* was upset by more than his father's death. "Is Hans here?" he asked.

Catherine walked in. "Hans left. We think he works for a printer in Reading."

"He doesn't know about *der Grossdaadi*?"

"Unless he hears it from a neighbor," Catherine said.

"Maybe I go tell him."

The next morning at breakfast, Dieter said, "*Daadi*, I ride into Reading Town now. I come back in a few hours and help plant."

"*Gross Dank*. Yesterday was the first day since we come to America I do not work." Adam shook his head slowly.

"We make it up," Dieter chuckled. "After all my studying, I'm ready for man's work. Is there anything you want in Reading?"

"Not now. Maybe we go later."

Dieter put the horse to a gallop on Tulpehocken Road, eager to see how people in the town were reacting to the Lexington skirmish.

Dieter had been in Reading several times before. He sensed a mixed feeling of sorrow and excitement today — groups of men on street corners wearing black crepe in mourning for the slain in Lexington, others showing their anger, vehemently raising their arms, talking boisterously. After tethering his horse to a hitching post, he walked up and down Penn Street and listened in on conversations — two companies of foot being raised in the town . . . every township to have at least one company.

As he walked, Dieter spotted a sign for a print shop. He entered, and there was Hans in his printer's *Schatz*, bent over setting type. Hans' head flew back, his eyes big as saucers when he looked up and saw Dieter.

"Hans, I'm glad to see you. *Wie gayt's*?"

"*Zimmlich.*"

"I don't know whether you heard. *Grossdaadi* in Frankenthal died."

Hans said nothing.

Dieter waited. "Don't you say anything?"

"I know nothing about him."

"You never heard how he encouraged *Daadi un Mamm* to leave home and come to America?"

"I heard them tell you, but they never tell me. They never tell me anything."

"If *Grossdaadi* had not encouraged them to leave Germany, you would not be in America now."

"*Ya*, but no matter where we live, you are the favorite." Hatred dripping from his lips, he said, "You are the *college boy*. I like my sisters but I don't like you."

"Hans," the printer called out in a gruff voice, "I don't pay you to talk. I am ready for the next pressing."

"All right, I leave." Dieter said. "Hans, you break their hearts. Please go home and make up."

Catherine was waiting for him. "Did you see Hans? Is he all right?"

"He works for a printer. He looks the same."

"*Guud.* Maybe soon he comes back."

"I go out to the back field now." Dieter smiled. "We come in for dinner at *genau* noon."

Dieter did not expect his father to ask about Hans, and he didn't. As Dieter began harrowing, his mind wandered. He thought of the long hours he spent in college browsing through hundreds of books in the open stacks of the library. He read widely, including world affairs. He believed that war between Britain and the colonies was inevitable. He felt strongly about the American cause and would certainly enlist for military service when that time came.

Should he sign up with a company of associators or the militia or the federated army? His three years of college and his fluency in English might qualify him to be commissioned as an officer. Or should he stay home and work on the farm and enlist as a private for three-month terms? Or should he finish college before he enlists?

As they plodded in for dinner, Dieter shared his apprehensions with *der Daadi*. "That shot at Lexington," Dieter said, "certainly means war comes."

"*Ya*, for sure."

"One of my professors says Pennsylvania Germans do not take sides."

"*Ya* well, we live like foreigners here. But we choose to come to America. So, *ya*, we support America," Adam said.

"I guess I have three choices: enlist for a short term in the militia, enlist in the federated army, or stay home and help work the farm."

"*Nay, nay, verdamptsei nay* — you don't stay home."

"But how do you manage the farm?"

"I manage. You have one more choice — finish college."

"But you must have help with the fields."

"I hire help. And Rebecca and Tillie are as strong as you boys. Even Ruth and Rachael help." Suddenly he paused and looked down. "It wonders me — what does Hans do about the war?"

For the next six weeks Dieter worked long hours in the fields. Adam smiled. "College does not make you *schwach, gell?* You do more work than me."

On Thursday night Adam and Dieter went to the tavern. These days the Kurtz gang talked about nothing but the crisis. Bully Lenhardt's voice meant no more than anyone else's. In spite of his youth and being a college student, Dieter Staudt was accepted.

"What a *schayni Yuni Daag*," Sam Fidler said. "I get a lot done." He took a big gulp of his rum then paused for attention. "Yesterday I was in Reading. Congress wants eight Pennsylvania companies of riflemen to march to Boston as First Defenders."

"Who told you that?" Bully shouted.

Sam ignored him. "I hear Captain George Nagel's Company moves out soon."

"I don't believe this crap," Bully snickered.

"I hear the Second Congress meets in Philadelphia," George Riegel said. "Peter, what does the *Gazette* say?"

"Adam and Dieter took the produce to Philadelphia last week. *Verleicht* they know."

"*Ya*, we brought the paper with," Adam said. "It says John Hancock was elected president of the Congress. The men in the Old Plough Tavern near the market were all worked up about the war."

"What does the Congress do about it?" George Riegel asked.

"*Ya*, that is *wichdich*," Adam said. "They create a Continental Army and name George Washington commander."

Heads nodded. "*Guud, guud.*"

"They say Washington did not want it," John Lamm said.

"I know for a fact Hancock wanted it," Bully said.

"Get out," Henry Warner said. "*Du liegscht.*"

Michael Kintzer asked, "Do I have it right that Attorney Edward Biddle from Reading is a delegate to the Congress?"

"*Ya, sel iss recht*," Adam said. "Here, you read it."

"Biddle is my lawyer," Bully said and swaggered to the bar for a refill.

"Does the paper give anything about Bunker Hill?" John Lamm asked.

"*Net viel*," Adam said. "It gives two hills there, Bunker and Breed's. *Ennihau*, I guess the lobsterbacks won, but they lost more men than we did."

At 10 o'clock George Riegel and Paul Stiely left. "I guess we go too," Adam said to Dieter. "*Die Mudder* likes to hear what we talk about. You tell her and I go to bed."

TEN

THE SUMMER OF 1775 FLEW BY, DIETER WORKING long days in the field and short evenings reading. Once a week he rode to Charming Forge to catch up with Michael. The highlight of the summer at the mansion would be a party the Eges planned for *Fraa* Ege's sister's family, the Morgans of Lancaster, and guests from Philadelphia. As Michael's best friend, Dieter was invited. He accepted but was concerned about not having the right clothes.

"We go in Reading and order from Ritter the tailor," Catherine said. "You need them anyway for church . . . and for college when you graduate."

Dieter came in from the back field early on Saturday, giving himself time to dress and be at the Ege's by 5 o'clock. "You look handsome, Dieter," Catherine said. Ruth sashayed up to him. "Oh, I must dance with this handsome young man." He mounted the best horse and waved goodbye to the giggly sisters and to Catherine and Clara.

The guests had arrived at the mansion in four stately carriages. When Dieter arrived, they were in the drawing room, the women resplendent in brocade and satin, the gentlemen, their wigs powdered, in party clothes and buckled shoes. Dieter suppressed a giggle when he saw Mr. E*ge* in a wig. Not to be outdone in style was *Herr* Ege's uncle, the famous glass designer all Philadelphia knew about, Baron Stiegel.

A gloved servant moved about the room with glasses of Madeira and a tray of cheese and grapes. *Fraa* Ege introduced Dieter to the Philadelphia guests — the Shippens, the Smithtons, and the Rittenhouses. Dieter was wowed by the young beauties, especially the petite one with dark eyes, blond hair, and a pleasing figure. Her name was Lucy. Had Little Burr been here, Dieter reflected, he'd be delighted with all the beauties — and they with him.

After an hour of socializing, the guests were ushered into the large dining room, the walls a pale yellow above a walnut wainscot, sconces and candles on the walls, a large candelabra hanging over the table. His humble home just a few miles away, Dieter had never imagined anything so sumptuous. The table was set with fine china, silver, and glassware from Europe and the East, Dieter assumed. A Philadelphia mahogany china closet displayed fine porcelain figures. Two uniformed waiters stood like sentries at their places, ready to serve. The incongruity of high fashion and style here on the Tulpehocken frontier brought a wry smile to Dieter's face.

The guests were led to their places. Michael's cousin Barbara, at home in the party scene, was seated next to Mr. Rittenhouse, Dieter next to Lucy Smithton. On his other side was Mr. Edward Shippen. To Dieter he looked like who he was, a prosperous proprietor used to getting his own way.

"I have had the pleasure of doing business with Mr. Ege for years," Shippen said to Dieter.

"Is your business in the city?" Dieter asked.

"Yes, on Fourth Street." He paused. "Did you know that Philadelphia now has 40,000 residents. We are ahead of Boston."

Shippen was a smooth talker, probably a Tory, Dieter speculated. He anticipated a lively conversation, perhaps a debate. Remember what you learned in Whig Club, he told himself. And whatever you do, don't neglect lovely Lucy.

"I understand you and Michael will be seniors at the College of New Jersey," Shippen said. "What do you think of the education you are receiving?"

"I'm pleased with it."

"Have you had a course in world affairs?"

"Not as such, but from our debates on the campus we know what's going on."

"You do, do you? Well, what did you think of the news from Lexington?"

"I was shocked, but I realized the tension in New England would some day lead to violence." Dieter leaned over to say a word to Lucy.

Interrupting their conversation, Shippen became feisty. "That Sam Adams is a rabble rouser. He's not half the man his cousin John is. He talks forever about taxes."

"I agree with him that we should not be taxed unless we are represented in Parliament."

"No, son, we are getting all the privileges of the British empire and must pay for them."

Conversations up and down the table slowed down as the Eges and their guests discretely listened in on what was becoming a lively debate. *Herr* Ege was becoming uncomfortable. He and Shippen were compatible in their business relations, their political views never discussed. In his frequent visits to Charming Forge, Dieter observed *Herr* Ege's heavy involvement in politics. It would not be surprising, Dieter thought, if he became a delegate to Congress or a judge.

"Sir, is it not true," Dieter said, "that our colonial assemblies can do nothing about laws they consider illegal because the governors veto their efforts?"

"Where are you getting these ideas, son? Of course the governors represent the Crown." His tone became derisive. "And the colonies can't get around that with their so-called 'Committees of Correspondence' and 'Committees of Safety'. Read John Dickinson's letters."

"I have read them, sir. I remember he wrote that those who are taxed without consent or representation are slaves. And he wonders why we should pay to defend dominions like Florida, Canada, and Nova Scotia."

"Dickinson never wrote anything of the sort. He advised the colonies to act with caution. 'Anger produces anger,' he said. He told us to behave like obedient children."

"My grandfather in the Palatinate encouraged

my father to think for himself, I am told, and my father encourages me to do the same. I believe it is wrong not to speak out against injustice. Sir, you don't agree with Dickinson, do you, when he predicts that independence would bring centuries of jealousies, hatreds, and devastating wars?"

Shippen reddened. "You are getting . . . getting off the track. Before dessert is served, we end this discussion and share conversation with others."

Relieved, but not disappointed in himself, Dieter turned to Lucy. "I suppose you heard some of that."

"Every word." She spoke softly. "I was intrigued by how you handled him. His daughter Peggy" — she nodded toward her — "is a good friend, but *he* is a windbag. Oh, I mustn't say that, must I? You won't tell on me, will you?" She giggled and put a hand on his arm.

The dinner ended with cake and coffee. Dieter never dreamed of being entertained so elegantly in a mansion so close to home. *Herr* Ege and his male peers retired to the parlor to smoke; Michael and he and the young ladies returned to the drawing room. Earlier in the evening, Dieter noticed the pianoforte. His eyes grew wide when he saw Lucy approach the instrument.

"Please take seats, everyone," Anna Marie Ege said. "We will be entertained by our young and talented guest Lucy Smithton."

Wunnerbaar! Wunnerbaar! Dieter mused as she began. Playing without printed music, she dashed off a movement of a Haydn sonata. She went on to a piece he didn't recognize. He'd heard about the Austrian prodigy Mozart. Could it be his? Stunned, Dieter was the last guest to rise and take his place at one of the two whist tables. Michael's partner was Ann Rittenhouse. Dieter smiled. He'd be Lucy's partner.

The evening of delicious food, stimulating conversation, and congeniality wound down. It was late when Michael and Dieter climbed the stairs to Michael's bedroom. Dieter's sumptuous adventure in the life of the wealthy would end tomorrow. Of all the beautiful memories he will have, he mused, a lovely girl playing Haydn will be the brightest.

After breakfast the next morning, Dieter approached Lucy. "I want to tell you how pleased I was to be your partner for whist, and especially to hear your little recital."

"Thank you, sir," she said with a sly wink and a stylish curtsy. "Perhaps we will meet again."

"I hope you won't think me bold, Miss Lucy, but may I write to you?"

She smiled slyly. "I was expecting you to ask." She opened her handbag and pulled out a paper with her address on it. "I look forward to hearing from you."

Dieter was back at work on the farm with his *Daadi* in the middle of the next morning. Some chores tedious and repetitive, his mind wandered to Lucy. The decision he must soon make about returning to college, joining the militia, or staying home was now even more complicated. Is he in love? he wondered. He knew this—he wanted very much to see her again.

He felt strongly that he must join the inevitable fight for independence. The colony of Pennsylvania, reluctant earlier to authorize militias, he'd heard, would soon require every male sixteen to sixty to swear allegiance and sign for military service as an associator, a militiaman, or a reservist in a Flying Camp. He caught a rumor about the formation of seven Pennsylvania battalions. He hoped his college education would qualify him for a commission.

Dieter wondered what Michael was thinking. They talked together every Sunday after church. "Soon we head back to Prince Town," Michael said. "I'm ready. How about you?"

"Just about. We're up to our necks in the harvest, but by then the work will slow down." If he decided not to finish college, he knew, he must inform *Herr* Ege soon. How would he react?

"I'll miss not seeing our friend Aaron. We must find out what he's been doing since he graduated," Michael said.

The following week Dieter told his parents he

made his decision—he would return to college. They were relieved.

Three weeks later Dieter and Michael were busy checking in at Princeton, registering for courses, greeting friends. At the end of the first day, Michael said, "There's a different attitude around here."

"There is certainly much war talk. I notice there aren't as many registering this first day. Some may have already enlisted."

The two quickly fell into the study routine, the curriculum of courses a variation of the first three years. A special treat for seniors was lectures by the college president on history, law, philosophy, criticism, and composition. Dieter visited the library every evening, losing himself amid wonderful books.

One evening at dinner, Michael and Dieter overheard the name "Burr" at the next table. They walked over and inquired. A student from Burr's town told them that after Aaron graduated from college a year ago he studied for the ministry. When war broke out he volunteered in Col. Benedict Arnold's battalion. "In the march from Cambridge to Quebec," the student went on, "they said Burr showed such amazing leadership that Gen. Montgomery made him a captain and aide-de-camp. They said that when the general later was wounded and lay dying, Burr acted with great valor."

When they walked away, Dieter said, "Michael, this is hard to believe—our little Burr, the skinny weakling making captain and acting with valor."

"I'm happy for him."

Dieter wrote home every other week. And he now had a more zealous correspondent. When they began their correspondence, Lucy knew only that Dieter was German, a student at the College of New Jersey, and his father was a farmer. Dieter knew only that Lucy Smithton was English, lived in Philadelphia, and attended Mrs. Brodeau's Boarding School on Walnut Street. In their letters, they wrote about their families, their interests, their hopes for the future. But they already knew the important thing—they liked each other very much.

In her last letter Lucy wrote, "I talked with Mamma about this today. We want to invite you and your friend Michael to our home for Thanksgiving Dinner. We can send a carriage to Princeton for you early in the morning. I can hardly wait to see you again."

There would be no classes on Thanksgiving Day at the College of New Jersey, Dieter learned. He dashed off an acceptance.

November brought cold days. Dieter could hardly believe in another week he'd see his sweetheart. On Thanksgiving Day he and Michael went out onto the campus early. Soon the Smithton carriage arrived, and a few hours later they pulled up to the Smithton house on Chestnut Street.

The Smithtons—parents, Lucy and two sisters—were hospitable and gracious. Because of distance to travel, the visit would be short; Dieter relished the precious time. Dinner was traditional and delicious—turkey, corn, sweet potatoes, salad, and mince pie for dessert.

Lucy and Dieter were excited to be together, smiling, talking without end, holding hands slyly at the dinner table. After dinner she took his hand and led him into a parlor where they could be alone. Wisely not overstaying their time together, they returned to the drawing room. But not before Lucy gave him a lusty kiss. "I love you," he said and returned the kiss.

On the ride back to Princeton, Dieter relived every minute of the wonderful day. Michael said, "I guess you know her parents liked you."

"I think it went well. By the way, I noticed how sister Sally kept her eyes on you."

Two weeks later Dieter was overjoyed to receive a letter from Lucy, sealed with her ring signet. He ripped it opened and smiled. Her words were gushy.

Dieter Dear,

    I probably shock you by writing so soon. And perhaps I shocked you with my kiss. Did I? I am so happy. That was the best Thanksgiving Day ever. I love you, Dieter, and I can't wait to see you again.

    Everyone likes you so much. And they all like your European accent. You can imagine the teasing my sisters give me, imitating your accent. Sally says she'll take Michael if he waits till she grows up a bit more. As for Father and Mamma — well, Father said you look as though you'll have a future. It takes a lot to impress him! And I can tell Mamma really likes you. Peggy Shippen and Ann Rittenhouse are envious!

    Here's the big news. My parents invite you to visit during the Christmas holiday. The invitation is for your parents as well. We will be at our house in Paoli over the holidays, so there is plenty of room for overnight guests. I know it will take weeks to write home and get an answer. If it takes too long, maybe you can just write and say you are coming.

    We must see each other soon. In the big house there is more room to hide.

Love and kisses,
Lucy

    Dieter returned to his room, a strange uneasiness grabbing him. He reread the letter slowly. He was delighted by her candor and thrilled by her words, but when he came to the phrase "big house," reality struck, suddenly and hard. Is there a future together for the daughter of a rich Philadelphia merchant and the son of a German farmer? At the start of a war, are the families on different sides? Is Tulpehocken a world too far from Philadelphia?

    A leveler between them is the education he is pursuing, he believes. But he will always be the son of proud Palatinate German farmers. Would his parents accept their invitation?

    Anguish turned into malaise. For the first time, Dieter Staudt ignored his nightly study. He spent an hour composing a letter to Lucy turning down the Smithton's invitation. Weary, he went to bed early.

ELEVEN

BACK AT COLLEGE, DIETER WAS DEPRESSED. Christmas service at the Church on the Hill had been devout and inspirational with special music and liturgy. Parson Waldschmidt had delivered an appealing sermon, drawing a distinction between passing happiness and Christian joy. But at the Staudt house after church there was a pall over the holiday. Without saying a word, everyone hoped against hope that Hans would be home for the holiday.

Just as distressing, Dieter acknowledged, was that he missed Lucy terribly and longed to know how she reacted to his letter. Two or three times a day he checked the college mail room.

The letter arrived a few weeks later. She wrote Dieter about her holiday, festive as always, she said, *but all I could think of was that we weren't together to share it. I miss your voice and your handsome face. I miss all of you. We must see each other soon.*

Here's the good news. Father has agreed to have Zeke drive me and a friend to Princeton! We would stay at Nassau Inn for a couple days and hope to have dinner with you and a friend. Please write soon and tell me when it will suit. Ben Franklin told Father he is setting up a postal system that will speed mail to Boston in three days, so maybe we won't have to wait as long for letters.

Anyway, Liebschdi, I love you more than ever. (Did I spell it right?)

Love and kisses,
Lucy

Dieter folded the letter with care. No, no, he thought. The idea of her visiting didn't seem right. He replied that evening.

Dear Lucy,

I received your letter today. Thanks for your kind words and thanks for offering to visit me. It's hard to believe I am actually writing this, but I don't think it's a good idea. From now until graduation I will be studying hard for final exams. Also, with all the war talk going around, the campus is not the quiet, sedate place it was just a few months ago. Everyone is talking about Tom Paine's pamphlet **Common Sense**. We hear it is showing up all over the colonies. Have you read it?

I think of you many times every day, and I am very eager to see you. I have this idea. If you invite me after I graduate, I will ride to Philadelphia to visit you in late May or early June. I could stay in an inn and visit you again the next day. Am I being too forward?

Lucy, we must see each other soon because I am uncertain about my future. I have several choices, but if war breaks out I will definitely serve. After that we may not be together for a long time.

I regret writing in such somber tones. If times were different, we would be talking more definitely of the future. But I earnestly hope we will stay together through our letters. Our love can survive whatever the future holds.

All my love,
Dieter

Excitement had filled the Princeton campus when copies of Paines's *Common Sense* arrived. Paine's straightforward but passionate premises quickly found their way into the Whig and Cato debating clubs. Dieter and Michael read the forty-seven pages fast and agreed that Paine's arguments were more persuasive than any earlier document they'd examined in class. "Did you note," Dieter said, "how Paine takes advantage of anti-Catholic sentiment in the colonies when he compares George the Third to the pope in the practice of succession by heredity."

"Yes," Michael said, "he is clever. On the title page he states, 'written by an Englishman,' asserting his right to reply directly to the king."

"I thought George III was influenced by his ministers, but in his proclamation he denied that and asserts that dangerous and designing men in the colonies were the culprits."

"Let's go to the Whig meeting tonight to see what others make of Paine," Michael suggested.

Club members got into their discussion without preliminaries. "I learned in class today," a newer Whig member said, "that Paine came to America from London only a few months before the Lexington skirmish. Does anyone know more about him?"

"Professor Eaton told us," the club president said, "he considers Paine unqualified to write on the subject. He put him down as a failure at everything he pursued in England—corset maker, teacher, grocer, even husband."

That brought laughs.

"But let's consider the substance of the pamphlet," the club president said. "Are there flaws in his rhetoric?"

"I find none," Dieter said. "I agree completely with his main theses—that government by heredity is wrong, and that equality of the rights of citizens must be defended by a just government."

"That's good," Michael Ege said. "But we've heard these arguments before. It's really his forceful language that excites the reader. His tone is straightforward and simple, not scholarly or statesmanlike. Listen to this. *All men being originally equals, no one by birth could have a right to set up his own family in perpetual preference to all others forever.*"

Michael went on, "He even goes so far as to say we should not be burdened by maintaining contact with

England. He writes, *Our plan is commerce. I challenge the warmest advocate for reconciliation to show a single advantage that this continent can reap by being connected with Great Britain. Our corn will fetch its price in any market in Europe, and our imported goods must be paid for, buy them where we will.* I wonder how this uneducated man was able to think so clearly and write so well."

The president said, "I heard somewhere, probably in Professor Eaton's class, that Paine impressed Ben Franklin in London and the great man spoke highly of him. Paine soon established himself as a journalist, even writing scientific articles. He also caught the eye of Dr. Benjamin Rush. Some say Rush himself wanted to write a pamphlet promoting independence but deferred because of his profession and connections. Instead, he asked Paine to do it."

Hugh Brakenridge, the seer of the club, rose to speak. "About Professor Eaton. He is open about being a Loyalist. It's not surprising he talks about Paine's past, including his going bankrupt. Even Patriot John Adams criticizes the piece because Paine doesn't propose alternatives other than independence. One thing we know about John Adams—he always speaks his mind."

The club session broke up and Michael and Dieter walked back to Nassau Hall. "So Michael, what do you think of all this?" Dieter asked.

"I think this is the spark that will set the colonies ablaze. And at only two shillings a copy, we'll see it everywhere."

"I wonder if the Kurtz Tavern gang has seen it. I wonder what *der Daadi* thinks. I'm glad he reads English," Dieter said.

"You can predict your father's reaction better than I can my father's," Michael said. "I've never heard him discuss his views on independence. He does business with both sides."

The New Jersey winter was long and hard. Dieter missed his family, and he looked forward to spring on the farm, to working the soil. Until then, letters were the only way to share thoughts.

Dieter's love for Lucy grew. Perhaps because he was German, he mused, his words were less nuanced, less personal, than hers to him. He stayed away from writing about marriage, but he thought about it often.

But Lucy's letters became less and less inhibited. *I think of you so often. At school I find myself dreaming of being together, really close together. You know what I mean. A couple stolen kisses are not nearly close enough. (Am I embarrassing you?) In my bed every night my thoughts are only on you. I dream of our wedding night. There will be one for us, won't there?*

She wrote several times a week, each letter more sensual than the last. His thought ran to a growing fear. Philadelphia, now the largest, most important city in the colonies, was the most social city as well. Blond, petite, well-shaped, dark eyes, face of a doll — Lucy Smithton would be noticed anywhere — out shopping, out at dinner with her family, at the concert hall, at plays in the Southwark Theatre. Certainly she attended balls and galas, Dieter assumed, escorted by male partners. She never wrote about that. No point thinking about it, he mused.

Every second or third week Dieter received a letter from home, *die Mudder* always the writer. More and more he realized how strong and resourceful a Christian woman she was. He knew a bit — not as much as he wanted to know — about how they left the Palatinate to settle in the New World. He inferred that in her self-effacing way she was the one who sustained the family in the early years. Strong faith, love of family, unselfishness — the perfect helpmate to a salt-of-the-earth German farmer. Dieter loved them both.

Die Mudder's letters revealed the strain of trying to understand a black sheep son. She wrote about not hearing from Hans, not knowing where he was, what he was doing. Although she hadn't said as much, *der Daadi* was ready to disown him. *It breaks my heart,"* she wrote. *When you come home in the spring, can we try to find him?* Was he himself wrong, Dieter wondered, to accept *Herr* Ege's largess in paying for college? Is that the barrier between Hans and him?

There was little else in *Die Mudder's* recent letters. Dieter understood, the winter a time of less activity. But she never closed without a word of pride in him. Four years of close association with English students here at Princeton led him to treasure his German character.

Dieter responded to his mother's letters within a week, usually in English. For this one he needed German.

Liewer Mudder,

Thank you for your letter. I will certainly do my best to locate Hans. Maybe he is no longer working for the printer in Reading. Try not to worry. He is capable of taking care of himself.

I have news about graduation. Ceremonies will be held on Sunday, May 12, at 1 in the afternoon. I have never asked anything of Herr Ege, so now I will make a request that he kindly use his two coaches and drivers so all of us can be accommodated on that day.

I can anticipate der Daddi *will say the event will be too fancy for him. He might say he can't converse easily in English, and he doesn't have the right clothes. Mamma, none of that matters. Wear your church clothes. If you don't know what to say or how to say it, let the others talk. You and the Eges get along well and they will be with you all the time.*

The Eges are kind, wonderful people, and after the war, if there is a war, I will pursue a career and pay back the money they lent me. I owe them something else. You remember the day I was invited to a party the Eges had for Fraa Ege's family and friends from Philadelphia? I never told you this, but at that party I met a girl I am in love with, and I want you both to meet her. Her name is Lucy Smithton. She and her mother will be at the graduation ceremonies.

Children sometimes neglect to express their feelings toward their parents. I want to say that you and der Daadi *have been the best parents a son could have. I will never let you down. My wish is to become the man* der Daadi *is. I love you both.*

Dieter

TWELVE

THE PRINCETON TRIO OF AARON BURR, DIETER Staudt and Michael Ege were known as the "Triumvirate," as much for their academic achievement as their togetherness. The notoriety of the two German students from the hinterland continued through graduation. Both were announced at commencement ceremonies as *summa cum laude* graduates. Unfamiliar with the term, the Staudts nonetheless felt the pride. The loudest applause came from them.

After the ceremony, graduates and their guests were ushered into the dining room. Catherine gasped at her first glimpse of the splendor. A band from Philadelphia made the occasion more festive.

The Eges suggested the seating arrangement at their table. Catherine was pleased to have Lucy on one side, Mrs. Smithton on the other. Adam felt secure between the Eges. Dieter sat between his sweetheart and Michael. The dynamics were right.

Catherine was struck by the Smithton mother and daughter—their clothes, their elegance, their graciousness. She couldn't take her eyes off the beautiful young girl her son was in love with, she and Dieter a picture of young love overjoyed at being together.

"They seem well suited, don't they?" Mrs. Smithton said.

"*Ya.* Your daughter is lovely."

"Thank you. She was so eager to see Dieter." Mrs. Smithton chuckled. "Oh my. Can you remember the feeling?"

"*Ya,* in Germany Adam and I do not live in the same town, but I can't wait for summer when I stay with my aunt in Frankenthal where Adam lives."

"Are your parents still in Germany?"

"My father died. My mother came with us. Adam's father stayed in the Palatinate. He died just a year ago."

"I'm sorry." She waited. "I so admire the Germans who settled in the wilderness. And the countryside where you live is beautiful—green fields of corn and brown fields of wheat."

"Yes, but not till summer. When did you see them?"

"Last summer when we visited Charming Forge. That was when we met your son."

"Then you rode right past our farm. It is where the little Cacusi Creek runs across the road." She paused. "*Ya,* but when we first come it gave nothing but big trees here."

"You know Mr. Smithton is a grain broker. He believes the Tulpehocken wheat is the best in the Middle Colonies, always the first bought."

"*Ya,* we work hard for good crops."

"He regrets he can't be here; he's in Boston on business."

On Mrs. Smithton's other side, George Ege and Adam chatted about the forge. Unaccustomed to social conversations at mealtime, Adam nevertheless knew a word of thanks was called for. "*Gross dank* for all you have done for Dieter." Catherine had told him not to bring up repaying the loan, but his German character won out. "We pay you back."

"*Dank, awwer* that is not necessary. It was our pleasure to have your son be Michael's companion. We are proud of what they have both achieved."

"Will Michael work for you at the forge?"

"*Ya wohl.* What will Dieter do?"

"*Ich wayss net, awwer* if it gives war, he fights."

Lucy and Dieter heard no other conversation but

their own. "I wrote," he said, "about riding down to visit you." He stopped and smiled broadly. "But we're seeing each other now."

"Now, Dieter dear, seeing and talking isn't all there is." She chuckled. "I think you are kidding about not coming, but I want to be sure. I want you to come to Paoli on June 12. See, I memorized the date."

The luncheon ended and the college president rose to address the graduates. "We trust your education has made you each a better man. You leave the College of New Jersey during turbulent times. Whatever the future holds for you and for our colonies, we pray you will be safe and well and that the colonies will be united and will prosper. Come back to the campus whenever you can."

Early the next morning three carriages started the journey home. At Trenton they ferried across the Delaware River and continued on. When they reached the outskirts of Philadelphia, the Eges and the Staudts said goodbye to the Smithton women and headed to Plymouth Meeting to take the Tulpehocken Road north.

Die Grossmudder, Ruth, and Rachael sat on the bench outside the house awaiting the carriages. The first time they had ever been away from their farm overnight, Adam and Catherine jumped off and hugged their family. "We knew you would be starved," Clara said, "so it gives a pot of *Supp* cooking."

"*Guud*," Catherine said. "We take only a minute to get ready."

One by one Sarah, Rebecca, and Hans had left their parents' home, Rebecca most recently. At 21, she and her husband moved into his father's farm. The gradual reduction in the household struck Dieter as he returned home during his years of college.

There was still enough springtime light for Dieter to wander out into the front field. He reached down and grabbed a handful of soil. This is home, he mused. He'd be up at first light to get an early start with the plowing.

At breakfast on Thursday morning, Adam said, "Dieter, do you want to go with to the tavern tonight? It gives big Kurtz crowds these days. John Lamm said they are anxious to hear what the Princeton people say about *Common Sense*. Take your copy along."

After a good day's work and a good supper, Adam and Dieter walked to the tavern. It was crowded and noisy, an excitement they hadn't felt before. Dieter recognized only half the men. He was surprised to see George and Michael Ege.

"*Wie gayt's?*" Ege greeted them.

"*Guud, guud,*" Adam said. "I am surprised to see you here."

"*Ya well,* these are exciting times," Ege said. "I wonder what people are saying."

Rolf Ludwig greeted them. "Glad to see you and your son, Adam," he said. He put out his hand to Ege. "My name is Ludwig. Your son and Dieter Staudt just graduated from college, *gell? Verleicht* they tells us about Tom Paine's pamphlet."

"Let's have a drink," Adam said to the Eges. "I buy." Adam looked around. He spotted all the regulars except Bully Lenhardt.

Soon Ludwig stood on a chair, an arm raised, a mug in his hand. "*Allrecht, Buwe,*" he shouted, "listen to me. Adam Staudt's and Herr Eges's sons are here. They tell us about *Common Sense.*"

Dieter gave Paine's main arguments, at times reading excerpts. Shouts of *Ya, ya,* and *verdumptsi* rang out. "Hold it down," Ludwig said. "John, what is your question?"

"No question. I hear the printer in Reading is running off copies in German."

"*Guud, guud,*" Sam Fidler said. "I want to read it myself."

Leroy Gerhart asked, "Does it give war? What do your professors say?"

"Most believe war comes," Dieter said. "There is no declaration yet, but fighting has started."

Kurtz Tavern newcomers also asked questions.

"What did the professors say about Ticonderoga?"

"General Arnold and Ethan Allen won that battle," Michael said, "because the fort had only forty-eight old soldiers. The attack on Montreal was different. Arnold led a thousand volunteers on a long march from Cambridge. Only six hundred made it. He fought a delaying action that prevented the British from invading the lower colonies."

Cousin Peter spoke up. "The *Pennsylvania Gazette* has articles about that. But I don't understand why we even fight in Canada."

George Riegel said, "I guess we think the French people there join us as the fourteenth colony. After all, they don't like the British any more than we do. I hear it was the Catholic bishops who swung it the other way by getting their flocks to remain loyal to the king. *Ennichau*, we were driven out."

"*Ya*," Dieter said, "then our troops marched to Boston. The British won the Battle of Bunker Hill but lost twice as many men as we did."

"If the British won, why did they abandon Boston?" someone asked. "That makes no sense."

"Michael," Dieter said, "you know about that."

"*Ya*," Michael said. "This is a good story. A fat colonel by the name of Henry Knox takes his troops to Fort Ticonderoga to bring back artillery pieces. Oxen pull sixty pieces on sleds to Dorchester Heights through 300 miles of the Berkshire woods. British General Howe can't raise his artillery high enough to bomb the position, so he decides to abandon the city for good and fight in New York."

Michael continued, "Without Colonel Knox, we might have lost the revolution right there."

"Tell them," Dieter said, "what the professor who is a friend of John Adams said."

"Adams called what was going on 'half a war.' He is impatient to declare independence and get on with it."

Paul Stiely asked if Michael knew how people in the colonies feel about independence.

"It's the question," Michael said, "that delegates to the Second Congress are debating in Philadelphia. In a lecture to the senior class, the college president said opinion was split between reconciling and breaking away. He said John Dickinson and the moderates proposed one more petition to the king. Dr. Forry added that Britain is trying to destroy our economy, and the king threatened to crush the rebellion, calling us traitors. Rumors from Europe, he said, tell of German mercenaries being enlisted by the British."

That caused a stir in the tavern.

"Dr. Forry told us some feel it is too late for reconciliation. When soldiers from the Middle and Southern colonies marched to Boston, he said, compromise left with them. Congress then opened trade to every country but Britain. Some colonial legislatures instructed their delegates to declare the colonies 'free and independent states.' "

Peter Staudt said he read in the *Gazette* that Congress was considering a motion by Richard Henry Lee to do that. Jefferson, Franklin, and Adams and two others were appointed to write a declaration of independence. "But," Peter added, "Dr. Forry said both sides agreed Pennsylvania and Maryland were not ready to break with Britain, and a vote on the motion was postponed."

"*Ennichau,*" George Riegel said, "the *Karichleit* know whose side they are on. At Hain's church we cut out the word *Keenich* from the tablet above the door."

The long meeting was about to break up. George Ege sat back, a warm feeling of pride in his son and in Dieter.

"It's getting late," Rolf Ludwig said. "Before we leave, we thank our two Tulpehocken *Buwe* for their information."

Loud applause and huzzas followed. Adam and Dieter left, a father's heart filled with pride.

THIRTEEN

TILLIE AND RUTH WERE WEEDING THE KITCHEN garden. A shot rang out. "What is that? Tillie asked.

"Someone's hunting."

"It can't be *der Daadi* and Dieter. They work in the back field."

A few minutes later, a second shot, then a third and fourth and more. "Let's run to the field and find out," Tillie said. As they ran they heard shots from the opposite direction.

"This is a funny one," Ruth said.

The air was filled with shots from all directions. Out of breath, Tillie asked, "*Daadi, Daadi, w*hat is it?"

"We never hear anything like this. Your brother thinks he knows," Adam said.

Before Dieter could explain, they heard horse hoofs and saw their Welsh neighbor, Hugh Jones, riding up. "Huzzah for liberty! Huzzah! Huzzah!" he cried loudly.

"*Ya*," Dieter said. "I believe it's the day everyone waits for. It comes sooner than expected."

"Quick, quick. What is it?" Tillie asked again.

Jones got off his horse. "A rider from Pottstown came through with the news," Jones said. "Congress passed a motion to separate from Britain. Huzzah! We are going to be a country of our own!"

"*Ya, ya,* Jefferson's declaration," Dieter said.

"No more work today, Dieter," his father said. "We go to the Kurtz Tavern and celebrate" He paused. "First we go in and tell *die Mudder un die Grossmudder*. They must be scared."

The two were walking toward them. "It is something to do with the men in Philadelphia, *net?*" Catherine said.

"*Ya, ya,*" Adam said. "This is big news. The men go to the tavern to find out. Maybe the *Weibsleit* get together at the *Karich* to see what it gives. You and the girls and *die Grossmudder* go, then Dieter and I come when we know more."

As they hurried to the tavern, Dieter said, "The *Bauere* should stop shooting and save their shots for the militia. "*Ennichau, Daadi,* I guess I made the right decision to enlist, *gell?*"

As Adam and Dieter strode to the tavern, they heard church bells chiming in the distance, the bells drowned out by a raucous din as they entered and spotted the regulars and a few they didn't know, all with glasses raised high, Amos Kurtz and Minnie besieged behind the bar. Bully Lenhardt, staggering, wiggled through the crowd to greet them. "We was wondering where you were. *Kumm rei, kumm rei.* We show those Goddamn lobsterbacks who runs this country."

Dieter chuckled. "Bully got an early start on the rum."

"*Ya,* like always. It gives many *Gsoffners* before this night is over," Adam said.

The tavern became overcrowded, the men boisterous, nearly out of hand. "I hope," Adam said, "it doesn't give Tories in here." He chuckled. "They maybe get tarred and feathered and ride the rail."

After ten minutes of near mayhem, Dieter had enough. "I can hardly hear you, *Daadi.* I think I join the family at the church."

"*Ya, ya,* we go."

They walked up the cart path. As they reached the crest of the hill, Hain's bell greeted them. "*Wunnerbaar!*" Adam said. "*Besser wie* gunshots."

Adam and Dieter walked into the stifling hot church

and saw a scene of serenity and prayer. The pews were crowded with women and children and a few old men. Consistory president Johann Gernert was seated in the last pew. He motioned to Adam and Dieter.

"*Ich denke* people would like to hear the news but they think it is wrong to do anything but pray in the *Karich*," Gernert said. "Maybe I tell them."

Herr Gernert walked to the front of the church. "This *Karich* is a sacred place every Sunday. But when important things happen in the colonies, it is *allrecht* for *Leit* to meet in *die Karich*. Dieter Staudt knows what happens. I ask him to say."

Grossmudder Christman and the Staudt *Weibsleit* smiled broadly when they saw their Dieter walk to the front. "Earlier," he began, "when you hear gunfire you are scared and puzzled. Some have guns for the militia. Some *Bauere* fire theirs in the air to celebrate when they hear our leaders in Philadelphia act to separate us from Great Britain."

The people looked around in amazement, murmuring to their neighbors. Dieter gave them time. A hand shot up. "Does this mean it gives war?"

"*Ya*, already there are battles. But now our leaders have told Britain we separate from them."

"Why do we do that? We come from the old country to get away from war," one woman said.

"*Ya*, that is true," Dieter said. "The colonies have mainly English people, but there are also Welsh, Scots, Irish, and others. Like us. Remember when we pledge allegiance at the dock in Philadelphia? Even though we are English citizens, we are like strangers in a foreign land. The English settlers do not like the way the king treats them. After years of putting up with him, they are ready to fight."

"But," the questioner said, "we come here for land. We farm the land, and every year it gives more crops. We don't want to fight."

"But," Dieter replied, "the British abuses affect us too—taxes without consent, British soldiers take over houses, houses searched without warrants. We are all in the same boat."

Hettie Lamm raised her hand. "Dieter, I understand

what you say, but what happens to bring this about now?"

"You know about Tom Paine's pamphlet *Common Sense.*" Many nodded. "That gives a big effect on the people. Representatives in the Provinces and then in the Congress pass motions that 'we are and ought to be free.' Congress appoints a committee to write a declaration to be sent to the king. The messenger who rides up from Pottstown today tells us the sheriff will read the declaration in front of the court house in Reading."

"When?" a woman called out.

"The rider did not know," Dieter said.

The people squirmed, talking excitedly. When they quieted down, Dieter was shocked to see his mother's hand up. He waited. "This lady has her hand raised," he said, smiling. "*Mamma*, what is your question?"

The people laughed.

"I read the delegates in Philadelphia are talking about 'free and equal.' Do they mean they want the country to be free and equal, or do they mean the people should be free and equal? What about the blacks? What about women? Why can't women own property and work at jobs or trades? If their husbands vote, why can't the *Weibsleit?*"

The women of the congregation knew Catherine Staudt was outspoken, but when they heard this they gasped, putting their hands to their mouths.

"*Ya*, this is a difficult question, *Mamma*. I can't answer. Maybe the declaration says something. The rider said the State Board of Safety sends the Committee of Berks County a copy of the Declaration so we soon know."

On the walk home, Dieter thought about Lucy Smithton. His sweetheart lives on Chestnut Street, only a few blocks from Congress Hall. What a pleasure it would have been to be with her yesterday, to hear the city's church bells ring all day and most of the night. He would write tonight. But there were a few hours of summer daylight left. He knows *der Daadi* will want to get back to work.

After a late supper, Dieter takes up the quill.

Carl Frey Constein

July 6, 1776

Dearest Lucy,

Today we received word that Congress passed a declaration of independence from Great Britain and that the bell in the State House was ringing all day and night. That must have been exciting. Did the church bells keep you awake during the night? Here in Tulpehocken word of the declaration arrived just after noon today. I thought of you immediately. But at times like these we must think of our country first.

Still, mixed in with these thoughts are my dreams of you, dreams of us together in a settled world after the war. Of course I will serve. If I had a choice to make earlier, I no longer have one now.

We are told the sheriff will read the declaration in front of the Court House on Penn Square on Monday. I will ride into Reading early so I can be up front. I am eager to hear it and study it. After that, I will stop at the print shop to see if the printer puts out German translations for the people. Dear Lucy, the war will separate us, perhaps for a long time. I am worried that we may not be able to get married right away. Even if we could, would that be fair to you? In a few days I will visit the recruiting office in Reading. I hope my education qualifies me to be an officer.

We must see each other before I leave. Please write as soon as you read this and tell me when I may visit. If I don't hear from you and must leave for the service, I will ride to Philadelphia anyway. If you are in school, maybe your mother will intercede for us.

I will write again as soon as I know more. I love you and I need you, now more than ever,

Dieter

The next morning Adam and Dieter went out to the field early. They spoke about the events of yesterday but soon concentrated on their project of erecting a fence. The bond between them grew even stronger as they worked long days together. "I'm glad," Dieter said, "I had a chance for an education, but I think I was meant to be a farmer."

"Nay, *nay*. When the time comes you put your education to use. You don't stay on the farm." Adam paused and hung his head. He said, almost to himself, "What I do for you is nothing compared to what my *Daadi* did for me."

His future, his career, his life with Lucy—all would have to wait, Dieter knew.

Word spread from farm to farm in the Tulpehocken Valley that the declaration would indeed be read at 12 o'clock noon on Monday. Excitement had died down a bit since yesterday, but neighbors visited neighbors to keep up with the news. Inns and taverns expected brisk business late into the night. Church bells were silent but would ring out tomorrow to announce special services. Occasionally throughout the day a few eager patriots could not resist sending up gun shots. In Womelsdorf there were more visitors than ever in the borough's short history as word got out that a large, elaborate Liberty Pole was being erected.

After breakfast on Monday morning, Adam told his family, "This is a day we remember." He shook his head slowly.

"I ride to Reading now so I can be up front," Dieter said "You can't all fit in the carriage. Maybe Cousin Peter has room."

"I ride over and see," Adam said. "Tulpehocken Road will be crowded with horses and carriages and many walkers. We leave early too."

"Wave to me when you see me up front," Dieter said as he mounted his horse. Even at a slow gait, he would be there four or five hours early, he knew. He was surprised that even before the sun came up he was not alone on the road. Cart path roads from settlements north, east, and south would also be crowded.

In a few minutes, directly ahead the sun rose, a huge bright ball announcing a glorious day, Dieter mused. How many lives would be changed today? he wondered. Certainly his. He thought of Lucy. He came up behind a large wagon carrying a dozen lively, chattering children. There was no room to pass, the four-foot wide single-lane road hemmed in on both sides by towering two-to-three-foot wide chestnut, oak, and walnut trees—the forest primeval.

Up ahead he saw a clearing in front of a farm house. He passed the wagon but soon caught up to families walking.

The day was cloudless, foretelling another in a string of what people said were the hottest, most humid days ever in the colony. The *Gazette* reported the heat in Philadelphia was taking a toll on delegates to the Congress, even delegates from the South.

People in the yards of every farmhouse waved vigorously to the stream of riders and carriages. "Huzzah! Huzzah! Huzzah!" they yelled. "Liberty! Liberty! Liberty! Huzzah for Liberty! Huzzah for Liberty! Huzzah for Liberty!" Dieter spotted a life-size effigy of King George the Third, crown and all, hanging by rope from a tree. A few miles farther on, he spotted a second effigy of the hated monarch, this one held in a stream by a huge rock. A few farmers were working on their Liberty Poles and Liberty Trees. Defying the order not to waste gunshot, a few farmers peppered the sky with shots. Many had a good start on their liquor.

Dieter forded the Schuylkill and rode up Penn Street. From every direction he heard church bells in a resounding chorus. People were in the street, talking excitedly, huzzahing to walkers and riders streaming into the town, cheering the new arrivals. Federal Inn, the Green Tree Tavern, and smaller taverns on King Street close to Penn overflowed with customers, many bringing their drinks out onto the street.

As he rode on, Dieter spotted the speaker's stand erected in front of the courthouse on Penn Square. Riders on their mounts had taken the choice spots up front. He had planned to hitch his horse to a post but abandoned that idea. He took the closest place open and joined the celebration. For reserved Germans of Reading and Berks County, today, July 8, 1776, was a day to be friendly and open to strangers.

By the middle of the morning, the square was completely filled with people and horses and carriages. Most folks were well-behaved; some got out of hand. Were there, Dieter wondered, any brave enough, or foolish enough, to speak out for the other side?

At 11:30 a sudden hush fell over the crowd as the

Court House bell rang and a cortege of perspiring, dressed-up officials climbed the steps to the speaker's stand. Gawking, people moved and pushed to get a better look. The most portly among the officials was in charge, seating the others. I hope they aren't all going to speak, Dieter thought. There'd be a riot.

Dieter guessed it was the mayor of Reading who rose to address the crowd. "Welcome to this *wunnerbaar* event. We are gathered to hear the Declaration of Independence read. This is done at the direction of the State Board of Safety in pursuance of the resolution of Congress on July 4."

"We can't hear you," someone yelled from the back of the crowd near South Queen Street.

"*Allrecht*, I speak louder," the mayor said. He cupped both hands around his mouth. "Is this better? First I introduce the officials and guests present on the stage." As they stood, the crowd cheered loudest for Dr. Bodo Otto.

"Now," the mayor said, "I introduce the official who will read the declaration, Mr. Henry Vanderslice, sheriff of Berks County. He will read it first in English then in German."

"IN CONGRESS, July 4, 1776

THE UNANIMOUS DECLARATION of the
thirteen united STATES OF AMERICA

When in the Course of human events it becomes necessary for one people to dissolve the political bands which have connected them with another . . . . We hold these truths to be self-evident, that all men are created equal, that they are endowed by their Creator with certain unalienable Rights, that among these are Life, Liberty, and the pursuit of Happiness . . ."

If only he could record these words for study, Dieter thought. These are certainly Jefferson's words, no one else's on the committee. And how amazing, he reflected, that *Mamma* predicted his words on equality.

After the preamble came a long list of abuses by the

British Crown on the American colonies. The committee and the delegates, Dieter assumed, had written them. He knew the main ones, but the list went on and on, perhaps two dozen, he guessed.

Next came a few paragraphs on Petitions for Redress made to "a Prince marked by every act which may define a Tyrant, unfit to be the ruler of a free people."

"WE, THEREFORE, The Representatives of the UNITED STATES OF AMERICA . . . ." Coming to the end, Dieter hoped for more precious words from Jefferson himself. He heard them: " . . . with a firm reliance on the protection of divine Providence, we mutually pledge to each other our Lives, our Fortunes and our sacred Honor."

A thundering cheer rose from the square as the sheriff finished. It would be an hour or two, Dieter guessed, before the crowd dispersed. Tulpehocken Road would be jammed. Now would be a good time to go to the recruiting station.

A line of young, gawky recruits waited to sign up, some much too young, Dieter thought. They spilled out onto the street. Dieter stepped to the end of the line.

An hour later he reached the table where several officers were buried in enlistment forms, shouting to one another. "Next," Captain Hiester called out. He shoved a form at Dieter. "If you can read English, fill this out. If you can't, get in that other line."

"Sir, my name is Dieter Staudt. I have a question and a reference letter from *Herr* George Ege."

The captain laid down the forms and looked up. "What is your question?"

"Will my degree from the College of New Jersey warrant an officer's commission?"

"See that major at the small table in the corner? Go over there."

Dieter repeated his question. "The College of New Jersey is a first-class institution. When did you graduate?" Major Schlegel asked.

"May 10."

"Your reference from a prominent citizen like Ege will help. You will have no trouble getting a second lieutenant's commission. Fill out this form."

"I hear Captain Nagel's company is leaving soon for Boston as First Defenders. Will I have my commission by then?"

"Not likely. A messenger will deliver the papers to you in person. I will talk to Captain Lesher about you serving with him. His company will be dispatched to New York soon."

"Thank you, sir," Dieter said and left.

He mounted his horse and rode to Hamilton Street. He spotted the printer's sign, tethered the horse, and walked in. "*Herr* Jungmann, I believe you have an apprentice named Staudt."

"Not any more." He scowled. "I pay him one Saturday and haven't seen him since," he said.

"Do you know where he is?"

"I hear he works for printer Sauer in Germantown."

At least it's a lead, Dieter thought as he left. When he visits Lucy, he'll ride out to Germantown.

After supper that night the Staudts were eager to hear Dieter's news. Catherine shook her head slowly. "Will you be safer as an officer, *Liebschdi?* "

"*Ich wayss net*, but I believe I can do more than carry a rifle."

"*Ya*, Dieter, much more," his mother said. "I pray for you every day and every night."

"It seems funny," Adam said. "We are busy on the farm just making a living. I never think in the New World we want to be a country of our own."

"*Ya*," Dieter said. "It doesn't come to this if the king listens to reason from the colonies and some people in his own Parliament, like William Pitt and Edmund Burke."

"I pray for you and I pray for Hans," Catherine said. "I wonder where he is."

"I hear he may be working for printer Sauer in Germantown. I will try to find out."

His mother's mouth fell open. She lowered her head and said softly, "Thank God, thank God."

In bed after a long, eventful day, Dieter reflected on the momentous change his life is about to take. His last thoughts were on Lucy Smithton.

FOURTEEN

THREE OR FOUR WEEKS. THAT'S ALL THE TIME HE had, Dieter figured, before he left with the militia. Tomorrow he'd ride to Tailor Ritter in Reading to get fitted for a uniform. But there'd be time in the long days working the farm with *der Daadi* for bittersweet reflection. How lucky to be born to courageous, hard-working, loving German parents here in the New World, to have Cousin Peter to help them get started, and the Eges as neighbors. What were the odds, he asked himself, that a poor German farm boy in the colonies would receive a college education? Best of all, how lucky to have met Lucy Smithton.

"*Daadi*," he said one day as they ate dinner, "I think I'll ride down to Germantown tomorrow and talk with Hans."

"*Guud*," his father said. "I go with but he won't talk to me."

"He may not talk to me either, but I'll try."

Dieter had no trouble finding Sauer's print shop on the main street. "*Herr* Sauer, I am Hans' brother. May I speak with him briefly?"

"We are on a big job. Come back in an hour."

Dieter hitched his horse to a post and strolled around the town. He returned and went in.

"Go outside if you want to talk," *Herr* Sauer said. "But only ten minutes."

"Hans," Dieter began, "I know we have our differences, but I come to ask you to go home and visit *die Mamma un der Daadi, die Grossmudder* and the girls."

"I'm too busy," Hans snarled.

"They miss you and want to make up. *Mamma* prays for you every day."

Hans said nothing, not once looking at his brother.

Dieter was stumped. He remained silent for a long awkward minute. Then he played the only gambit he had left.

"In a few weeks," he said, "I join the militia. Maybe you will come home if I am not there."

"Maybe." Hans said and stumped into the shop.

Dieter shook his head. A day of riding for a five-minute conversation! Still, the *maybe* was more than he ever had before. He left for the long ride home.

As he rode, his thoughts turned to his uncertain future. He had no misgivings about joining the militia rather than accepting *Herr* Ege's invitation to work at the forge. He thought about Lucy. He had no doubts about their love for each other, but they might not see each other for a long time. Would she wait for him? Desperate to receive her letter, he'd gone to the tavern every evening to check.

Dieter arrived home just in time for dinner. "You must be tired, *gell*?" Catherine said. "You go to bed early. Did you talk with Hans?"

He fibbed about how long they talked.

"Did he say he'd come to see us?" Catherine asked.

"I believe he will after I leave for the militia. I hope so."

As he walked into the tavern two days later, Minnie Kurtz greeted him. "Here it is, Dieter. The post rider just left." She chuckled. "It's from your sweetheart, *gell*?"

He sat at a table and unsealed the letter.

Liewer *Dieter,*

    I will make this short. Yes, sweetheart, I am very eager to see you too. I will be waiting for you on Saturday or the next. It must be a Saturday because I sometimes work for Papa during the week in the summer. Mamma and Papa invite you to stay overnight.

    We are in our summer home in Paoli. Ride to Lancaster then east on the Lancaster Road, about forty miles. Our house is on the right, the only one in the village with blue shutters and a blue door.

    Liebschdi, our house has extra rooms. I can hardly wait to be alone with you. By the way, how is my German? If you teach me your language, I'll think of something to teach you. Did you ever hear the saying "A kiss, a letter, or something better?"

                              Alles meiner Lieb,
                                      Lucy

    Dieter's pulse shot up. His Lucy is no shrinking violet. He tucked the letter in a pocket and left.

    He arrived home, took the horse to the barn, and dashed to the back field. "*Daadi*, I hope you can do without me on Saturday. I want to visit Lucy."

    "*Ya*, we finish the fence before." Adam paused. "Lucy is not German, but she is *en schayni Maedel*. And nice too."

    "*Danke.* It may be long before I see her again. This time I go to the summer home in Paoli."

    "Paoli is near Philadelphia, *gell?*"

    "*Ya*, they call it a 'dependency.' I ride to Lancaster then turn east. I allow about five hours."

    It was a long three days, but Saturday finally came. His sisters joshed with him at breakfast. "Dieter, take me with," Rachael said. "Nellie can ride two."

    "Don't be dumb," Ruth said. "You would just be in the way." She laughed. "But Dieter, behave yourself."

    Extra clothes packed in the saddle bag, he mounted the new young mare and galloped to the road.

    The hot spell still covered a big swatch of Penn's Woods. He stopped at inns along the way to rest and bait the horse. Just after noon he spotted a village he hoped was Paoli. He pulled into a barnyard and asked. "*Ya*, you have right. Paoli straight ahead," the farmer said.

Dieter was pleased to hear the dialect. "*Gross Dank*," he said.

He was amazed to see large, two-and-three-story stone houses. Dieter looked for blue shutters. There it was, the largest house in view. These are summer homes? he mused. Mr. Smithton's grain business is prospering.

He rode up, dismounted, and pulled the latch cord. He expected to see Lucy's maid. "*Liebschdi*, Lucy said. "I'm so happy to see you. Come in, come in."

He was shocked when she threw her arms around him and gave him a passionate kiss. And then another. "I expected to see your maid at the door," he said weakly.

She smiled broadly. "Oh I gave the servants the afternoon off."

"Aren't your parents home?"

She giggled. "No, I gave them the afternoon off too. Just teasing. They went to Southwark to see a new play. Aren't we lucky?" She took his hand and led him to the parlor. "You must be tired. Did you stop for something to eat?"

"No."

"While you wash up, I'll set the table."

He reflected about the situation. Here he was being propositioned by a beautiful girl, a girl he loved. He'd hoped they'd be alone for kissing, but suddenly there's more. This was exciting. But what if the Smithtons are testing their daughter and come home early?

He walked into the parlor. "Come to the dining room, Dieter dear. Lunch is ready." If he hadn't been to Princeton, he mused, he wouldn't know the word *lunch*. On his plate was something he'd never seen before, two slices of bread with something between them. This may be a day for new things, he mused.

"I hope you like what Chloe made for us."

"Oh, then she *is* here?"

"No, I asked her to prepare lunch before she left." He bit into the sandwich. "It's good. What do you call it?"

"It's a *sandwich*." She left and returned with lemonade.

"Lucy, do your folks go to the theater often?"

"Once a month or so."

"How long do the plays last?"

"Oh you're afraid we'll be caught." She smiled.

"Aren't *you*? Lucy, I love you and I want to marry you." He paused. "What if your parents don't like the play?"

She took his hand. "Oh Dieter, I love you too. I know my parents — they will not come home early." She led him to the stairs. "Wait here."

In a few minutes, she called, "Dieter, lover, come up."

She stood at the door of her bedroom, partly undressed. "You will sleep in the bedroom down the hall tonight. But for now, there will be no sleeping. Help me get undressed."

In that hour, Lucy Smithton and Dieter Staudt discovered a new joy. "Wasn't that better than a kiss or a letter?" she said softly.

"It was wonderful, Lucy dear. *Wunnerbaar!* Even, as the high Germans say — *Wunderbar!* I love you and I promise I will be faithful to you."

"I promise too. We'll get dressed now and go downstairs for a game of cribbage. Let them catch us at that." She smiled and gave him one last kiss.

When the Smithtons returned, the servants were at work and the household looked normal. After dinner Mr. Smithton said, "Let's get started at the whist table. You *do* play, Dieter?"

Lucy's parents were too good for them, winning handily. Mr. Smithton put the cards in their box and said to Dieter, "Here, take these with you. You will have time on your hands in the militia."

Mrs. Smithton said, "Dieter, will you go to church with us tomorrow?"

"Yes, but I want to leave after the service to get home before dark."

"We usually stay in the city for lunch at the City

Tavern. If you think you won't have time for that, we can take two carriages. Anyway, we'll have a big breakfast tomorrow. Good night. Hope you sleep well."

Breakfast the next morning was special—grapefruit, omelets, bacon, corn soufflé, toast, cookies, and coffee. One more thing to enjoy, an Episcopalian service at Christ Church. By tomorrow, Dieter mused, he'd come back down to earth.

After the service, Dieter said goodbye to the Smithtons. "Thank you very much for having me."

"It was our pleasure. I hope you enjoyed your visit," Mrs. Smithton said.

Lucy, an arm hooked in Dieter's, squeezed when he said, "Oh yes, I'll remember it for a long time."

"These are troubling times," Mr. Smithton said. "Our best wishes go with you."

"Yes," Mrs. Smithton added, "and if you are on leave, you are always welcome."

Lucy and Dieter climbed onto the rear seat of the carriage. They waved as the carriage moved out. The hour-long trip to Paoli was peaceful and silent. Arm hooked in arm, the young lovers needed no words.

———

In Tulpehocken, the Staudt family eagerly walked to church on this first Sunday after Independence Day. In a sermon even longer than usual, Reverend Waldschmidt preached on worldly justice. Eager to talk with friends about the war, the congregation squirmed. As always after the service, the women gathered in the front pews to socialize, the men in the rear.

Among members of the church were most of the Kurtz Tavern gang. "Do you know," John Lamm said, "printer Jungmann presses out copies of the Declaration in German."

"*Guud.* Tomorrow I get a copy," Sam Fidler said.

"Why spend your money?" Michael Kintzer said. "We know what it says."

"I buy a copy for Dieter. He studies it," Adam said.

"*Ya well*, I'm too tight to buy one," Kintzer said, half-smiling.

"How many signed it?" George Riegel wanted to know.

"I hear fifty-five," Lamm said.

"Did Lawyer Biddle sign?" Riegel asked.

"*Nay*, they say he was sick at home," Lamm said. "They say about twenty members did not sign."

The women started walking to the back of the church. It was time to go home.

Dieter arrived home from Paoli just as the sun was setting. Catherine, Clara, and the girls greeted him with hugs. "Tell us about it," Tillie said. "We want to hear everything."

"*Nay*," Ruth said, giggling. "He doesn't tell everything."

Catherine said, "You must be hungry and tired. We had our dinner after church, but I have *Supp* for supper. Did you have a good time?" She paused and looked at her son intently. "In the next days and weeks you do whatever you want."

"*Ya, awwer* I do the same thing I always do." He looked at *der Daadi*. "We have maybe two more weeks to work the land together. I am up early tomorrow."

In the field the next days, even fewer words than usual passed between father and son, the silence profound. In the house at night too, banter among the girls gave way to long periods of reflection. Memories that marked changes filled Dieter's thoughts—the girls growing up, the hard work of farming and building, Sarah and Rebecca leaving home for lives of their own, Hans' desertion, his own graduation from college. And now, not a memory but a foreboding—he'll be going off to war.

A military messenger galloped up to the Staudt farm one morning. "My brother's in the back field," Rachael told him. "Just ride back there."

The rider handed Dieter a rolled-up parchment. He

said, "You are to report to County Militia Headquarters in Reading tomorrow morning at 8 o'clock, ready for duty. Report to Colonel John Patton of the 4th Battalion. *Mach's guud.*"

Dieter opened the large parchment. The commission was signed by Samuel Morris, Governor of the Pennsylvania province. Dieter showed it to his father.

Adam nodded slowly. "*Ya,* you do the right thing."

The next morning Adam was awake early. An image of the Palatinate town of Erstein shot into his mind, a father standing on the wharf until the ferry carrying his son down the Rhine to Rotterdam faded from sight. This time it will be his turn to stay behind.

It was a bittersweet breakfast, Dieter in his brand new uniform, Sarah and Rebecca there early to say goodbye, the girls nervous.

After breakfast Adam said, "*Allrecht,* we go. I get the gig."

Dieter hugged them all — *die Mudder, die Grossmudder,* Sarah, Rebecca, Tillie, Ruth, Rachael. Ruth broke down, the others close.

"Dieter, we love you," Catherine said. "Write as often as you can."

"I will. Don't worry, I expect to be back in six months."

Tears flowing now, she said, "I pray for you every day. May God go with you."

When Dieter and *der Daadi* arrived at militia headquarters, Penn Street was overrun with carriages and families dropping off their sons. Dieter leaned over and embraced his father. "*Ich hab dich gaern,*" Adam murmured — the same nostalgic words, he recalled as he spoke them, from his father in Erstein twenty years ago.

"And I love all of you. I pray for you every day." Dieter jumped from the cart. Slumped on the seat of the cart, Adam waved slowly as he drove away.

Bedlam reigned as a motley swarm of levies milled around in the militia headquarters, seeking someone to tell them where to go. Some had muskets. None had uniforms. Red Coats versus No Coats. Is this the army that will bring down the mighty British military? Dieter mused. We need a miracle. Inside, when the recruits reached the head of the line, the recruiter shoved the enlistment orders at them.

Dieter bypassed the lines and sought out Capt. John Lesher. "The 5th Company is pleased to have you, Lieutenant," Lesher said. "Our other officer is First Lieutenant Jacob Rehrer. We have four sergeants, an ensign, a drummer, a fifer, and thirty-three privates. *Mir sin Pennsilfannisch* deitsch, all from the Tulpehocken settlement, so we get along. Some were collected together at Womelsdorf and join us this afternoon. Colonel Patton, our battalion commander, marches us out tomorrow."

The march north began the next morning, a raunchy military formation out of step, out of line. The drum was beating wildly, unevenly. The colors were flying and the fife was playing off key.

At sunset Capt. Lesher ordered the company to halt and set up tents in a field next to a peach orchard. Rather than a supplement to their supper, the recruits soon learned, peaches were the main course. The captain ordered Dieter to take a platoon and procure straw for their sleeping. As the men approached a farm, Dieter walked toward the house. "*Nay nay*, Lieutenant Sir, the Militia don't ask," the sergeant said, "we take. We go to the barn."

Before dawn the next morning the company responded to the reveille beat and broke bivouac in the tented field. They resumed the march, moving out helter-skelter as a sergeant called a feeble cadence. When they arrived in Bethlehem, Capt. Lesher asked Reverend Ettwein, parson of the Moravian church, to give his troops a sermon of reassurance. They entered the chapel and the parson preached in both English and German. When they reformed for marching, they were excited to learn they would lodge overnight at the Sun Tavern, the first time away from home overnight for most.

Capt. Lesher's 5th was the first company of the battalion to reach New York. Over the next two days all other companies arrived at Fort Washington, where the battalion was placed under the command of Gen. Thomas Mifflin. While they waited for the other companies to arrive, the three officers got better acquainted.

"*Wu wuhnscht du?*" Capt. Lesher asked Rehrer.

"Five miles west of the river, on the south side of Tulpehocken Road."

"I know the farm," Lesher said. "I live a little west on the north side. How many acres have you?"

"It gives about twenty under cultivation."

"*Wu wuhnscht du,* Dieter?" Lesher asked.

"You know where the Welshman Hugh Jones's farm is on the north side?"

"*Ya ya.*"

"I am right next," Dieter said, "at Little Cacusi Creek." He paused. "Captain, your farm is near Charming Forge, *gell*? Michael Ege and I are friends."

"*Guud. Ya,* I see *Herr* Ege on the cart path."

"I hear Colonel Patton owns a furnace," Dieter said. "*Verleicht* he and *Herr* Ege are acquainted."

Dieter had good early impressions of both Lesher and Rehrer as they talked about the disaster in the Boston campaign. Careful to play down his education, Dieter nevertheless added what he knew from Dr. Freyberg, particularly why the British abandoned the city after winning the battle. "We only assist the Continentals," the captain said, "but it does wonder me what General Washington's strategy will be." Dieter held off on his professor's criticisms of Washington.

"I don't see how New York can be defended," Lt. Rehrer said. "It is surrounded by water the British Navy controls. We have no navy to fight them."

"*Ya, awwer,*" Dieter said, "what choice do we have? We must make the Redcoats pay a price. What have we—19,000 troops on our side, most untrained? I hear they have 13,000 of their own plus 17,000 Germans they hire." He sighed. "I guess we fight against some of our own people. If we defend Manhattan, we dig ditches in the city and earthworks at landing sites."

"*Ya*, they call it 'soldiers of the spade.' But our bigger job," Lesher said, "is keeping the men busy and out of trouble until General Washington or General Greene calls for us."

———

The campaign for New York had begun two months earlier when American troops arrived and Gen. Washington set up headquarters at Number 1 Broadway. New York Island was a city of 20,000. After a third of the residents fled, American troops took quarters in the empty buildings and mansions.

The Command faced an unexpected problem — thousands of prostitutes in business near Trinity Church, a brothel area whimsically called "Holy Ground." A more menacing problem was the loyalty of many residents to the king. It came to a head when a plot to assassinate Washington was uncovered. The mayor and a dozen men were arrested, and one defendant was found guilty and hanged. Mobs of Patriots roamed the streets looking for Loyalists, mocking and beating them, tarring and feathering the unlucky ones.

Before he was transferred to the southern command, Gen. Lee had developed a strategy for defending New York. The city, he had reasoned, depended on the defense of Long Island, with Brooklyn Heights the key. Washington put trustworthy Gen. Greene in charge. Tireless, he built interconnected forts and entrenchments and erected barricades within the city.

It was the British Navy that Washington feared most. His fear was realized on June 29, the day after the hanging. Officers with telescopes sighted forty-five British ships dropping anchor in Raritan Bay! Intelligence confirmed that 10,000 troops that Gen. Howe brought from Halifax were camped on Staten Island. The firepower of five British warships, Washington knew, exceeded all the American guns in place. Panic gripped the American officers and troops and the city residents.

A respite from the fear had come four days later. Washington's army received sensational news — the Continental Congress in Philadelphia had voted to declare independence from England! Celebrations broke out everywhere. The officer corps retreated to taverns, and the enlisted men pulled out their hidden liquor. It was the wildest day of carousing any of them had ever seen, duplicated at Fort Washington farther north on Manhattan Island by the 4th Battalion and everywhere in the army and militia.

On Tuesday, July 9, at 6:00 p.m., on Gen. Washington's orders his troops were drawn down on the Commons and joined townspeople to hear for the first time: "When in the Course of human events it becomes necessary . . . we pledge to each other Lives, our Fortunes, and our sacred Honor." Mobs rushed down Broadway to Bowling Green where they pulled down a huge lead statue of George III, severed the head and mounted it on a spike. The air was filled with deafening huzzahs.

Three days later the British Navy shattered the Americans' confidence. The British warships *Phoenix* and *Rose* left their moorings at Staten Island and sailed up the Hudson. American cannon opened fire. The ships returned fire, balls slamming into houses, causing panic among citizens and troops alike. Washington himself observed the cries of terrified women and children and the faces of his officers and men who stood by in shock, helpless. Washington's spirits sank when he witnessed their cowardice.

In Fort Washington in Upper Manhattan, Col. Patton's 4th Tulpehocken Battalion awaited orders. Capt. Lesher, Lt. Rehrer, and Dieter had their hands full managing the restless men of the 5th Company. Meanwhile, other units were in action.

On August 22 British General Howe landed 15,000 men on Long Island. The Americans guarded all the passes except Jamaica. Early on August 27 the enemy feigned a noisy action on the western end of the Heights. On a signal from Howe, Red Coats on the left flank broke through the lightly-guarded Jamaica Pass. The Hessians took the center and the Americans were trapped. Some escaped to Brooklyn, many were taken prisoner, many savagely bayoneted by the

Hessians. On the American right, however, Continentals from Maryland and Delaware facing Gen. Grant fought back. Some broke through.

When the battle ended that afternoon, two American generals and 1,000 troops were taken prisoner. Both sides suffered casualties in the hundreds. Fortunately and inexplicably, Howe did not pursue his advantage.

Washington was persuaded by his council of war that his position was now indefensible. On August 28, small American units quietly and secretly crossed the East River to Manhattan.

On September 14, British frigates sailed up the East River and engaged several regiments of Connecticut militia at Kipp's Bay. When they faced the 4,000 British and Hessian forces, the militiamen ran without firing a shot. Dismayed, angry, Washington nonetheless had the presence of mind to send orders to troops in the city to leave. In the fracas that followed, for the second time in his military career, young Aaron Burr, Princeton classmate of Dieter and Michael Ege and now an officer on Washington's staff, acted courageously, leading several battalions to safety.

In Germantown Hans Staudt and Christopher Sauer, publisher of a popular German newspaper and a minister of the Church of the Brethren, swore when they heard church bells announcing the Declaration of Independence. "They do not force me to pledge allegiance to their foolish notions," Sauer said. "I tell them a thing or two in the next edition."

A few days later *Herr* Sauer talked with Hans about a British Ranger who went over to the American side as a double agent. "The Continentals caught him and jailed him in Philadelphia. They say Washington gets involved in the spy business and personally interrogated him."

"What's his name?" Hans asked.

"Major Rogers. He's a tough character from New Hampshire who fought in the French and Indian Wars."

Hans was silent for several minutes. "I wonder . . . maybe I could help him escape."

"Suit yourself. I don't get involved, but if you do I give you time off."

Hans rode down Front Street to the home of prominent Tory Joseph Galloway. They planned Rogers' escape. Bribes to two guards greased the way and Rogers made his escape. That was easier than he expected, Hans reflected. He met the major at their rendezvous and together they darted stealthily into the thick woods between Philadelphia and Germantown. They lived off the land, foraging the countryside. After a week, Hans put his life into Roger's hands and the scroungy pair headed for New York harbor.

At the harbor they awaited their chance to climb up the anchor chain of a British flagship. The ships officers welcomed the charismatic Rogers, who introduced Hans as the accompanist who made his escape possible.

General Howe was pleased. He promptly promoted Rogers to Lieutenant Commandant and ordered him to raise a battalion to be called the Queen Anne's American Rangers. With ample bribe money, Hans obtained hard intelligence from zealous Tory informants.

The Americans had their own spy in the area. Just before the battle of Harlem Heights, Gen. Washington had asked for a volunteer to move behind enemy lines and obtain certain intelligence. Captain Nathan Hale stepped up. In the guise of a schoolmaster, he left camp and made his way to Long Island. Learning that Gen. Howe and the British had begun the invasion of Manhattan and that Washington was abandoning New York, Hale rushed to the city. When he slipped across the sound, he entered Col. Roger's domain.

The British learned from locals about a schoolmaster asking suspicious questions. Roger's Rangers got on his trail. They spotted Hale scribbling notes as he walked. That night Rogers watched him enter a roadside tavern. He followed him in and struck up a conversation, befriending him, claiming also to be an American spy. They toasted the Congress. Rogers invited him to dine with him at his quarters the next day.

The next afternoon, Hale and Rogers entered a

public house close to Rogers' camp. Already there imbibing heartily at a rowdy table was Hans Staudt. Rogers ordered ale all around and the men talked heatedly of the Revolution. On a signal from Rogers, a platoon of Rangers rushed in and seized Hale. He was hustled to Howe's headquarters at Beekman Mansion.

After breakfast the next day, at a park next to the Dove Tavern, Hale was hanged. Hans Staudt left with no regrets. He knew Dieter's battalion had been ordered to New York. In this battle, he mused, he got the better of his college-educated brother.

Meanwhile, Col. Patton's 4th Battalion finally got its marching orders. They joined a formation of 5,000 Continentals and militia facing the British Black Watch detachment in Harlem Heights. Dieter's platoons came upon an American party of artillery struggling to move a twelve-pounder in the sand. They pleaded for help but Dieter acted with discipline and moved his platoons to his assigned place. For the first time the men of the 5th Company heard the muttering of cannon shot. Then enemy fieldpieces rained grape down on them. Some troops were injured by musket balls. The first sight of broken arms and legs and bloody heads was devastating to Lesher's company. They suffered their first casualties. The battle was tight, but the British prevailed. Howe fortified his positions then moved again, this time to White Plains, an apparent strategy to cut off American escape routes. But Washington's forces beat him there.

The battle lasted only an hour. Dieter said to Capt. Lesher, "How do we handle our dead?"

"Nasty business. We bury them as soon as possible. James Lamm was in one of your platoons, *net*?"

"*Ya*, their farm is about a mile from ours." Dieter paused. "Will there be a Christian service?"

"I should have appointed a chaplain."

Dieter recalled *der Daadi's* stories of *die Mudder* holding burial services aboard the *Neptune*.

"I will conduct a service," Dieter said.

"*Gross Dank.* Will you do the same for Sergeant

Ludwig?" Lesher asked.

"*Ya*, I do the same for both. I hope the sad news gets to the Tulpehocken quickly."

Ya, it is supposed to give a chain of military riders for this. I assign two squads to dig graves."

Washington had left 2,800 men at Fort Washington on Manhattan Island to hold the Hudson. The garrison was under the command of Col. Robert Magaw of the 3rd Tulpehocken Battalion. Magaw, a lawyer from Carlisle, and General Greene, area commander, assured Washington the fort could be held. But the fight went against them and the British summoned Magaw to surrender. Knowing of Lieutenant Staudt's facility in German and English, Magaw requested Dieter be ordered *absent on command* from his battalion to assist him at the surrender parley.

The next morning Washington came to Fort Washington from his headquarters in Fort Lee to consult with Magaw and Greene. Dieter spotted a familiar face among Washington's aides entering the fort.

"Aaron Burr!" Dieter burst out. He put a hand to his mouth and looked about apologetically.

"Dieter! I can't believe my eyes!" Aaron turned to Gen. Washington, "Sir, forgive our outburst. This is my college friend Dieter Staudt from Pennsylvania. He is detached here to assist in translating."

Washington smiled and nodded. "I am pleased to meet you, Lieutenant. I hear good things about the Pennsylvania German battalions."

"Thank you, sir," Dieter said, his voice shaking. "It is my honor to meet you . . . and to serve under you." He couldn't believe he was in the presence of the great man. His appearance—tall, imposing, regal—matched the image he'd had of him. Tonight he'd write to Lucy and to his parents about this exciting news.

The surrender session was pro forma, Gen. Greene straightforward. "Gentlemen," he said, "there will be no surrender." Dieter returned to White Plains with his master sergeant.

Just after dawn the next morning, the enemy came on hard in a three-pronged attack. After two hours of fierce hand-to-hand resistance, men stumbling over their dead and dying, the Americans were overwhelmed and forced into a fort built for no more than 1,000. The enemy rained twelve-pounders on the fort. Hessian Col. Rall demanded surrender. This time there was no option. Magaw and 2,500 defeated, distraught Americans were marched solemnly to captivity. Washington's party, halfway across the Hudson, looked on in sorrow and despair as the colors were lowered from the fort's flagstaff.

At the end of a battalion briefing for company commanders a few days later in White Plains, Col. Patton asked Dieter about the surrender parley. "It was a weird experience—both sides talking about surrender while both sides stood down." He shook his head. "War itself is weird. *Ennichau*, our General Greene said no and we left."

"I find it strange," Col. Patton said, "that a day after the parley Magaw gave in."

"Me too," Dieter said. "I overheard something between Greene and Magaw about the adjutant not being there. Greene was very upset. Do you suppose the adjutant revealed crucial information?"

"*Verleicht*," Patton said. He paused. "Being a prisoner. That's one thing I dread."

Howe pursued Washington into New Jersey, cutting him off from the other half of his force stationed in White Plains and Peekskill. Again Howe's decisions were baffling—sending 6,000 Red Coats to take Newport rather than finishing Washington off then and there! Returning to New York City, Howe offered amnesty to Loyalists and deserters. Hundreds accepted.

In late November Lieutenant Staudt and Patton's battalion and what remained of the defeated American forces broke camp and trudged wearily southwest, the British and Hessians in pursuit. The American Army reached Trenton on December 3 and four days later crossed the

Delaware into Pennsylvania. British armies did not conduct campaigns in the winter; Cornwallis gave up the pursuit. Leaving Hessian troops to hold British outposts along the Delaware River, Gen. Cornwallis marched his British troops back to New York.

FIFTEEN

THERE WOULD BE NO FIGHTING FOR PATTON'S Tulpehocken Battalion until spring. The battalion was quartered in Pennsylvania on the west bank of the Delaware River across from Burlington, New Jersey. Other units of Washington's weary, broken 3,400-man army of Continentals and militia were stretched out in New Jersey in locations past Bordentown and northwest past Trenton. "At least here," Capt. Lesher said, "the men won't be sneaking out looking for women."

Lt. Rehrer laughed. "Want to bet?"

When they were not in battle or on the march, the men had no responsibilities, no drill, no training. Their main assignment was falling out at reveille beat. They spent their time playing cards, gambling, arguing, fighting, drinking. To relieve the boredom and to annoy the officers, they frequently fired off their muskets at night. When their mess became meager, they adventured out without leave to forage for food. The officers had no scruples about this, for when the British took over a town, they consumed whatever was on the property.

Capt. Lesher became aware early of the different styles of his two subalterns. Lt. Rehrer was lenient on his platoons, overlooking their absences and violations. Unless assigned barracks duty, he spent his nights with officers of other companies.

Dieter spent time with his platoons and got to know the men well. He enjoyed their easy style, their creative use of the Pennsylvania German dialect, their German sense of responsibility and work. Most were farmers like him. He disciplined them when necessary but he had their respect and never feared the fate of officers who were shot in the back. Difficult though it was, Dieter conducted a nightly roll check.

Used to working hard on their farms, many enlistees were surprised there was so little to do. A few saw humor in everything, Dutch Boyer chief among them. He talked about the time he and his buddies fighting in New York discovered a wine cellar near his quarters on Stone Street. "We took the grate off a window and entered the cellar and helped ourselves to the Madeira. It was delicious. The owner discovered us and decided to let soldiers in and buy flasks of the wine for a dollar. Things got out of hand and the owner rushed to General Putnam's headquarters nearby, threatening to hang us all. I took my flask back to camp and enjoyed it. I never heard any more about being hung."

Dutch always drew a crowd. One night Dieter overheard him talking about a lieutenant he had served under in Brooklyn. He said the battle was raging and they saw broken arms and legs, broken heads everywhere. The lieutenant was ready to call them into the fight but he didn't because he was more scared than we were. He ran around talking to himself. "We can be thankful we have Staudt," Dutch said.

Dieter wondered how the battalion officers would react when they learned he'd met the commander-in-chief. Within the 5th Company, Capt. Lesher was proud that one of his officers had that honor. But Dieter's relationship with Rehrer became chilly.

Junior officers were inclined to gossip about their commanders. They held Washington in awe and revered him for his leadership, a symbol of personal courage and hope in dark times, but they spoke openly about how he was outmaneuvered in every battle. They quickly added, but he is a master at withdrawing troops with minimum loss. They thought of him as a "good loser" who could maintain morale and was always ready to fight another day in what he called "a war of posts."

With the approach of the enemy to Philadelphia, Congress moved to Baltimore. Before leaving, members gave Washington power to act independent of the Congress. He sent Thomas Mifflin, his quartermaster general, to Philadelphia to recruit. Inspired by the stunning "summer patriot" words of Tom Paine's new pamphlet *The Crisis,* a couple thousand militiamen and Philadelphia Associators signed up. Washington now had 6,000 troops to strike back.

Dieter spent his nights writing letters, reading, and making entries in his journal. New York, Dieter had discovered, supported more bookshops than Philadelphia did. He bought copies of *The Wealth of Nations* by Adam Smith, *Moll Flanders* by Defoe, and *Essay on Criticism* by Pope. In one shop an attractive chess set took his eye. Earlier he had tried without success to interest officers in whist, breaking out the cards Lucy's father had given him. Dieter was happy to find a chess player in the 4th Company. Not involved in real battle strategy, Capt. Bowers and he fought their nightly battles on the chess board.

Dieter wrote to his parents and Lucy every week, but as he had feared, the army mail delivery to civilians was unreliable. Surely *die Mudder* and Lucy were writing to him, he believed, but in five months he had received only one letter from each. He treasured them and read them several times a week. But he yearned for more. Mail calls, infrequent though they were, became a dread.

He received Lucy's first letter shortly after he had arrived in New York. He reread it every night, nearly memorizing it.

August 14, 1776

Liewer Liebhawwer,

How do you like the salutation? A teacher at school helped me with it. It may be hoch Deitsch *rather than* Palatinate, *but you are my lover in any language! It may also be redundant, but I want to emphasize my love for you.*

I was so relieved to get your letters, two so far. Have you received mine? I know you can't reveal exactly where you are. I know there are Loyalists and maybe some spies in Philadelphia. But the Gazette *gives us an idea of where the armies are. I am so worried about you. Even the word armies makes me shiver. As an officer, must you be out front leading your men? That sounds worse than being a private.*

Papa believes there will be fighting around Philadelphia sooner or later. If that happens and you are near here, maybe you can get a leave to get married. I realize Mamma and Peggy and Ann and others expect a big wedding, but I don't really care, one way or another. I just want us to get married. Think of how wonderful that will be. I'm glad we had a taste of the joy we will share. The war will end sometime and we can be together forever. If you can't get a leave maybe you can just get a day off to visit me. Getting Papa and Mamma out of the house might not be as easy as it was in Paoli, but we'll work it out.

There is not much news to report. School will begin in a few weeks. I look forward to meeting new girls and seeing the old ones. Do you know French? Maybe we can write love words in French. I will take my first French course in the fall.

I realize you may not know, but I hope everything is all right in the Tulpehocken and that your family are all well. I hope you get their letters and mine too in good time.

Take care of yourself and don't take unnecessary chances. I think of you often during the day and I pray for you every night. If it happens that your unit is near here in the future, try to get a night off. I long to see you.

I will write every week. Love and kisses,

Lucy

Dieter replied immediately, complimenting her on her German, wishing her well in her new term in school, concurring in her idea of a simple wedding. He couldn't tell her where he was encamped, ironically only fifteen miles northeast of her home. A vague sense of something big about to happen pervading the battalion, this was not the time to request leave.

He wrote instead about slow mail delivery. But he expected, he wrote, that her letters would eventually reach him. *I love your letters. They are all I have to cheer me. If the fighting comes to Philadelphia and my battalion is sent there, I will do all I can to get a leave.*

All my love,
Dieter

Dieter pulled from his bag the only letter he had received from home.

August 18, 1776

Liewer Sohn Dieter,
Every day we talk of you. We wonder where you are and are you well. We talk about how you did this and how you did that. Der Daadi *tells of how good and strong a worker you are. He says he could not farm so much land without you. The girls like to say how they tease you about Lucy. Sarah still comes on Wednesdays to help with Bible school. She talks English often and says* dank *to you. She says she writes to you in English. At night we get quiet. I believe we all think of you at the same time.*

There is not much new to say. Der Daadi *bought a horse to replace Nellie. She was old and sick. On some days a farm hand comes to help. I love church and do my best to help.*

We are all healthy, awwer *Cousin Peter does not feel good. He goes in Reading to see Doctor Otto. We worry about Hans.*

We pray for you every day. Write and tell us what you can. We write again soon.

Mir hab dich gaern. *God bless you always,*

Daadi, Mamma,
Grossmudder, Sarah, Rebecca, Tillie, Ruth, Rachael

Thursday sessions at the Kurtz Tavern were somber since July 4, the men greeting each other without the usual banter. When Adam arrived one November evening, Sam Fidler, Rolf Ludwig, and Michael Kintzer were having drinks at the bar. Adam joined the others at a table.

"Have you had letters from your son?" George Riegel asked Adam.

"*Nay*. It's hard. We don't know where he is."

"When Leroy comes, we ask. Your son and his are the only ones from here in Lesher's company, *gell*?"

"*Ya*, there were three, *awwer* . . . ."

Bully Lenhardt made his entry, quietly for him. He shook the snow from his coat. "*Ei, ei, ei.* This is the coldest day yet."

Conversation continued at the bar. "The *Gazette* says we lose all the battles," Ludwig said. He chuckled. "But it gives Washington credit for holding down the losses."

"*Ya*, none of our generals know much about strategy," Bully said. "But we don't argue tonight."

They took seats at the tables. Silence pervaded the tavern. Finally Adam said, "No one wants to bring this up, but we must talk about John Lamm's son. Does anyone know what happened?"

Leroy Gerhart entered and took a seat.

"Leroy, do you know anything about the Lamm boy?"

"*Nay*. Maybe I find out when Milton comes home."

"*Ya* , this is so *bedauerlich*. Some of us have boys in that battalion. It *verleicht* comes to us too."

Adam's thoughts went back to death on board the *Neptune*. He said, "It is hard to lose a son in the war, but then not to give him a decent burial, not even to see him. At least the people who died at sea got Christian burials. Catherine saw to that."

Bar business for Amos Kurtz was light. At nine o'clock the men finished their drinks and left.

Gen. Washington's audacious plan to strike back was about to unfold at Trenton. Receiving reports from his spies that the hated Col. Rall and his 1,200 Hessians might be drunk and off guard on Christmas Day, Washington planned an attack using three contingents. His detachment would make crossings of the Delaware at McConkey's Ferry. Patton's Tulpehocken battalion was assigned to this contingent. Gen. Greene would come down from the north and Gen. Sullivan would attack along the river road. The attack was planned for midnight when the Hessians would be in bed and the guard would be light.

Patton's men were among 2,400 troops loaded in flat-bottom *Durham* ore boats, the first wave led by Washington himself. Assigned to the lead boat, Dieter was thrilled to see the commander standing tall and erect. Broken ice on the river and heavy snow delayed the crossings for four hours. Only the first wave made it across. Even so, the three-pronged operation completely surprised the Hessians in their barracks and in the town. There was no contest. After an hour the Hessians threw down their arms.

For the Hessians it was a bloody defeat — 106 killed, including the hated Col. Rall, many wounded, 900 taken prisoner. Dieter learned later they were held in Reading. The Americans lost four dead, two killed in action, two frozen to death. The Tulpehocken 4th Battalion suffered no losses.

When the 5th Company stood down at the end of the grotesque Second Christmas Day, Dieter sat back and reflected, proud that his platoons performed well in Washington's first victory after four defeats. Would it be enough to keep alive the struggle for independence? he wondered.

His thoughts turned to Lucy. Would the battalion remain here near Philadelphia for a time? Would he be able to get leave? Could there be a wedding?

The only misgiving in Dieter's elation came when he thought of men they had killed. Ironic, he mused, that in fighting for independence from England, German blood was spilled on the enemy's side . . . and so many drunk, unable to defend themselves. Did they not have families in the old country, as he did? Had the devastation of the Thirty Years War not brought them to America, as it had brought him?

Five days later Washington crossed the river again, this time not to fight but to offer a bounty of ten dollars to every soldier in his army who would reenlist. Cornwallis moved his troops south from New Brunswick and Princeton to engage the Americans at Trenton. Leaving 400 men in bivouac around campfires as a guise, during the night of January 3 Washington secretly led his main force to Princeton and engaged the British in a 45-minute battle. Although they lost forty killed or wounded, they were overwhelmingly victorious. Exhausted, the Americans spent the night at Somerset Court House.

Two days later, Washington's army moved farther north into winter quarters at Jockey Hollow outside Morristown. For Dieter, the Princeton skirmish was a profound moment—victory near the college that held many happy memories. In the ten best days of the war for the Americans, the Army had beaten Rall at Trenton then stopped Howe at Princeton. For the first time, Dieter sensed confidence in the outcome of the war.

He was confident and happy for another reason. Philadelphia was only a half day's ride from Morristown.

SIXTEEN

DREARY AND COLD, WINTER IN TULPEHOCKEN was a season of discontent. "Thank the Lord for Sundays and our beautiful Church on the Hill," Catherine said at least once a day, it seemed to the girls. As the evenings dragged on, silence reigned, the deaths in Dieter's Company in their hearts. In the dense silence, deep fears lay beneath the surface.

The only worry the family had at home, beyond Hans' absence and Rachael's persistent cough, was Cousin Peter's failing health. Eighty-two now, tired all the time, he was no longer able to work. He missed the ministering care of Dr. Otto, who left to serve as Surgeon General in the Continental Army's Middle Department.

"*Ya*," Adam said, "a good man, trained in Germany. His sons are doctors too in Reading. Maybe Peter sees one."

"There are still two boys at home working Peter's farm, *net*?" Catherine said.

"*Ya gewiss*," Ruth sighed. "That William makes a good husband."

Tillie turned to Ruth and smiled. "Too bad you're so young, Sis."

"Stop this right now," Catherine snapped. Staring at Ruth she said, "You are *mannsleitnarrish*. You know you are cousins. If you are not so *partickler* you have somebody by now."

Adam changed the subject. "It wonders me," he said, "if Dieter's company was with on Christmas night when Washington crosses the Delaware at Trenton. We follow these things at the tavern. *Verleicht* someone knows."

"*Ya*, we won that fight," Catherine said, "but it was not a Christian thing to do, *abaddich* on Christmas and it was not fair because many of the Hessians were drunk. The Bible says love your enemies."

"I don't like Germans fighting Germans," *die Grossmudder* said.

"*Grossmudder* Christman, how old are you?" Tillie asked.

"I don't tell, but it ain't eighty yet." She smiled and sat back.

Adam rose to light his pipe. "It wonders me where Dieter is now. The *Gazette* talks about Morrisville in New Jersey."

"Morristown, *net* Morrisville, *Daadi*," Tillie corrected him.

"*Ennichau*, it is not far," Adam said. "They don't fight in winter, so *verleicht* it gives a leave to come home. He said he comes home in six months."

"*Ya, awwer* Morristown is closer to Philadelphia than Tulpehocken," Tillie said. She put on a wry smile. "Does he go first to get married or does he first come home to us?"

"I would get married first," Ruth said.

"If you want to get married," Tillie said, "stop fighting with every boy you see." She looked at her mother. "I wonder if we get invited to the wedding."

"I don't like this talk," Catherine said curtly. "What Dieter does is his business." She paused. "Lucy Smithton is a fine girl. I hope they don't wait till the war is over."

"*Ya well*," Adam said, "at Kurtz they talk that the war goes three years more."

"It gets late," Catherine said. "Before we go to bed, we think of our sons. Bow your heads. 'Heavenly Father, watch over sons Hans and Dieter no matter where they are. Keep them true to Christ's teachings. Give them courage to do thy will. War separates them from us and each other. Show us all the light to see and act the right way. When they are in danger, put your loving arms around them. We love them both. In Christ's name we pray. Amen.' "

———

After arriving in Morristown, Col. Patton's 4th Battalion built log huts for their winter stay, the work a pleasant change from the boredom and idleness of non-combat duty. Dieter's platoons were first in the battalion to finish their huts. Every soldier's objective now was simple — keep warm.

The time seemed right for Dieter to request a leave. Waiting for approval, he made plans — first ride to Chestnut Street and ask Mr. Smithton's permission to marry his daughter. If he consents, set a date for the wedding, ride home to make arrangements for the family to attend, ask Michael Ege to be his best man.

The next day a messenger came to Dieter's hut. "Leave approved. Seven days beginning tomorrow. Report to quartermaster for horse and saddle." He dashed to Capt. Lesher's quarters.

"You are free to leave after the reveille beat, Dieter," Lesher said. He smiled. "Have a good time. *Un mach's guud.*"

"*Gross dank!*"

Up before dawn, Dieter scampered to the quartermaster. He packed clothes and a few apples in the saddle bag and dashed off. At 10 o'clock he rode down Chestnut Street and came to the Smithton house. Chloe came to the door.

"Oh, Master Staudt!"

"Are Mr. and Mrs. Smithton home?"

"Mr. Smithton left for the office."

Lucy's mother came to the door. "Why Dieter, what a surprise! Come in. Have you ridden far? Let us get you something to drink. How are you?"

"I'm well, thank you. How are you and your family?"

"We are all well. Does Lucy know you are coming?"

"No, but I wrote to tell her I applied for a leave."

"Wonderful. Where did you come from, or should I not ask?"

"It's all right. The enemy knows as much as we do. We are in winter quarters in Morristown, New Jersey."

"You look fine. Has it been hard?"

"Our battalion has been in only a few battles."

"Lucy is in school. I'll ask Zeke to take us to Mrs. Brodeau and bring her home. Maybe we should stop by Mr. Smithton's office."

"I hope I'm not too bold, Mrs. Smithton, but has Lucy told you we want to get married?"

She laughed. "Many times."

Raising an eyebrow he asked, "And you approve?"

"Oh I do."

"And Mr. Smithton?"

She hesitated briefly. "He admires you for your education and your intelligence and predicts you will be a success in whatever you do after the war."

"But Mrs. Smithton, does he approve of our marriage?"

"He wonders whether you should wait."

Dieter dropped his head. Recovering quickly, he said, "I understand. I love Lucy deeply and had the same misgivings earlier. But Lucy does not want to wait. Please don't think me forward, but we want to marry now during my leave. I have only seven days."

"You should talk with Mr. Smithton as openly as you have with me. Let's go see him right now."

Alan Smithton was in his office with the door closed. Soon he and his visitor came out. "Dieter Staudt! Lieutenant Dieter Staudt! What a surprise! Does Lucy know you are here?"

"Not yet."

"Good to see you. How are they treating you?"

"The battalion—fine. The British—not so well."

Smithton chuckled.

"Dear," Mrs. Smithton said, "Dieter has a seven-day leave. He was candid with me about his thoughts. I think you two should talk before we go to Mrs. Brodeau's to pick up Lucy."

Smithton held the office door open for Dieter.

"Yes," Mr. Smithton said, "I believe Lucy is very much in love with you. Both Mrs. Smithton and I consider you two a good match. The only question . . . the only question is, is this the right time?"

"I've asked myself that question." Dieter paused. "I'll speak openly. I am sensitive to the differences in our family circumstances. And Germans are not held in high regard by some in Philadelphia, mostly because of our dialect." Dieter smiled. "I believe I lost some of my broad vowels in college. I hope so."

"No Dieter, that is not a consideration. People in business like to hear foreign accents and admire the German character. No, the only hesitation I have is . . . well, the war." He waited. "I knew this was coming but I haven't faced up to it."

"I understand." Dieter broke the awkward silence. "If you will excuse me now, I am eager to see Lucy."

Emily Smithton rambled on as she and Dieter rode to Mrs. Brodeau's. "Well, here we are," she said as they turned onto Walnut Street. She chuckled. "Lucy is going to be one surprised girl."

They entered the school and spotted Mrs. Brodeau in the hallway. "Mrs. Smithton, how nice to see you."

"Thank you. May I introduce Lieutenant Staudt, a friend of Lucy's. He is on leave, so Lucy will miss classes for a few days."

"Certainly. I will fetch her."

In a few minutes Mrs. Brodeau and Lucy came hurrying down the hall. When she saw Dieter, Lucy ran to him, hugged him tightly and gave him an effusive kiss.

Her mother put a hand to her mouth. "Dear me," she said under her breath.

Tight-lipped, Madam Brodeau turned away.

"Oh Dieter! *Liebschdi!* How long is your leave?"

"One week."

"We'll make the most of it! I am ecstatic. Every night I dream of us together."

Again a hand went to her mother's mouth.

"What comes next? We *can* get married, can't we?" Turning to her mother she said hurriedly, "Mother, I know you approve. Do we have enough time? Who knows when we will be together again."

"Slow down, Lucy. Go get your suitcase."

In the carriage Lucy snuggled up to Dieter. He too was embarrassed by Lucy's ardor, Mrs. Smithton thought. Only a young girl's desire? A one-sided affair? Suddenly Dieter seemed much older than her daughter, she thought.

When she could get her eyes off Dieter, Lucy asked her mother, "What does Father say?"

"Well dear, he approves of the marriage, he just isn't sure this is the right time."

"Mother, it may be the only time."

"I had a chance to speak with your father at the office," Dieter said.

"What did he say?" Lucy hurried to ask.

"He is concerned about what the war may do to marriage. You remember I too asked that."

"No, we don't even think those thoughts." Lucy paused. "All right, the three of us in this carriage believe the wedding should be held now."

"Yes," her mother said, "but I guess it won't be the big wedding every mother wishes for her daughter."

"I don't care about that." She paused. "All right, we must plan our strategy to convince Father the time is right."

Dieter laughed. "Planning strategy sounds military. Seriously Lucy, I'm not sure that would be proper."

"No, Dieter," Mrs. Smithton said, "Lucy is right. I'll start. On the way home we'll swing over Fourth Street and you drop me off at the office. Zeke can take you two and I'll come home with your father."

Lucy and Dieter had the same quick thought—are we going to be alone? They dropped Lucy's mother off and rode on. Ignoring gawking pedestrians on the busy street, they embraced in the carriage and kissed lustily. As they approached the house, she said, "Do you think we dare go to the bedroom? We'll just ignore the servants."

"No Lucy. If your father agrees, we'll have only a few days to wait."

"All right, but if you change your mind . . . ."

In the house, he said, "You'll laugh at this but the only thing I want from you right now is a piece of string. I must measure your ring finger."

His reason trumped her passion. They restricted their love to amorous petting. Lucy's parents pulled up a half-hour later. Her mother's smile and quick wink told the story.

"We have much to do," she said excitedly. "Dieter, I don't know when you plan to visit your family, but certainly you'll stay here tonight."

"I want to leave before sunrise tomorrow."

"All your family are invited to the wedding, of course. We have ample room."

"You met my parents in Princeton but you haven't met my sisters. Do you have room for them?"

"Yes certainly. They are all invited."

"My father is the only one who may be reluctant. He doesn't like things he calls 'fancy,' " Dieter said.

"Oh I like both your parents so much. Mr. Smithton will too," Mrs. Smithton said.

Before dinner the three of them worked on details. First, the date? Dieter had to report back to Morristown by 4 o'clock on Monday. They agreed on Saturday.

Mr. Smithton came home at six and the wedding conversation continued over dinner. Lucy and Dieter talked on their own as the Smithtons worked out the guest list. After dinner, Mr. Smithton and Dieter went to the parlor and Lucy and her mother discussed the maid of honor, the dress, the music, the food and drink, the flowers, the favors.

By 10 o'clock, Dieter was exhausted. "It's been a long day," he said, "and I will be on my way tomorrow before you folks are out of bed. Goodnight." He gave Lucy a peck on the cheek and walked up the stairs.

She smiled. "Good night, dear. Sleep tight."

Early the next morning Dieter saddled up and headed home. He rode west to Germantown to visit the print shop of Christopher Sauer. Dieter knew Sauer favored the Tories in his *Germantowner Zeitung* and Hans was caught up in the same anti-Patriot fervor.

Dieter found the shop on the main street. As he pulled up, he saw someone unlocking the door. "Good morning. I was told Hans Staudt works here. Is he here?"

"*Nay*, he works late last night. He comes in later." He looked Dieter over head to foot. "What do you want with him?"

"*Nix wichdich.* I come back later."

There was much to do at home to get ready for the wedding, but seeing Hans was also important. He recalled seeing the town's shops and buildings when he was here last year. A little further advanced than Reading, he mused, certainly more shops.

He walked past a shoemaker's shop. Suddenly something about that struck him. *Die Mudder* spoke often about Mennonites from Germantown being so kind to them when they arrived in Philadelphia. What was their name? Dieter asked himself as he walked on. A common name — maybe Klein. He chuckled when he caught himself. No, no, not Klein but the exact opposite — Gross! There it was on the sign.

He walked into the shop.

Herr Gross greeted him. "*Hallo. Wie bischdt?*"

"*Guud. Wie gayt's mit der?*" Dieter paused. "Is your name Gross?"

"*Ya gewiss.*"

"Do you remember the Staudts? This was twenty years ago."

"*Ya, ya.* I made them shoes. You are their son, *gell?* Are they well?"

"*Die Grossmudder* is nearly eighty. But still spry."

"I remember her well. *Un der Maedel un der Daadi un die Mudder?*"

"They are well. I have four American sisters and one brother."

"Sehr gut!"

They talked for a long time. "My parents and Sarah will be glad I stopped to see you. They speak of you often. Thank you for your kindness to them. Dieter turned and left.

He walked back to Sauer's. Hans was not there. There was nothing more he could do. He mounted his horse and left, riding north to the Tulpehocken Road, putting the horse to a hard gallop.

At noon he reached Reading and forded the Schuylkill. A few more miles and he'd be home.

Rachael, coming from the barn, was first to see him. "Dieter! Dieter!" she cried. He dismounted, ran and hugged her. They entered the house and he was mobbed by *die Grossmudder, die Mudder,* and the girls, jumping and shouting. He hugged them all.

"Where is *der Daadi?*" Dieter asked. "He's not out in the fields on this bitter cold day?"

"*Ya,* I don't know what he does," Catherine said, shaking her head.

"I come right back," Dieter said.

They soon returned, Dieter's arm firmly around *der Daadi.* They sat at the kitchen *Disch,* two girls on the floor before the fireplace.

"How is Cousin Peter?" Dieter asked.

"About the same. He loses more weight and looks tired," Catherine said "Before we do anything else we offer a prayer. Hold hands. 'Heavenly Father, we ask you to sustain and strengthen our dear cousin Peter, who has been our rod and our staff here in the New World. He is with us in spirit as we rejoice in the return of our son Dieter.

'Father, this is the day we wait for, the day you provide for our comfort. We thank you and praise you for bringing Dieter back to us and for looking over him in battle. He looks older and wiser. If he must leave again for the war, look over him and all sons who go into battle. If it is your will, spare them to see a better day. We pray in Jesus' name. Amen.' "

Rachael brought him a cup of warm cider. "Dieter, in

your uniform you are more handsome than ever."

"*Mamma,* can we clean up the uniform?" Dieter asked. He chuckled. "I've lived in it for half a year."

"*Ya,* we do it. How long are you home?"

Before he could answer, the girls bombarded him with questions about army life, the fighting, the men, the food, about what comes next. *Der Daadi* sat back, smoking his pipe, beaming in pride. Dieter answered modestly, keeping Catherine's answer for last.

"*Ya Mamma,* I report to winter camp in Morristown on Monday."

"I hoped it would give a wedding," Catherine said softly.

"*Ya,* now for some news. There will be a wedding in Philadelphia on Saturday and you are all invited."

The girls looked at each other with open mouths, their faces etched in shock. "Saturday?"

"*Ya,* we must work fast," Dieter said. All eyes were on him as he laid out what must be done before they left for Philadelphia on Friday. "But first." He said, "I ride over to Charming Forge to ask Michael to be best man. Lucy's mother asked me to invite the Eges too. When I return I must go to Reading to buy a ring. Will you go along, *Mamma*?"

After he left, the family collapsed in silence, stunned. As the news sank in, the girls wondered—all invited to that fancy house overnight? We don't have good dresses. How do we act? We know a little English but conversing with upper class Philadelphia people?

"I don't go," Tillie said. "I am embarrassed."

"Me too," Ruth said.

"It would be hard on me to travel that far," *die Grossmudder* said.

Adam chimed in. "A farmer does not mix with *schtolsich Leit* in Philadelphia."

Catherine had heard enough. She stood up. "*Sie schtill!*" she exclaimed. "I am ashamed of the lot of you! You are selfish. You think only of yourselves, not Dieter. Lucy Smithton is a fine girl and so are her parents. Adam, you remember how kind Mrs. Smithton was to us at Dieter's graduation in Princeton."

Catherine paused a long minute, staring at the girls. "*Ya*, the trip is too much for *die Grossmudder* and *verleicht* for Rachael." She waited. "It was God's will that Dieter and Lucy meet last summer at the forge, not far from here. I pray that God blesses their marriage and keeps them safe through their lives together."

She paused, looked down, and shook her head slowly. "I go to this wedding if I have to go alone." She turned and left the room.

Early on Friday morning a caravan of three carriages carrying the Staudts and the Eges headed east on the Tulpehocken Road. Dieter rode behind on his army mare. For the Staudts it was the start of two breathtaking days.

Catherine was right—the girls, Adam, Catherine, all were made to feel comfortable. Only Lucy's friend Peggy Shippen seemed cool.

It was thrilling, especially for the Staudt girls, to be in the big city of Philadelphia, to be guests in so grand a home. They had never dreamed of a scene like this—seated at a large dining table with women stylishly adorned in magnificent dresses beset with jewels, made up in fashionable hair styles. It was a new experience to taste a delicious and varied wine and food, to enjoy the music, to marvel at the luxurious gifts Lucy opened to the delight of the females.

Topping all was the simple beauty of the bride, dressed in a gown with a bouffant skirt and revealing neckline. After the meal ended and the cake was served, Lucy ran tiny pieces of the cake through her wedding ring and gave them to her sisters and every girl there as a gracious wish for their future.

After more conversation and sociability, the guests crowded around the front door as the bride and groom left on their honeymoon in George Ege's handsome cabriolet. They would spend the night and the next day in the Inn at King of Prussia.

Early Monday morning the happy couple returned to Chestnut Street. After a leisurely breakfast, Dieter said goodbye to Mrs. Smithton, saddled his horse, gave Lucy one last tender kiss, and headed north to Morristown.

SEVENTEEN

DIETER REPORTED TO CAPT. LESHER. "I GUESS I don't have to ask . . . but did you have a good time?" Lesher said, smiling broadly. "I'm glad you're back. We have a problem."

"Oh?"

"Men are deserting, even some who got the ten-dollar bounty to stay another six weeks. It's an epidemic."

"Any of my men?"

"No, but I want you to go help Rehrer with his platoons."

"*Ya,* but you know he has it in for me."

"All right, we go over together. I lay it out that he works with you or I put him on record."

"This is funny," Dieter said. "There are more desertions than ever, yet Congress wants new battalions."

For the rest of the week Dieter visited Lt. Rehrer's men in their huts, appealing to their patriotism. Even more than homesickness, boredom of camp life took its toll. For relief Dieter recommended to Capt. Lesher a generous policy of *per diem* leaves into the small town of Morristown.

Dieter was surprised one day to see Aaron Burr ride up to 5th Company Headquarters. Dismounting, he said "Haven't seen you since Manhattan, Dieter. How's it going?"

"Just back from leave, so I'm fine." Pointing to Burr's light colonel's insignia, he said, "I see you're doing well."

"Didn't really expect that, at least not yet."

"What brings you, Colonel?" Dieter said, grinning.

"Do you have duty tonight? I'd like to go to the tavern."

"I'm free. We'll celebrate your promotion."

"All right. About six o'clock."

The Nassau Tavern was busy. They found a table and ordered rum. "Here's to the Colonel," Dieter said, raising his mug.

"Thanks for not including 'Lieutenant' in front. What about you? With your degree and flawless record, you should be more than a second lieutenant."

"I lack time in grade."

"People get around that. I'm thinking about the regulars, not the militia. You'd probably be a captain and get a company right away."

"No, Aaron, I plan to leave the military as soon as the war ends. I don't want any restraints." He paused. "Now that I'm a married man I have responsibilities."

"You're married? Since when? Who's the bride?"

"We were married in Philadelphia last week. Her name is Lucy Smithton."

"Ah, an English bride." Aaron paused. "Is she pretty? Tell me about your honeymoon."

Dieter ignored that.

"Congratulations. I hope I meet her soon. Anyway, you know you can resign your commission after three years. I have *my* eyes on politics in New York. Think over what I said about the Continentals. It's altogether different from the militia. If you prefer a staff position, I'm sure General Washington will remember you."

"Thanks, Aaron. I'll let you know."

"One other possibility. As a German you'll be interested in this. Have you ever heard of General Peter Muhlenberg?"

"Everyone knows about the Lutheran cleric Henry

Melchior Muhlenberg." Dieter said. "I believe he lives in Trappe, near Philadelphia."

"Peter is Henry's son and also a clergyman. This is interesting. In the pulpit after his sermon one Sunday, in Woodstock, Virginia, Peter shocked the congregation by removing his robe. There in all his glory stood a Continental Army Colonel in full regimentals! We hear that General Washington and Patrick Henry urged the Virginia House of Burgesses to appoint him to head an all-German battalion. I believe they will deploy here to Morristown in the spring. Maybe you'd prefer to serve with him."

"It would be an honor."

The two spent the rest of the night reminiscing about the college "triumvirate," their professors and courses, and the happy years at Princeton. Dieter left, ruminating about how a skinny thirteen-year-old-sophomore could have become a military hero, perhaps destined for greater honors.

After reveille the next morning Dieter approached Capt. Lesher, not only his company commander but now a good friend. "Last night I had dinner with Lieutenant Colonel Aaron Burr from Washington's staff. I believe you know we were college classmates. He thinks I should join the regulars."

"*Guud.* It is hard to fill your shoes, but you take advantage of that. The way you handle your men you are ready."

"That puts pressure on you, *net*?"

"I get a replacement from a Flying Camp." Lesher rose. "If you decide to leave, I give you best wishes."

Dieter longed for Lucy that night. If only he could see her before he made a decision. He took out his quill.

February 6, 1777

Dear Mrs. Staudt,

This is my first chance to call you by your new name. How do you like it? But as Shakespeare puts it, you would be sweet by any name.

How are you? Are your parents adjusted to having a

second married woman in their house?

A sage once said, "I can live for three weeks on one compliment." Well, I can live for three months, maybe three years, on the memory of our wedding weekend. I can hardly wait to see you.

I wish I could visit you to get your opinion about a decision I may make soon. It's this. Aaron Burr is here in Morristown on Washington's staff. He believes if I join the Continental Army I would become captain and command my own company. I would prefer that to serving in the Pennsylvania Militia because I notice the Regulars are better organized and prepared for battle. The problem is this: I would be expected to serve for three years before I could resign my commission. That is why I so much want your opinion.

I don't know what I want to do or can do as a career after the war, but I feel I must continue to serve our Glorious Cause. My friend Peter Ege is working with his father at Charming Forge. I suppose I could serve in a somewhat similar way. I am ambivalent about this, but I lean toward staying in military service. I wish I knew how you feel. Mail deliveries to this camp are practically non-existent so I must probably decide before I get your letter. The only possibility, and I can't count on this, is to get a day off base and ride down to see you. If I do, the leave would be for a Saturday, so please keep the next few Saturdays free. Do you think your parents could handle giving their daughter and son-in-law some daytime privacy?

Lucy, I love you completely. It may have been fate that I was stationed close enough to Philadelphia to marry you. I pray that fate will be as good to us in the years ahead.

My best regards to your family. Tell your parents I think they raised a marvelous daughter.

All my love,
Dieter

After a long four weeks of no mail from Lucy, Dieter applied for the one-day leave. Capt. Lesher said yes immediately. Early Saturday morning he mounted a quartermaster horse and left for Philadelphia.

As he rode, he considered the situation. Yes, he thought, he should take advantage of Aaron's help. If he joined the Continentals, his commitment would be for three years. But which offer—a staff position or a command position? The first offered more security, more safety, but that, he believed, should not be a consideration. Besides, Aaron said he could probably have his own company in Muhlenberg's German battalion. That appealed to him. And *der Daadi* would be proud.

He arrived at Chestnut Street earlier than he'd figured. Sure enough, Lucy was home. After a big hug and kiss she said, "*Liebschdi*, nothing on earth could have taken me out of this house on a Saturday."

Lucy's parents were disappointed that his leave was only for the day—not nearly as disappointed as he and Lucy were. After dinner, they took a stroll through the city, out-of-doors best for a private conversation.

Yes, Lucy told him, she received his letter, and yes, she had an opinion—join Gen. Washington's staff. He admitted he leaned toward joining Muhlenberg. "Whichever choice I make," he said, "you will support me, won't you?"

"Of course, Dieter dear. I love you." She waited until the street was empty then gave him a peck on the cheek.

They arrived home and had a bit of privacy. He was anxious to leave to avoid night riding. After a string of sweet kisses, he mounted the mare and left.

Back in camp, Dieter was still ambivalent about his decision. Finally, coming down on the side of Muhlenberg's Battalion, he walked to headquarters and applied for a commission.

Activity in Col. Patton's Tulpehocken Battalion and in the whole camp slowed to a crawl. Controlling the men was tougher than ever. But at least the desertion issue passed. This would be, Dieter reflected, the perfect time for training. But in this rag-tag militia there was no close-order drill, never any training at all. Even among the Continentals on the base he saw few formations.

Until his replacement reported, he spent time with his own men. At night he read, played chess and occasionally backgammon with Lt. Gring in the 2nd company. And he wrote letters.

When his battalion had been in New York, Dieter had the notion to keep a journal. He enjoyed writing, and he had many ideas. Why do the armies fight the illogical way they do? How many gun shots hit anyone? How can an army win battles without being trained? What are the odds of the colonies defeating the world's greatest military power? But he procrastinated. What should have been daily entries became weekly, at best. With so much time on his hands now, he resolved to get back to the journal.

Dieter's application for a commission was handled in Washington's headquarters on the base. The day after Dieter turned it in, Aaron walked into the 5th company. "*Viola*, Dieter, here's your commission."

"Thank you, sir. That was fast."

"I'm curious to know whether you decided on a staff or a command position."

"I lean toward serving with Muhlenberg."

"All right, your orders will read, '. . . to remain in place until the Eighth Virginia Battalion is deployed to Morristown, New Jersey.' Chuckling, Burr said, "You're going to have time on your hands."

An eager newly-commissioned second lieutenant arrived at Morristown to relieve Dieter. After a week of reading, writing in his journal and going off base to the village of Morristown at will, Dieter tired of the freedom. He hurried to general headquarters.

"Tell me what you think of this, Aaron. Could orders be cut to assign me to the headquarters staff until Muhlenberg arrives?"

"Good thinking, sir," Aaron joshed. "You must have a degree from the College of New Jersey. Yes, yes, that will work. General Washington will be glad to have a bright supernumerary, especially in planning. What you learn in these few months will serve you well when you command your own company. I'll look to it right away."

Two days later a courier rode up to the 5th Company

and called out Dieter's name. "Sir, orders for you."

Dieter rushed to Washington's headquarters for duty. He was assigned fill-in tasks, mostly mundane, a few substantial projects. He gained more than he contributed, he mused. Every now and then he caught sight of his Excellency George Washington.

———

It was March and the long winter lull in fighting was coming to a close. Dieter had learned much in army headquarters, particularly about the imminent Philadelphia campaign. And he learned about Parson Peter Muhlenberg.

More on his leadership qualities than his military experience, it was believed, Muhlenberg had been appointed to command a battalion to serve under Gen. Lee at Charleston. After he returned to Virginia, he determined he was of more service in the army than in the pulpit, and in January, 1776, dramatically announced his decision. Promoted by Congress to Brigadier General, he and his 9th Battalion deployed to Morristown and reported to Maj. Gen. Nathaniel Greene. Dieter was assigned to command the 6th Company.

In what turned out to be valuable rehearsal for battle, Dieter's company engaged the Redcoats in minor skirmishes in the New Jersey countryside. Fearing that Gen. Howe planned to attack Philadelphia, Gen. Greene crossed the Delaware River and on July 31 marched toward Philadelphia. But Washington was filled with doubts about the enemy's strategy. The large British fleet carrying Howe's army had sailed out of New York Harbor and later was spotted in the Delaware Capes. Was Howe's objective Philadelphia, or was this a diversion to draw Washington away from New York?

On August 1 the Americans marched west and camped between Germantown and the Schuylkill Falls. The weather was intensely hot. Officers of Muhlenberg's Battalion were ordered to meet at Cross Roads Tavern to consider a growing discipline problem—sutlers selling liquor to the troops.

Finally, on August 22 the British fleet was seen in the

Chesapeake Bay, approaching Philadelphia from the rear. For the Americans, there could be no further delay. They broke camp and proceeded to Nicetown, below Germantown. Two days later Washington and his 11,000 men marched through Philadelphia en route south to meet Howe, Cornwallis, and the Hessians' Baron von Knyphausen. The Muhlenberg battalion was first in line in the showy parade. After two weeks in Delaware, Washington moved back across the Pennsylvania line, taking positions south of the Brandywine Creek at Chadd's Ford.

The Battle of Brandywine was a disaster for the Americans. The Redcoats they saw in front of them were diversionary. The British crossed upstream fords and attacked from the right rear. Gen. Muhlenberg's Virginians slowed down the British rearguard long enough for other battalions to retire toward Dilworthtown, once engaging in fierce bayonet combat.

Dieter's 6th Company was the last to leave the field. The Continentals suffered 1,200 casualties, 400 taken prisoners. Dieter's company lost three killed, including one by shot, two by bayonet, and five seriously wounded. The battle was Dieter's first look at the young General Lafayette, also wounded in the action.

Howe moved into Chester, fifteen miles from the new capitol. On September 18 Congress evacuated Philadelphia, moving first to Lancaster then to York. The Liberty Bell was sent via army baggage train to Allen Town, to be stored in Zion Reformed Church. Earlier, anticipating Philadelphia's fall, the army evacuated crucial military stores to the main Continental depot in Reading.

Washington retreated to Pottstown, still determined to hold off the British conquest of Philadelphia. Howe moved his main body across the Schuylkill, and on September 23 Cornwallis marched triumphantly into the city with four British and two Hessian units. He set up camp in Germantown, five miles north of the city.

On October 4, never admitting defeat, strengthened by additional militia, Washington led his forces from Pottstown during the night, boldly attacking the British in a four-pronged surprise attack on Germantown. Early-morning fog caused great confusion, resulting in friendly fire against Wayne's column. The British confiscated the Chew House on Germantown Avenue for its headquarters. Rotund Gen. Henry Knox failed to destroy the house with his big guns.

Dieter's Company led Muhlenberg's Battalion south of town, driving into the enemy's position, taking 100 prisoners, then turning to fight their way out. The situation everywhere deteriorated fast. The troops knew their generals' plan was too complex, doomed to failure. Panic set in. Soldiers left the fight and rushed out of Germantown. The battle was lost. The American Army withdrew to Whitemarsh.

Gen. Washington's management style open to the views of his staff of general officers, he asked for recommendations for a site for winter encampment. Muhlenberg recommended a less settled upcountry location between Reading and Lancaster or between Reading and Easton. Washington chose a different site. He chose Valley Forge.

EIGHTEEN

Hans Staudt returned from New York pleased with himself for his contribution to the Tory cause on Major Rogers' mission. Hans foresaw intriguing possibilities for more secret exploits.

He rode to Germantown and entered the print shop, surprised to see a new man at the press. Hans turned to Sauer. "Good morning. I see we have an extra man."

"*Wie gayt's*, Hans?"

"*Gunz guud*. But I'm glad to be back."

"Hans, it went longer than I expected. I'm sorry but I had to get another apprentice," Sauer said.

"You mean you let me go?"

"Fulltime, *ya*. I'll call you when we need help."

"But you were the one who talks about Rogers. You say I could have time off."

"I don't know how busy I get."

Hans eyed the new man top to bottom. Then he strode to the case and retrieved a few tools and his *Schatz*. He stared at Sauer. "These are mine," he said as he tramped toward the door. He stopped. "One more thing. You and I are on the same side on this war. Someone will hear about this." He banged the door and left.

In spite of his showy remonstrance, Hans was not disappointed to be fired. On the long trek home from New

York, meditating on the amazing feat with Rogers, it came to him there are many ways to make a living during a war. He could perhaps be an agent for the cowboys and skinners busy stealing cattle to sell to the Tories.

He was surprised to see so many camp followers, some there to boost morale, some to be useful in little ways like washing clothes, some to nurse the wounded and sick. Some were wives. But there were hangers-on whose motives were selfish—sutlers supplying at steep prices whatever the soldiers' hearts desired, and spies and counterspies digging out scraps of information about troop movements. Hans saw his future. He could serve his cause and make money doing it.

He had learned valuable pointers from Maj. Rogers, the no-good New Hampshire roughneck. He pictured himself skimming off the top of bribe money allotted to paying spies. He would always be on the opposite side from his brother. Even so, there might be times when the Patriots would pay more than the British.

He learned how easy it was to live off the land, with the occasional lifting of a housewife's bread or pie. Both armies, he mused, do their share of raiding and foraging. Finding a place to sleep was no problem in a landscape dotted with farms and barns. When his work would take him into a town or city, he'd rent a room or stay in a tavern or ordinary, perhaps picking up a printing job or two.

Hans acknowledged he would never be a family man. He took his pleasures visiting Philadelphia's notorious bawdyhouses. He found a new source of income—pimping for his favorite girls. He was excited about the prospect of devious income from both citizens and soldiers. He began his new life by skipping out on the overdue rent.

On December 19 the American Army went into winter camp at Valley Forge, northwest of Philadelphia. Washington was criticized in Congress for choosing an area so exposed to the elements, a site he chose for its strategic location between Philadelphia and York, Congress' current home. Dieter had the same misgiving about exposure and learned later Gen.

Muhlenberg warned Washington of the potential problem, recommending scattering the troops in the wide-open frontier to the northwest.

The troops, especially the militia, were in dire circumstances. Clothing and shoes, provisions and food were scarce. Some men had not eaten in days. Here in the midst of a plentiful country, many soldiers believed they were in danger of perishing.

Men fell ill to smallpox, dysentery, thyroid ailments, and other diseases. They had come to their winter quarters late, weak and exhausted. Living in drafty tents for weeks, they rushed to finish their small log huts. Dieter wasn't surprised that the Pennsylvania German soldiers of his battalion were in their huts in four days. A few lucky squads ordered by the Quartermaster to forage for food in the countryside were quartered for the winter in the village of Downington.

An even bigger concern was that in the camp many soldiers were rioting, drinking heavily, marauding or violating General Orders. The number of deserters was growing. Outside the camp, near the pickets, strangers without papers, some potential spies, hung around.

Washington saw a solution: he persuaded Congress to provide a Provost Corps to enforce the Articles of War. Early in June, sixty-three officers and men were assigned the duty. He confided in Gen. Muhlenberg. "The Pennsylvania German troops," Washington said, "are the most dependable, hardest-working troops in the Army. For this assignment I want an all-German contingent."

Washington ordered the men recruited from the Reading-Pottstown area. He appointed Bartholow von Heer, an experienced European military police officer, to commad what he called the *Marechausee*.

Gen. Muhlenberg's battalion's area was nearest the enemy, a mile or two from Washington's headquarters in the village. At least, Dieter thought, he was only twenty-five miles from his Lucy in Philadelphia. For all the good it did him, it may have been a thousand and twenty-five miles. In the three months since the British entered the city, he received no mail from her or anyone else. Desperate to see her, he went to General Headquarters to talk with his friend Aaron.

"I don't know how I can help you this time, Dieter. Some battalions are granting extended leaves and furloughs, but that still wouldn't get you into the city."

"How tight is security in Philadelphia? Could I get through disguised as a civilian?" Dieter asked.

"No, no, Dieter. An officer in disguise caught by the enemy can be hanged without a trial." He waited. "But if you want a leave to visit your family in Tulpehocken and Muhlenberg turns you down, maybe I can help."

Dieter immediately walked to Battalion Headquarters. He was in luck: no company commanders were on leave. Permission granted.

Horses were scarce at Valley Forge, so many starving, but Dieter was able to sign out a Quartermaster mare.

Before turning north on Tulpehocken Road, Dieter paused and glanced longingly toward Philadelphia. How will this all work out? he wondered. When will he see dear Lucy again?

———

As Dieter rode toward home, his brother was busy in Philadelphia plying his new trade—mining information about patriots, information he sold to his English contact. For patriots in Philadelphia, even food was hard to obtain, some farmers—even some patriot farmers—paying agents like Hans to sell their products to wealthy Tories. Hans' biggest payoff came when he revealed American movements to the British.

Dieter arrived in Reading and rode down Penn Street. Memories of the glorious day of July 8 flashed into his mind. Was it really a year-and-a-half since he signed with the militia? In quick succession vivid images flashed by—Lucy in Paoli, battles in New York City and Harlem Heights, Aaron Burr, His Excellency George Washington, Trenton, Princeton, Morristown, the wedding, Brandywine, Germantown, Monmouth, the Paoli massacre. And now,

Valley Forge. He forded the Schuylkill and smiled broadly as he put the horse to a gallop, his thoughts concentrated on *die Mudder, der Daadi, die Grossmudder, un es Maed.*

As he turned into the farm, the horse left distinctive tracks in last night's thin layer of pristine snow. Dieter yelled, "Hallo! Hallo, Staudts! Is anyone home?"

The sisters rushed out. He dismounted and hugged them hard and kissed them. "Dieter! Dieter! Oh Dieter!" they cried.

"It's cold. Go in. I'll be right in." He led the horse to the barn.

He trotted to the house. First in line was his mother. She held him in a long embrace, falling silent and closing her eyes in prayer. Tears came to her eyes. She stood back and looked him over head to foot. "We are so grateful you are not injured. You look stronger than ever."

Der Daadi gave him a long hug and vigorous handshake. Then came *die Grossmudder.*

"Come, you have dinner now," *die Mudder* said. They all sat around *der Disch*, eyes fixed on him. They couldn't wait to ask their questions—how is Lucy? How long is your leave? Is it as bad in Valley Forge as the *Gazette* says?

"Now girls, let him finish dinner," Catherine said.

After he left the *Disch*, Tillie took his hand and pulled him to the best chair. "You get more handsome every time we see you," she said. "Next time bring a couple of your officer friends."

"None of that nonsense, Tillie," Catherine said. "Are you tired, Dieter dear? Do you want to rest?"

"No, I'm anxious to find out what's new." Rachael looked thinner, her breath more labored. "You all look well," he fibbed. "First I want to know about Cousin Peter."

They all looked to Adam. "I am glad you are here, Dieter," he said. "We go see him today."

"My turn to talk," Ruth said. "You surprise us. We have no idea you are coming."

"Yes, Ruth, we should start at the beginning. You know the British occupy Philadelphia." Dieter paused, looked down, and swallowed. "I can't get into the city to see Lucy. We can't even exchange letters." He paused again. "I'm worried that someone learns her husband is an American officer."

"That is *schlecht*," Catherine said. "But her parents take care of her, *net* ?"

"Yes, but the neighbors may not like this. Our spies tell us feeling runs high in the city."

"When we meet the Smithtons," *die Mudder* said, "I try to see how they lean. It's toward the English, *gell?*"

"It may be mixed," Dieter said. "*Ennichau*, about my leave. Officers take turns during the winter lull. So here I am."

"How long do you stay?" Ruth asked.

"Ten days."

"Ten days! *Wunnerbaar!*" Ruth said. "We do things. We have a good time. Maybe we go to Reading. We go neighboring."

"You don't mention the important thing," Catherine said. "We go to church."

Adam and Dieter took the buggy to Peter's farm. What they saw seated in a large chair, a shawl on his lap, was a man half Peter's normal weight, his checks sallow, his expression gaunt. "Come here and let me shake your hand," he said to Dieter in a soft voice.

"I'm so glad to see you, Peter."

"You look good. The service hasn't hurt you." Peter shook his head slowly. "I remember the day you were born."

Adam was used to his cousin's turning back the clock. "I remember leaving the homeland, going to Schoharie, then coming here to the *wunnerbaar* Tulpehocken. It was a good life." Peter smiled. "I own the land."

"Without your help, I don't know we make it that first year," Adam said.

Breathing hard, Peter said, "But we look ahead. John Lamm stops in to see me. He says we now have a constitution in the colony." Peter sat front in the chair, his voice stronger. "John says it favors the common people."

The sentence amazed Dieter: Cousin Peter was an Enlightenment idealist to the end. Dieter swallowed hard as they said goodbye, as true, as faithful a friend they would ever have, sharing to the end. On the ride home, Dieter and *der Daadi* were silent.

The days sped by. The weather was mild enough to work in the fields and building fences. Dieter was still a man of the soil, enjoying every chore.

He and the family got around to doing everything Ruth had proposed. The girls and Dieter rode into Reading one afternoon to see the sights and to buy soft goods at the White Store Post. "At Valley Forge," Dieter said, "we hear Philadelphia merchants come to Reading for the social season. Anybody know about this?"

Tillie giggled. "Dear me yes. Not a week goes by I don't get invited to their balls."

"Get out," Ruth said. "You haven't been in Reading for a year."

On Sunday the proud Staudt family rode to church. The Eges waved to Dieter as they walked down the aisle. After the service Dieter rushed up to Michael. "Good to see you, Michael. What day would it suit for me to visit?"

Two days later Dieter rode to Charming Forge. Anna Marie Ege greeted him with a smile. "I wanted to tell you in church, you look wonderful, Dieter. George was sorry to miss you. He's away on business."

"I can't tell you, Mrs. Ege, how many times I've thought about your generous gift—more than a gift, an education. When I'm settled after the war, I will pay back the loan."

"No, no. We are pleased Michael has so faithful a friend."

"What's going on down the road, Michael?" Dieter asked. "What are all these men doing?"

"We need stronger water current for the mill, so we hire Hessian prisoners to dig a channel from the Tulpehocken Creek to supply the slitting mill. They sleep on the top floor of the mansion."

"How many are there?"

"Thirty-four. They are good workers, worth the 1020

pounds we pay the government."

"I can see you enjoy the business, Michael."

"*Ya, ya. Der Daadi* has a job for you too after you leave the service. Or do you plan to stay in?"

"I haven't decided. I'm eligible to resign my commission next year. As you remember, I was always interested in politics and government in college. But I don't consider the future until I resign. My big concern now is the present. How do I get to see Lucy? How can I get a letter to her?"

"I wonder . . . *der Daadi* maybe can help. We supply the Continentals with cannons and shot, but we also do business with the English in Philadelphia. We have no difficulty moving about the city. Maybe we can deliver a letter to Lucy. I will talk with *der Daadi.*"

"*Danke.*" He waited. "I don't believe I told you—this is not to brag—but I met General Washington and served on his staff for a little while. I learned he never gives up. It would not surprise me if we move to take Philadelphia back. I pray we do."

"That must have been an honor. *Wunnerbaar!* You seem to enjoy the military life. I don't believe I would."

"It's different from what you think. We spend most of our time keeping the men fed, clothed, and out of trouble. Some officers spend little time with their men, but I enjoy working with them.

"Michael, one reason I came to see you is to hear about the new Pennsylvania constitution. I believe this happened at the time our company left for New York."

"*Ya, ya. Der Daadi* was elected a delegate to the convention. This was funny. They met in the West Room of the Statehouse at the same time members of the Continental Congress met in the East Room. *Der Daadi* said he caught glimpses of the famous men. Benjamin Franklin did double duty—president of the Pennsylvania Convention and delegate to the Congress."

"How long did the Pennsylvania Convention delegates meet?" Dieter asked.

"Eight weeks," Michael said, going on to give a full analysis of the legislation. Dieter was surprised when his friend said he considered it the most liberal constitution in the colonies.

"Thanks for all that, Michael. I must head home now, but I'll come once more before I go back to Valley Forge."

On Thursday night Adam and Dieter went to the tavern. Kurtz greeted Dieter like a hero. His daughter Minnie hugged and kissed him openly, a few of the Kurtz gang raising their eyebrows. "What a uniform," she exclaimed. "What a man! What are you doing later tonight?"

All the regulars rushed to shake Dieter's hand and vied to buy him a drink. He saw only one newcomer, Martin Sheidy, who, he learned, had moved in from the Maxatawny Settlement.

The gang talked about farming and the other regular subject, local politics. "I guess you know Peter Staudt is pretty low," John Lamm said. "He surprised me when he asked about the constitution."

"*Ya*, we had the same feeling on our visit," Adam said.

"I'm like Peter," Leroy Gerhart said. "I want to hear more about the constitution."

"I know the delegates voted for a legislature with only one house," Lamm said.

"I guess the other colonies," Gerhart said, "have two houses. Maybe we save some money."

"*Ya verleicht*," Sam Fidler said. "But the best thing about that is everybody in the Assembly is equal. There is no House of Lords. Dieter, do you know any more about this?"

"Peter Ege knows about it because his father was a delegate. He told me the legislature would be stronger than the executive branch."

"How did they get that passed?" Henry Brucher asked.

No one seemed to know.

"What about the right to vote?" Brucher asked. "Must you own land?"

"No, you just have to be at least twenty-one, a resident for one year, and pay taxes," Dieter said.

"*Wunnerbaar!* I wonder what the upper class thinks of that?"

"George Ege said the draft was printed in the *Pennsylvania Evening Post*," Deter said. "It brought strong criticism from the anti-constitutionalists. You have to give these delegates credit—they had the debates and votes printed in English and German."

The discussion moved on—taxes, the war, and the loyalty of some neighbors. As Dieter reflected on the next big step in his life, a year or so ahead, a prior thought returned—perhaps he'd get involved in politics.

As usual, Bully Lenhardt put in his two cents.

Taking their drinks from one table to another, the men gossiped a bit about neighbors. "Haven't heard about your brother lately," Bully said to Dieter. "Anything new with him?"

Dieter hesitated. "I believe he's still working for printer Sauer in Germantown."

The party broke up about 10 o'clock. On the way home, Adam said, "I overheard what you said about Hans. Were you telling the truth?"

"A white lie, *Daadi*. I tell this to you but we must not tell *die Mudder*. I hear Hans may be active as a spy."

Adam waited, his head down. He said softly, "Oh Hans, Hans. Why are you so different?"

No one was in bed when Dieter and Adam arrived home. "We must take advantage of having you home," Catherine said. "Sit and tell us about the war."

He described army life—mostly trying to stay warm and alive in camp. He talked about the men of his company—some funny, some morose and dejected, most trustworthy.

"I'm lucky to be in General Muhlenberg's battalion." He smiled. "He's from Hanover, so we Low Germans don't understand some of his words, but we get around it." Dieter chuckled. "Once he told a raiding party to bring back *Kartoffel*. Someone called out, 'He means *Grummbeere*.' "

"Did you serve under any other generals?"

"We served in General Nathaniel Greene's division

in the battle of Germantown. Next to Washington, he is the general we respect most. And Henry Knox is a good strategist. But no one matches Washington as leader. I try to be like him."

"Is he haughty? Does he speak to privates?"

"As freely as with generals. He is so tender-hearted he can't stand to see a man flogged."

"I hope he is religious," Catherine said.

"*Ya, Mamma*, they say when he is in his field tent he has services every morning and evening. They say he hates to hear the men swear."

"Do you carry a rifle?" Rachael asked.

"No, officers carry pistols."

No one asked about the fighting, but he felt they wanted to know. "Fighting is horrible, especially close-in fighting." The terrible bayonet fight at Paoli flashed into his mind. He paused for a long minute. He said softly, "No one who lives through it will ever be the same."

The eyes of the Staudts were moist. Catherine broke the silence. "We have prayed together often, but this one is special. Join hands.

"Our Father in Heaven, we thank you for the good men and women who helped bring us to where we are in this new world. Deep in our hearts is Cousin Peter, our right hand here in the wilderness. We pray for his soul. We know he will dwell with you.

"We pray for the souls of all soldiers on both sides who die in this war and for comfort for those wounded and in prison. Be with their families. We thank you for the lives of the selfless men in Philadelphia who lead us in our cause to set men free. If it be your will, may we be victorious and may we proclaim justice.

"We thank you tonight for looking over son Dieter in his times of trial and danger. Keep him safe. Keep all soldiers safe. Be merciful to all who fight.

"Thank you for our family. Look out for son Hans. We look on him with love and kindness and hope for his early return.

"We pray this prayer in Christ's name. Amen."

NINETEEN

Back at Valley Forge, Dieter inspected his company. All his men were accounted for, only two on sick call. As he moved from one platoon to the next, he observed that spring had brought renewed spirit, renewed animation.

Spring fever struck Dieter too. He dreamed of seeing Lucy. It was clear the army would soon break camp. The word among field officers was that the council of Washington's generals was debating either retaking Philadelphia or moving against New York. British General Clinton made the decision for them. On June 18 he evacuated Philadelphia, moving his 10,000 troops and a covey of Tories and camp followers out of the city toward Haddonfield, New Jersey. But not before Clinton and Howe were treated to the gaudiest party ever seen in Philadelphia. They called it a "Mischianza".

After a sumptuous dinner, guests floated down the Delaware River to a meadow set up for a staged medieval tourney, fireworks in the background. Drinks flowed freely as contestants and spectators toasted the king and queen and the Royal family. After the chivalric display, the party of would-be knights and their ladies sailed back and danced the night away.

Lucy watched with excitement as the Continental Army marched into Philadelphia like conquering heroes. What the soldiers observed was a volatile mix of Patriots, Loyalists, and neutrals who had remained during the nine-month occupation. Lucy exulted in one thought—she would soon see her husband!

Washington gave the order to pursue the British, shattering Dieter's dream of an early leave. The enemies met at Monmouth Court House and fought to a draw, both sides suffering casualties of more than 300 men, including some felled by sunstroke on the hottest day on record. The 6th company lost four killed, seven wounded. Dieter suffered a bullet wound of the left shoulder.

Washington put Brigadier General Benedict Arnold in command of the city. Philadelphia the capital of both the Colony of Pennsylvania and the United Colonies, he'd have his hands full. Beyond an injury that kept him from field command, Arnold was troubled by personal demons. Impatient, restless, he aspired to wealth and luxury, power, and fame. A dark demon gnawed at his soul—he had been passed over for promotion.

Keeping angry civilian patriots out of the city longer than anyone expected, Arnold commandeered expensive goods of Tories fleeing with the British army. He confiscated military supplies and medicine left behind by the British army and shipped all the goods to Wilmington. When his thievery became known, gazes of admiration turned to glares of contempt.

Arnold fell deeper and deeper into speculation and shady deals. In exchange for a two-thirds share, he offered New York merchants goods and properties the British left behind. He and his partners arranged for the confiscated British ship *Charming Nancy* to leave port with the loot. When the British menaced the ship at Egg Harbor, New Jersey, Arnold dispatched twelve army wagons to return the stolen cargo to him.

Arnold and his partners needed intelligence to carry out their schemes. "I know just the man," Robert Shewell said "—the German who freed that Major Rogers from jail."

"What's his name?" William Constable asked.

"He goes by one name—Hans."

———

With a handsome payoff from the Nathan Hale case, Hans Staudt found a niche with more pay than he made as a printer—and more excitement. Wanting to be where shipping and business deals were made, he rented a room on crowded Front Street near Market. The London Coffee House was across the street, a beehive for news and gossip, business, and theatre tickets. He was close to his regular business with girls, and he had his choice of clubs for drinking and carousing. For meals there were the "glutton" clubs.

Shewell knew where to find him. Without preliminaries, he said, "I have work for you."

Hans walked to the window and scanned the street. "How do you know about me?"

Shewell chuckled. "You're not the only one with secrets."

More firmly, Hans said, "I must know who told you about me."

"A friend from Germantown."

"What's his name?"

"*Herr* Sauer. Are you interested or aren't you?"

"Tell me about it."

Shewell's narrative became long and redundant. "Are you in?" he said finally.

"From what I hear from you, I see three jobs—selling stolen cargoes in Wilmington, delivering and returning secret messages to merchants in New York, and bribing an army wagon master. I'll consider it. Come back and we talk again."

In two days Shewell was back.

"All right, what will you pay?" Hans asked.

"Two hundred dollars. But only after everything is to our satisfaction.

"*Nay nay.* Half now and half when I finish."
"I am not authorized for this."
"You have partners. Who are they?"
"Never mind. You deal with me."

After Shewell left, Hans sat and reflected. For the first time ever he felt important. He needed to act the part; he needed better clothes. After this job, he reflected, he'd move on. First he had to know where his brother was stationed. Sister Rachael would tell him.

———

Arnold, meanwhile, was imposing himself on the social scene in Philadelphia, and in the eyes of Joseph Reed and the Pennsylvania Council, not for the better. They accused him of condoning gaudy scenes of debauchery in city theatres. On the night before the execution of two Tories convicted of collaborating with the British, he audaciously gave a party attended by Tory wives and daughters.

The Council had had enough. It ordered Arnold and his partner Clarkson to testify on their private use of army wagons. Their defense was surprising—they were accountable only to Congress. After long debate, Congress approved a court martial.

Amid the turmoil and charges came the shocking announcement of Arnold's pending wedding to Lucy's friend Peggy Shippen. "Why would she marry a man like that, and twice her age?" Lucy asked.

"I guess you're not disappointed she didn't choose you as bridesmaid," her mother said.

"No, no, Ann may have the honor if she wants it."

Philadelphia society expected the wedding to be the big social event of the year. Attending, the Smithtons supposed, would be men of the Continental Congress, top brass of the Army, governors of several colonies, the mayor and high society of the city—all adorned by their ladies in sumptuous dress. Would such notables as Jefferson, Adams, and Madison be there? people wondered.

Everyone was shocked to learn that the wedding was already held, apparently attended only by family. Gossip had it that Edward Shippen would do no more for

Peggy than he had done for a sister who recently married Edward Burd. The scandal was too much for Lucy and her sisters and friends to ignore. Ann Rittenhouse invited them to dinner to gossip.

"You won't find a prettier bride anywhere than Peggy," Ann said.

"Yes, and except for a limp from his injured leg, old Benedict's not unattractive," Lucy said. She added, "But he's nothing compared to my Dieter."

"He has icy eyes and a swarthy complexion," Sally Smithton said. "He looks like a mystic."

"Peggy herself is a little strange at times, don't you think?" Ann said.

"I heard she was shy as a little girl. I didn't know her then," Lucy said.

"Shy and at times hysterical," Ann said.

"She seems to have an unusual interest in money and business." Sally paused and chuckled. "I hear she pursued him."

"This isn't nice to say, but I think he looks old enough to be her father. When she's sixty he'll be eighty."

"You're right, Ann, that wasn't nice. Let's just wish them the best," Sally said. Smiling, she added, "Maybe they deserve each other."

"Here's a bit of scandal I heard at school," Lucy said. "A young British major by the name of Andre was captured and interned in Lancaster. En route, the guard convoy stopped in Philadelphia for a few days. Apparently Peggy and Becky Franks met him at a social."

"They say Andre's rather effeminate and likes music and art. I hear he drew miniature ovals of them," Lucy said. "And . . . I hear Peggy Shippen openly flirted with him." Eyebrows around the table shot up.

"Let's change the subject," Ann said. "Has anyone heard how the Whig society folks made out when they exiled themselves to Reading for the season?"

"Reading is at the edge of the Tulpehocken Settlement where Dieter's family lives," Lucy said.

"What I heard," Sally said, "is that Mrs. Grayson entertained at a house on Queen Street. The other hostess who competed with her was Mrs. Biddle, who set up her salon at the Crown Tavern." She chuckled. "They say the small cakes she served were popular."

"I heard," Lucy said, "the young folks of Reading were delighted to have fashionable Philadelphia society people with them. I heard it was a grand mixture of Whigs and Continentals, Tories and British, with some Hessians thrown in."

"I know of a few prominent local men," Ann said, "who were seen at parties there—George Ege, Colonel Bird, Colonel Nagel, Captain Hiester. And Mr. Hall, the printer, was one of the favorites. He was popular because he brought his press to Reading from Philadelphia to turn out Continental currency."

"But they're all back in Philadelphia now, I guess," Lucy said. "Thanks for inviting us, Ann" She smiled broadly. "The dinner was delicious, and the gossip even better."

The first suggestion that the Arnolds might defect to the British came from his bride. The surest way to the ear of British commander Sir Henry Clinton, she told her husband, was through his aide, handsome British Captain John Andre. She kept from her husband the flirtation she'd had with the captain when he was in Philadelphia as a prisoner.

Besides Andre, one more collaborator was needed as go-between, the Arnolds concluded. They contacted Hans Staudt. Hans was moving up in life. With the payment for his work for Arnold's machinations in Philadelphia, he bought a quality suit of clothes he'd never dreamed he could afford. Robert Shewell hinted at more work to come. People who saw Hans on the streets and in the taverns of Philadelphia could not imagine he was once the backwoods character who helped British Major Rogers break out of jail. Meanwhile, he was not without steady income, involved as he was with his girls. Even more lucrative, he hung around taverns and clubs to collect intelligence on troop movements, numbers and conditions of forces, changes in command, field personnel. He sold it to the highest bidder. Who needed a college education for this? he mused.

He left for New York immediately, slipping through the lines to contact Andre. He returned to Philadelphia with a reply. Clinton was willing to pay two guineas a head for each American soldier Arnold led into a trap. But when Arnold demanded an additional 10,000 pounds, negotiations broke down.

Arnold found it difficult to live with the failure. At the same time he was losing influence in the city, and his prosperity vanished. He determined to revive the plot. Through an unsuspecting New York congressman, Peggy planted doubts in Washington's mind about the competence of the commander of the fortress at West Point, recommending Arnold for the post. Washington ordered the change. Preparing to hand the fort over to the British, Arnold set about weakening its defenses.

Details of the plot took shape. Andre, in civilian clothes, would assume the name John Anderson. He and Arnold, who used the code name *Moore*, would be transported up the Hudson by the British sloop *Vulture*, with Hans accompanying them as guide and messenger. They would then trek to a secluded spot in the woods for a late-night rendezvous.

The conference lasted into the dawn. Their plans were disrupted when suddenly the following morning the *Vulture* was attacked by an American squad. Arnold issued passes to Andre and Hans to get by the American guards, and they left for White Plains. They were apprehended by the militia, who were suspicious and detained them. Hans escaped into the woods. Andre was captured near Tarrytown and sent to Continental headquarters, where detailed plans of West Point and other secret papers were discovered in his shoes. He was tried, convicted, and hanged at Washington's headquarters at Tappan.

Hans brought the news to Arnold in the Robinson House, Arnold's headquarters across the river from West Point. Washington was scheduled to visit the same day. Agitated, flushed, Arnold rushed to the bedroom and told Peggy the terrible truth. The couple said their emotional goodbyes, not knowing when they would see each other again.

Hans watched from the shadows outside the house as Washington's party entered and saw a disheveled Peggy Arnold in her morning gown, hysterical, pleading with the accusers to spare her baby, falling on her knees to pray. In her histrionics, Arnold escaped.

―――

After Clinton abandoned Philadelphia, his army retreated to New York. Winter was approaching and Washington sought his generals' opinions on winter quarters. This time Muhlenberg's point—that the forces should be scattered rather than concentrated as they had been at Valley Forge—won out, and camps were ordered set up in New Jersey, New York, and Connecticut. The sides balanced, the war was at a standstill. The American army went into a stand-down mode, observing the enemy, reconnoitering, at times raiding and foraging.

General Putnam was in command. When he was away on detached service, Muhlenberg was in command. In his headquarters at West Point he showed a lighter side, entertaining officers and their guests with lavish dinners, some of fourteen courses. The music and dancing increased Dieter's longing for Lucy. Since the battalion was not going to be engaged during the winter, this was his opportunity, he reasoned, to request a leave.

The request was approved. The ride to Philadelphia was long and cold; Dieter allowed himself only two stops. Finally he entered the city, rode down Chestnut Street, and hitched his horse in front of the Smithtons.

Chloe came to the door.

"My oh my. It's Master Staudt."

Lucy heard the voices and ran to the door. "Oh Dieter! Dieter! What a surprise!" She hugged him and showered him with passionate kisses.

She turned to Chloe. "You and the others take a long walk, go to the market, go anywhere, all of you. Don't come back till four o'clock."

"Your parents aren't home?" Dieter asked.

"They're away. Isn't that wonderful?"

He picked her up and swung her around. "*Ya, ya.*

Wunnerbaar! I have so much to tell you, Lucy."

"We'll talk later, dear." She grabbed his hand and dragged him to the stairs.

"Give me a minute to take care of the horse."

She laughed. "But only a minute."

After hours of beautiful lovemaking, they dressed and went down to the parlor. Seated discretely on the sofa, they awaited the servants and dinner.

Pointing to his new major's insignia, she asked. "What's next — colonel?"

"We'll talk about that, but you go first. How's school? Tell me about the occupation."

"All right, but you haven't said — how long is your leave?"

"Seven great days."

"And nights!"

"Are your parents away?"

"They'll be back on Thursday. I can't believe our good luck. I may wear you out by then."

Lucy talked non-stop, her pace speeding up when she described the wedding. "That Arnold is turning out to be a terrible man. And I believe Peggy Shippen is no better. I don't know when I'll ever see her again." She paused. In a lower voice she said, "My father and I had words about that."

"Oh?"

"I can't believe this, and I don't believe Mother can either, but Father has a good opinion of Arnold. Of course you know Arnold favors the Tories."

Dieter didn't respond.

"Father even urged me to accept invitations to their parties." She waited. "We still haven't made up."

Dieter had detected the tension. Does his father-in-law's Tory leaning result merely from his business dealings? Dieter wondered.

After a long monologue, Lucy stroked Dieter's shoulder. "We were too busy earlier for me to mention it, but I noticed the scar. You didn't write about that. Were you hit?"

"Yes, but it's minor. It doesn't bother me."

"You've been so patient, dear. You must have a great deal to tell me."

"Yes, but let's just relax. I wonder . . . could we have a glass of wine?"

"I'll call Chloe."

TWENTY

THE LOVERS SLEPT LATE LAST NIGHT. HE AVOIDED talking about the future. After breakfast, the weather pleasant, he said, "I'd like to see where the Congress meets."

She smiled broadly. "*Ya wohl, Herr Major.* It's just a couple blocks away."

The sun shone brightly as they left the house hand in hand and strolled down Chestnut Street. At Sixth and Chestnut they saw a building under construction. "What will this be?" he asked.

"The future home of Congress. I believe they'll call it Congress Hall."

They came to a large red-brick building with a bell tower and a clock. "And this building?" he asked.

"This is Pennsylvania's State House." Reveling in her role as docent, she added, "This is where Congress meets now. Pretty building, don't you think?"

"Even grander than Nassau Hall."

They strolled to the court yard. "Right here is where Mother and I stood to hear the Declaration read. What a day that was."

"Wasn't your father with you?"

Lucy shrugged.

"Our celebration in Reading came four days later on

Penn Square."

They walked on to Fifth and Chestnut. "This lot seems to be laid out for a building," Dieter said. "Another government building?"

"I'm not sure of this one, but there's talk of moving the Town Hall here from cramped quarters at Second and Market."

They continued on and turned right into Fourth Street. "This is Carpenters' Hall. The First Congress met here before the war."

"I'm confused. This isn't a government building, is it? Why didn't they meet in the Pennsylvania State House where they meet now?"

"Because the Pennsylvania Legislature was in session in their own capitol. Carpenters' Hall is owned by a company of builders and architects. They lent it to Congress for its first session in 1774."

He pulled her to an alcove beside the steps of the hall and gave her a kiss. "That's for being such a good docent."

She kissed him back. "And that's for being a good lover."

They returned to Chestnut Street. As they crossed Third Street Dieter said, "This looks familiar. Isn't the City Tavern near here? George Ege took Michael and me to the tavern on our first trip to Princeton."

"Just a block down," she said, pointing. "Shall we have lunch? But it's a bit early to eat. We'll come back later."

They turned north onto Second Street and walked to High Street. "Down there near the river is Bradford's London Coffee House. Maybe you'd rather eat there."

"Perhaps another time. I'd rather eat at City Tavern again."

Continuing on Second Street, they passed Christ Church. "Your church is magnificent inside and out. How different from my little Church on the Hill back home."

"Yes, very different. Did I tell you when we worshipped there that Washington and Franklin have their pews. Sometimes they bring their black slaves."

They crossed Arch Street. "I'll show you the alley

where Elfreth has his tailor shop," Lucy said. They strolled the alley, admiring the little houses.

"Looks like a nice place to live," he said.

"You're having a good time in the big city, aren't you, Dieter dear?"

"W*unnerbaar*. What is the population?"

"Father believes it's forty thousand. He said Penn's Green Town doubled in the last decade. Some brag about it as the biggest and finest in the colonies."

"It's impressive the way Penn laid out this city so neatly. It would be hard to get lost," he said.

"And the parks in the four sections of the city are very pretty. Look, there's the Library Tavern. You'd enjoy poking your head in there. Then we'll stroll down to Front Street and the grand Delaware River. A lot to see there."

She's right, Dieter mused as he spotted an array of tall ships in the docks and on the river. Hundreds of stevedores and seamen ran about shouting. " 'Busy as bees ben they,' as Chaucer put it," he said.

"Ah ha, showing off your education." She giggled and poked him lightly with a fist. "Only joshing."

He raised his sights toward the horizon and fell silent.

"What is it, dear? What's bothering you?"

"Something about staring east across the ocean and the old world beyond . . . . " He paused for a long minute. "When I think of Mamma and Papa, Sarah, *un Grossmudder* . . . leaving home forever, crossing the wild Atlantic . . . ."

Had he known his brother was living just two bocks from where they were standing, Dieter might have been even more somber.

Lucy put an arm around him.

Finally he said, "All right, I'm ready to go."

At City Tavern Dieter spotted the table where the Eges and he had sat. "This is special, dear — our first meal out alone. Isn't it wonderful to look ahead to many good times," Lucy said, stroking his arm.

"*Ya ya, wunnerbaar!*"

Back home, Chloe greeted them. Lowering her head,

a hand to her face, she said, "Missy Smithton, do you . . . do you want us to go for a walk?"

They burst out laughing. "No Chloe, but thanks for asking."

Relishing the happy, carefree day, they relaxed in the parlor, a long evening ahead for talk.

"Lucy, I have something important to tell you. I'm now eligible to resign my commission."

She jumped out of her chair. "Wonderful! I can't believe this!" She gave him a hug and lusty kiss.

"But . . . but what then?" he said.

"I can't even think of that now. All I know is we'll be together. Wonderful!"

"But I must think about what I'll do for a living. And we must talk about where we'll live."

"It doesn't matter. We'll be together."

"Lucy, my work matters a great deal."

She sat back in her chair.

He gave her time. "I have a liberal education, but even if I'd want to be a lawyer or doctor or parson, I'd need more education."

"My parents will support us."

He rose and turned directly to her. "Lucy, I don't ever want to hear that again."

For the first time, she saw a flash of anger in him.

"We will end this conversation," he said somberly.

Pouting, she said nothing.

He put on his coat. "I'm going for a walk."

He was back in fifteen minutes.

"I'm sorry," she said. "The wonderful news followed by uncertainty was too much for me." She gave him a gentle hug. "Forgive me. You know, dear, I've been critical of Peggy Shippen for being self-centered. I'm acting just like her. I'm sorry."

"Let's drop it now. I want to read the *Gazetette*."

At 9 o'clock Lucy rose. "I'm not used to all that walking. I'm ready for bed."

"I thought we could postpone this but I must get a

few things off my mind. Two possibilities. If your father has a place for me in the business for a year—I say if he does—we could save money and then go into our own business. Or, you know Mr. Ege offered me a position at the Charming Forge iron plantation. What would you think of living in Tulpehocken, or perhaps in Reading Town?"

"Oh."

He rose, walked to the window. Turning to her he said, "Lucy, did Mrs. Brodeau teach you about the Enlightenment?"

"A bit."

"Well, I believe every person in the colonies, including slaves, including women, should be included in the freedom we are fighting for, and if they wish, should be able to work for a living, own property, and vote."

"Oh that sounds wonderful."

"And I don't think wives should blindly follow their husband's decisions. You were shocked when I mentioned Charming Forge because you hadn't considered moving. Let's talk about that."

She sat silent for a few minutes. "It would take a while to get used to the change." She rose, walked to him, and kissed him gently. "Dieter, we love each other. We'll be happy wherever we live." She paused and smiled. "As for a career, I see you as a teacher."

"Hmmm. I hadn't thought of that." He paused. "Regardless, I want you to be as forthright as the other woman in my life, my mother."

"I'll try." She took his hand and led him to the stairs.

"One last word. My best opportunity may be to stay in the army. By the end of the war I'd probably be a full colonel."

She raised her eyebrows and stared at him. "Recently, very recently, a nice man told me to stick up for myself." She smiled broadly. "No no no. Not the army, dear. I need you. I want you home. I want to start a family."

She walked to the stairs. "I'm not sleepy, but it's bedtime, dear."

On the long road back to camp, Dieter ruminated about his wonderful week, but as he rode on, he felt uneasy about facing Gen. Muhlenberg, the away-from-home father figure he admired so much. He never thought seriously about the ministry as a profession, but if he had, he'd have the general as a model. After he arrived at the camp, Dieter checked on his company and called it a day.

The next morning he walked to headquarters. An aide ushered him into the general's office. "*Komen herin*, Major Staudt. Or maybe I say, *Kumm rei, gell?* But you understand my Hanover German."

"Dale."

"I have a *Gemisch*e of *Hoch un Pennsilfaanisch Deitsch.*"

"*Ya, ich wayss.*" Dieter waited. "Sir, there is a connection between us. I believe your mother is a daughter of Conrad Weiser, *net*? When I was six or seven *der Daadi* took me out to Weiser's farm to meet him. I was fascinated hearing him talk about Indians."

"*Ya*, I was in *Grossdaadi's* company only a few times, but I too was intrigued. Weiser was a very important man."

"When I heard about your German battalion in Virginia, I was surprised. I thought the Germans settled only in Pennsylvania."

"*Ya*," the general said, "my family lives in Providence, near Philadelphia. Some call it Trappe. When I went down to the Shenandoah to serve the Woodstock church years ago, I discovered many Germans had moved down from Pennsylvania. *Ennichau, sitzen sich.*"

"Sir, I came to tell you I wish to resign my commission."

Muhlenberg raised his brows and paused. "I regret hearing this, Major Staudt. Your company is my pride. May I know why?"

"Army life is tough, but I have no regrets about serving. And I am very proud to serve under you." He paused. "It's just that I came off leave to visit my wife in Philadelphia. Since our marriage we have been together only three times."

"I understand. I have the same problem getting home. When I joined the Army I left our furniture and effects in the glebe at Dunmore. I asked General Washington for leave to move the furniture out so as not to inconvenience the new parson. His Excellency asked me to defer my visit."

"Sir, I do not abandon the Patriot cause and will support it actively. When I joined the Continentals I expected the war to be over in three years. Maybe having France on our side will speed up the end." He paused. "My concern is to make a start in my career."

"What will that be? I know you are a graduate of the College of New Jersey." He waited. "You would be a fine prospect for the ministry."

Dieter chuckled. "My mother would be delighted to hear you say that. I wish you could meet her." He paused. "I'm uncertain about a career but I'm eager to get started."

"*Guud.* Send your resignation letter to Congress." The general handed him a paper. "Address it to this officer's attention." He paused and smiled. "And Major Staudt, *Mach's guud.*"

TWENTY-ONE

LUCY HAD BEEN WAITING FOR DAYS. FINALLY, there Dieter was, handsome in his uniform, smiling broadly. She hugged and kissed him.

"*Wunnerbaar!*" she said. This time you're home for good."

Mrs. Smithton rushed downstairs and greeted him. "Welcome home, Dieter. We're so glad to see you. We've arranged a little suite upstairs for you to share."

Dieter brought in his bag. "Have you told your parents we'll be staying only until we find a place of our own?"

"Oh, I forgot." She paused "You must be hungry."

"Hungry and tired. I was up before dawn."

"Lie down and rest. We're going to have a special dinner."

Dieter was still asleep when Mr. Smithton came home. Lucy woke him. "Dear, we'll be eating soon."

After he dressed, they went downstairs. Mr. Smithton rose and shook his hand. "Happy to see you, Dieter. You look as though you've survived well."

"Thank you, but the war goes on. I hope my whole company will be as lucky as I was."

"How long do you believe it will last?" Smithton

asked. "What is the next campaign?"

Dieter's head jerked back at the questions. He said nothing.

The dinner was sumptuous—lentil soup, greens, beef, turkey, sweet potatoes, corn soufflé, beans, apple pie. "Delicious. Never had a meal like this in the army," Dieter said, smiling.

As he had feared, conversation over dinner was somewhat strained. What could they talk about—how the war was going? his battle experiences? their life during the British occupation? Gen. Arnold's shameful management of the city?

"You were very quiet at dinner, dear," Lucy said when they retreated to their suite. "Are you tired?"

"No, it's just that it may take a while to get used to being a civilian." He waited. "Lucy, I wrote to my family about what's happening. I want to ride up to Tulpehocken tomorrow."

"Oh yes, let's. I'm eager to see them."

He kissed her. "Lucy, you have no idea how happy it makes me to hear you say this. Ruth and Rachael are the only sisters still home, maybe only Rachael. There'll be room for us."

"I'm more concerned about sleeping arrangements right here," she said with a little giggle. "The master bedroom is only thirty feet from ours. But we won't be as bad as Tom Jefferson. They say when his wife visited from Virginia, he went home from the Congress every afternoon for several hours."

"Good for them."

A week later, rested, fitted with new clothes, Dieter rented a livery stable carriage. A sharp "gidyap" and they were off.

"Tell me what's new in the family," Lucy said.

"Last time I was home, *die Mudder un der Daadi* were well. *Die Grossmudder* is close to eighty, but she's still spry. Tillie is married, and I believe Ruth has a man. The only one with a problem is Rachael. Some days she is so sick."

"What about your brother? I never hear about him."

When they came to a creek crossing the road he said, "Let's stop for a rest. There's a place to sit over there."

"I should have told you before, Lucy, but it never seemed like the right time." He held back nothing—the young boy who was lazy and troublesome, the jealous brother, the journeyman printer who can't hold a job, the son whose distraught parents pray for him every single night. Dieter fell silent. Then he said, "I'm embarrassed to tell you, but I've heard he pimps for the streetwalkers on Front Street." He shook his head. "Perhaps worse, he may be a spy."

"A spy for the British?"

"When they occupied the city, did you notice any Tory sympathizers?"

She hesitated. "A few girls in school talked about how their parents felt."

"Some merchants favor the British, of course. Will this be a problem for us?"

"I never heard this discussed at home. Mother and I are Patriots. I'm just not sure about Father. Could we talk about something else."

"Let's talk about my folks. We'll be there in a few hours."

They arrived in Reading, forded the Schuylkill and rode west on the final leg of the journey. In an hour they were home.

Rachael spotted them first. "Mamma, look, it's Dieter. And Lucy is with him! Lucy! Lucy! Lucy!" she cried.

The women came running. "Oh Lucy, we didn't expect to see you," Ruth said. "This is *wunnerbaar*."

They took turns hugging her, *die Grossmudder* last.

Dieter smiled. Guffawing, he said, "*Guck amol.* I'm here too."

"*Guck alliebber*, here's the driver who brought Lucy," Ruth quipped, laughing heartily.

After tenderly embracing her son, *die Mudder* said, "Ruth, quick go fetch *der Daadi*."

"*Nay*, I go and *verleicht* surprise him," Dieter said.

Adam saw him coming and rushed to meet him.

They hugged. "*Was iss es Gezewwel, Sohn?* What does it give?"

"They are excited to see Lucy. *Verleicht* they thought they would never see her here."

"*Ya well*, I am *verschtaunt* too, surprised *un frehlich*."

In a little while, the excitement settled down. After a supper of *Groombeera Supp, Brot, Kaes un Lattwarrick*, the Staudts spent the evening in lively chatter.

"I'm learning a few new words tonight," Lucy said. "I remember the word *Kartoffel* from school, but the soup was delicious no matter what it's called."

Die Grossmudder was more talkative than usual. "Lucy, this will be your first night in a log house, *net?* My first time was in the Gross's house in Germantown many years ago." Catherine and Adam smiled and the girls giggled as she related her oft-told story of being pushed by her son-in-law up a ladder to the second floor.

It was time for bed. "*Bauersleit* get up early," Catherine said, "*awwer* guests get up whenever they wish. We are so happy you are here. Sleep tight. I say a special prayer for you."

As soon as Dieter and Lucy climbed the ladder, he hugged and kissed her tenderly. "Lucy dear, you are *wunnerbaar!*"

"*Gross dank*, dear. That was sweet."

"In my heart I knew," he said . . . "I knew you would fit right in but what makes me doubly happy is that you sincerely enjoy them. Can you imagine your friends even visiting in the back country?"

Lucy and Dieter slept late. After breakfast, he said, "I'm going to ride out to Charming Forge to see Michael. Would you like to go along?"

"*Nay, nay*," Ruth said, "she stays here with us."

"You mind your manners," *die Mudder* said sternly.

"It's up to you, Lucy," he said.

"Will you be going to the Eges another time before we leave? I'd like to be with the girls today."

Since Dieter had last seen Michael, he had married

and had a young daughter. They had their own spacious quarters in the mansion.

Mr. Ege came home after dinner. "I'm glad to see you, Dieter. If you're here seeking work, the offer is open."

The next day Dieter put on work clothes and helped *der Daadi* in the back field. Without words, they reaffirmed their strong bond, Adam grateful that his son had returned home whole and sound. Men of the soil, their time together was precious.

On Wednesday Dieter and Lucy rode into Reading. "I have this idea. We build a two-story house, live on the second floor and have a business on the first."

"And what kind of business will that be?"

"Maybe a book and stationery store."

"Do most people read English? Is there a market?"

"There will be. But we will have German books too. Think of the pleasure we'll have reading the books before we sell them." Dieter chuckled. "I think of Henry Knox, the stout colonel I fought with at Germantown. He became an expert on fortification and artillery by studying British field manuals in the bookstore he owned in Boston."

"Where would this bookstore of yours be?"

"Of *ours,* not of *yours.* I'll show you." They rode up Penn Street and turned north on Callowhill. When they came to an empty lot on the east side, Dieter jumped off the carriage. "Right here!" he said, spreading both arms widely.

"All right, dear. But we better keep an open mind."

At dinner on Thursday evening Ruth said to her brother, "Don't you think the men at the tavern would like to see the pretty girl you married? If you're going to the tavern, take her with you?"

Catherine jumped on her daughter. "I am ashamed of you for even thinking such a thought. Women don't go to taverns."

Lucy smiled. "My husband encourages me to think for myself. I'd like to meet these men Dieter told me about."

"Maybe we could introduce you and then leave," Dieter said.

"*Nay, nay, nay!* We don't do this," Catherine said firmly. "I am surprised at all of you. If people want to see Dieter's bride, they come to church on Sunday."

Sunday dawned bright and clear. Attendance at the service was heavier than usual; the Staudts split up and sat in different pews. Catherine had been prescient—many church newcomers came to gaze at the Philadelphia beauty the neighbors were buzzing about.

The contrast between Hain's Church and Philadelphia's magnificent Christ Church was stark, Dieter mused. Yet, surrounded by his family, Lucy felt warm inside. She missed a choir but she enjoyed the hymns, giggling softly as she struggled with the German words. Parson Waldschmidt climbed the steps to the wine-glass pulpit. He was indefatigable and dreary, striving for points and lessons that escaped her. After an hour and a half, she whispered to Dieter, "How much longer?"

The service ended and many parishioners lingered. The neighbors rushed to meet Lucy. She was struck by their openness and simple charm, some girls bashful, most smiling. How different from Christ Church, she reflected.

Back home, *die Grossmudder* said, "Lucy, we call this being *Keenichin*, queen bee. You enjoyed, *gell?*"

"*Ya, Grossmudder*, I had fun," she said, smug in using the dialect.

Lucy knew that Sundays in the country were days of inactivity. She hoped a stroll down the lane and into the road would be all right. The girls busied themselves helping with the dinner. Rachael was given the honor of announcing, "Dinner is ready. *Kumm esse.*"

Early the next morning *der Daadi* hitched the horse to the carriage, and everyone came out to see Lucy and Dieter off. "Thank you for having us," she said. "It was a wonderful week."

On the ride to Philadelphia, Lucy and Dieter had a

long time to talk about the future. "You aren't reluctant, are you," she asked, "to work for Father?"

"I'm not sure. I certainly don't want a no-account position. I'd rather work outside an office. What I'd like to do is work for a year to save enough to get started on my own."

"I'm sure Father would lend us money to get started."

"Germans don't like debt. *Der Daadi* couldn't rest until he paid the patent on the land."

"Well anyway, let's enjoy ourselves living in Philadelphia. There's plenty to do."

"I look forward to it. If your father doesn't have a position for me, I'll find a job elsewhere."

"So long as we're together, everything will be fine." She kissed him.

TWENTY-TWO

DIETER AND LUCY STAUDT RETURNED TO Philadelphia to make their home. Even though they had their private suite upstairs, Dieter felt uncomfortable. He was concerned about finding employment. Lucy encouraged him to approach her father.

"Don't you believe if he needed someone he'd ask me?"

"Maybe." She chuckled. "I believe what we are seeing is a case of pride on both sides. Why don't you ask him if he knows of a broker or merchant wanting to hire a college graduate."

The next morning after breakfast Dieter caught Mr. Smithton at the door.

"The city is growing fast," Smithton said. "There will be many opportunities for you. If you're interested in the grain business, I've been considering adding a man to stay in contact with my farmers."

"Sounds interesting."

"Competition is keen, especially for quality wheat. Except for one day in the office, this new man would be out visiting and advising farmers every week."

"I know something about farming. I'd like that."

"I must leave now. Think it over."

Dieter took a seat in the parlor. He needed a good

job, he reflected, dependent as he was on his meager Army pension. If he could work for a year and save half the income, they could move to Reading, borrow money and start a book business. Until then, he would insist on renting a small house. Is Lucy prepared for this? he wondered.

The war would end soon, Dieter believed, but tension between Patriots and Tories, between wealthy merchant aristocrats on one side and poor or middling farmers and tradesmen on the other would continue. Would politics be a tension between him and his in-laws?

He went upstairs. Lucy gave him a hug and a big kiss. "What's that for?" he asked.

"That's to show you how much I love you. It's wonderful to be together all the time."

He laughed. "You showed me last night, but thanks anyway."

Lucy was overjoyed when Dieter accepted her father's offer. "It seems just right for you, dear. I'm going to miss you on the days you're away, but we'll make it up."

A month later they moved into a house on Elfreth's Alley, just off Second Street. The Smithton servants hauled furniture from their rooms into the house, and they went shopping for parlor and kitchen furniture.

"I don't want to embarrass you, Lucy, but can you cook?"

"Mamma told me we may have Chloe."

"No Lucy, no servants for us."

"But I don't know how to cook."

"We'll compromise. We'll have Chloe teach you. Or I'll help you."

"You don't mean you'd work in the kitchen? No one ever heard of that. But I'm so . . . I don't know . . . awkward."

Dieter laughed. "Back home we call that *dappich*. You cook English and I'll cook German. We'll keep that our secret."

—

Dieter fell into a routine in his job — in the office on Monday, up north in the back country the rest of the week. The old farms within forty miles of Philadelphia no longer productive, Smithton bought his wheat northwest of Pottstown in the rich Oley Valley and from farms surrounding Reading, especially in the Tulpehocken Valley and in Lancaster County. Having plenty of forest land to clear, some early settlers gave no thought to soil conservation, abandoning worn out fields for new ones. But German farmers, frugal and industrious, cleared no more land than they needed. Blessed with a limestone belt like the calcareous soil of the Rhine Valley they left behind, they learned the essentials early—prepare fields with care, rotate crops, abandon alternating fields for a season and plant red clover and grass in them. And manure generously.

As he worked his way from farm to farm, Dieter found only a few German farmers who confessed they had a problem with their crops. A generation younger than most farmers he visited, he felt awkward setting himself up as an expert. Jacob DeTurk in the Oley Valley asked him, "What is Smithton's idea? Is he worried about someone outbidding him?"

"Competition is becoming tougher, and he wants to be sure to work with you men."

"At this time I have no complaints. But I hear rumors that the Allens and other wealthy Philadelphia brokers have also sent their men out. Did you say your name is Staudt? I believe I met your *Daadi* at a *Versammling* once in Tulpehocken."

"I'll ask him if he remembers."

Dieter was eager to call on farms in the Tulpehocken Settlement. Karl Schneider was glad to see him. "*Ya*," he said. "I have some sick wheat. Do you know what to do about it?" He led Dieter to the back field.

"I see something sticking to the blossom," Dieter said. "This is your newest field, *net*?"

"*Ya*, the first crop."

"Maybe it comes from the shade of these trees close to the field. You can bolt it off, but I doubt that Mr. Smithton would accept it."

"*Ich wayss.* I guess we must trim out some of the big oaks. Over here I have some wheat with chess. But there's no shade here."

"Did you wash the seed before you planted it?"

"*Nay,* but I try that. *Danke.*"

Before leaving Schneider, Dieter said, "Do you know any *Bauer* unhappy with the price they are getting?" He got a few leads to follow.

By Thursday morning Dieter was ready to consult with a special farmer — *der Daadi.* Ruth spotted him as he rode up. "Dieter, Dieter," she cried. *Die Mudder, die Grossmudder,* and Rachael all took turns hugging their hero. "From your letter we knew you were coming," Ruth said, "but we didn't know when. I guess we are your last stop, *gell?* "

Der Daadi rushed in from the back field and shook Dieter's hand vigorously. "This time you come to give *mich der Rot, gel? Ya well,* I don't look for advice but maybe you know something I don't" He shook his head. "I can't believe they pay you for doing this."

"*So gayt's. Ennichau,* I came here first this morning. I must go next to the Hoch *Platz.* I will be back at dark." He chuckled. "Think of some questions to ask me."

"We make something good for supper," *die Grossmudder* said.

Dieter returned about six o'clock. "*Kumm hock dich mol,*" *die Mudder* said. "We think you don't get dinner so it gives *schnitz un gnepp* for supper."

"Dieter, catch us up on the news," Ruth said. "How's Lucy? I hope she comes soon back."

"Tell us about your house, *Sohn,*" *die Mudder* said. "Do you like living in Philadelphia?"

Dieter talked about Elfreth's Alley and the important buildings, the plays and musicals they attended, their friends, the Free Library. "There are stores for books and newspapers. I like that."

"It's Thursday." Adam said. "The Kurtz gang will be at the tavern tonight, *Sohn.* Bully Lenhardt promises us a new trick."

"New trick?"

Adam laughed. "I haven't seen it yet but I hear about it."

A half dozen regulars were already at the Kurtz Tavern when Adam and Dieter arrived. "Look who's here," Michael Kintzer said. "It's the farm expert."

"Don't do that," George Riegel said sharply. "Just be glad Smithton isn't sending out someone who doesn't know nothing."

"*Ya, ich wayss.* I was only having fun," Kintzer said.

Others drifted in. "I hope Bully gets here before dark," Riegel said. "He needs daylight for his trick."

"Dieter," Sam Fidler asked, "are you glad you're not in the army no more?"

"I might have stayed in, but the war was moving to the South. We heard our battalion would not be active."

"*Ennichau*," Sam said, "seems to me the war is winding down. Our boys did their part."

"Out here in the sticks," Leroy Gerhart said, "we don't get much about Philadelphia. What's this about Benedict Arnold stealing things?"

"He was in charge after the British left," Dieter said, "and he ran things for his own profit. You maybe know he was caught scheming to turn West Point over to the British."

"*Ya*, we read about that in the *Gazette. Ei, Ei, Ei.*"

"Where's your wife?" George asked. "We hear she's a beauty. I come special to see her."

Suddenly the men heard peals of children laughing and loud huzzahs. "*Uh, oh,* it must be Bully," George said. "This will be good."

The men hurried out. "*Guck emol do!*" Leroy shrieked.

Coming up the road was a steer gaily decorated with garlands, mounted by none other than Bully Lenhardt, tipping his hat to the children and boisterous followers. As he came to the tavern he dismounted and said, "You ain't seen nothing yet." He spotted Dieter.

"Hallo, Major Staudt," he called. "I'm glad you're here to see this rare act. Watch carefully."

Bully pretended to whisper into the steer's ear. "*Nay*, he is not ready yet to perform. Someone bring me a drink till he's ready."

The light was failing as Bully downed his third draught.

"Hurry up, Bully," Rolf Ludwig called out. "It gives dark."

Bully walked to his steer. "All right, Herman, I guess we do it."

He mounted, rode down the road forty yards, turned and came back, this time with Herman pacing like a show horse.

"*Huzzah! Huzzah!*" the crowd cheered. They had never seen anything like this.

"The best is yet to come," Bully said.

He rode back down, turned with a flourish, and paced back in the same gait as before. But this time he had Herman stop every five yards and hold up his front right leg. The crowd, swelled now to fifty men, women, and children, went wild.

On the ride home, Dieter said to *der Daadi*, "It was *wunnerbaar* being with these men. This is different from anything else I do. If we come back to live, I will go to the tavern often."

"You come back to live?" Adam asked. "*Wunnerbaar!* Wait till I tell *die Mudder*."

"*Nay, Daadi*, that slipped out. This is not definite. Can you and I keep this secret?"

"*Ya*, but you let me know, *gell*?"

At breakfast the next morning, Dieter announced he was going to the *Miller Bauerei*. "I'll be back for dinner and then leave tomorrow. *Allrecht?*"

Early the next morning Dieter said goodbye and left for Philadelphia. He arrived home as night fell. Lucy was watching for him. "I'm so happy to see you, dear? How was your week?"

"Good. And yours?"

"*Wunnerbaar.* All day I've been thinking of the first thing we'd do when you got home." Smiling slyly, she took his hand and led him upstairs. It was a good start for the weekend.

After they got dressed Dieter said, "I'd like to go out to eat."

"My parents belong to the Liberty Fishing Company. We could eat there. Or we could go to Peg Mullen's Beefsteak House."

"Could we just eat in a tavern, one that has the latest newspapers."

"Good. There are dozens to choose from."

They walked out, passing several taverns. They came to the Bunch of Grapes Tavern. "This is a good one, dear. Want to try it?"

During dinner Lucy said, "There are several new theaters springing up in Southwark. Why don't we see a play tomorrow night?"

"What is the play?"

"The American Company is giving *The Prince of Parthia* in their new theater on Cedar Street. Sarah told me her family enjoyed *The Tempest* in a new theatre in Society Hill."

"Are there musical productions?"

"I heard one company performed the ballad opera *The Paddock* last week. When we leave here we can walk to the London Coffee House to see what tickets are available."

Dieter was thrilled by everything the city offered. They went out to dinner and theatre with their friends Amanda and Charles Smith and exchanged evenings for cards.

The highlight of his week came on Saturdays for Dieter when he walked out to the Union Library Company on Chestnut Street. Among the collection he spied *Joseph Andrews, Paradise Lost,* and *Lives of the Poets.*

Dieter felt his excitement grow when he left the library and hurried next door to the bookstore of Henry Miller, who printed and sold mainly books in German. He planned to walk later to the Woodhouse and Hall shops, but it was with Miller that he felt most comfortable.

On his second visit there, Dieter had greeted him with, *"Wie gayt's?"*

"Where are you from, sir? I don't often hear that dialect in my shop."

Dieter related his Tulpehocken story. "My wife and I live in Elfreth's Alley, but we will plan to move back, probably to Reading." He chuckled. "Reading has no bookstores. I'm considering opening the first one."

"I have been to Reading. *Schayni Dorf.* Maybe I can help." Miller talked about the printing business in Philadelphia. The printers advertise their bookstores in newspapers, he told Dieter. Some import their books from England and Europe, but there is no copyright law, Miller explained, so they simply reprint popular English books of Defoe, Goldsmith, Gray, and other literary writers, and also some popular authors. "The Scotsman Robert Bell is our most successful bookseller," he said

"I notice you have newspapers and stationery for sale. Is that successful?"

"The seven papers add a little. I sell them just to get people in."

Busy weeks and months slipped by, Lucy and Dieter Staudt very much in love. A backdrop to Dieter's joy was one constant thought — a bookstore in Reading is feasible!

One night in bed Lucy had a surprise for her husband. "Dieter dear, I think you're going to be a father. See what you think." She put his hand on her stomach.

"Oh yes. *Wunnerbaar!* Do you feel all right?"

"A little funny some mornings, that's all."

"Have you told your mother?"

"I'll wait a couple weeks to be sure."

"I'm eager to tell the folks in Tulpehocken. They will be thrilled. Their first grandchild."

The baby was a boy. They named him Andrew. Mrs. Smithton was beside herself, visiting every day. Dieter raised no objection about having Chloe stay for a month or two.

With spring in the air, Dieter could wait no longer. "Lucy, remember when I talked about working here for a year? It's a year and a half now and I'm anxious to leave."

"I can tell." She waited. "It will be hard, but we must do it, I guess. Can we wait another month or so?"

"I must give your father notice. He has been fair with me."

"It has worked out so well I wonder why you want to leave."

"It's hard to explain — maybe returning to the land, maybe wanting to be part of Reading as it grows, certainly going home to the Tulpehocken. You understand, don't you?"

"Yes dear, I have those same feelings for Philadelphia."

The day came to leave. Mrs. Smithton held Andrew to the last. Her voice shaky, she said, "Goodbye and God bless you. Write often."

"We will," Dieter said. "At least the post is improving. And we aren't that far away."

TWENTY-THREE

DIETER AND LUCY STAUDT, BABY ANDY BUNDLED up in his mother's arms, headed for the Tulpehocken Valley. On this very road, Dieter reflected, his parents, their daughter, and *Grossmudder* Christman had walked to the frontier from Germantown thirty years ago and began a line of Staudts in the New World. Except for worry over Hans, life had been good. Soon Adam and Catherine would meet their newest grandson.

The road was improved since those years — a bit wider, fewer overhanging branches, fewer holes and puddles. And there were more taverns and inns for travelers. Their carriage, brand new, was comfortable and their horse was fast. They stopped to rest and refresh themselves and bait the horse at taverns along the way.

As they came closer to Reading, they chatted excitedly. "The Black Bear Inn is up ahead," Dieter said. "Do you want to stop?"

"Let's keep going. I'm so eager to show off Andrew."

They passed the summit of Neversink and came to Penn's Mount. As they started down the steep hill, Dieter kept a sharp eye out for the river, hidden by the thick forest. Dieter smiled. The Indians called it "the hidden river."

They caught a glimpse of shimmering silver. Dieter's

heart swelled. In ten minutes the road became Penn Street, wider, smoother. "I remember hearing at the tavern," Dieter said, "when Thomas Penn, Conrad Weiser, and the surveyors laid out the town, Weiser wanted to name this street 'Heidelberg.' But Penn the proprietor, he said, 'No, no. It will be 'Penn Street'."

Dieter marveled at how fast this inland town was growing. They passed Thomas Street and came to Callowhill, seeing houses everywhere, perhaps a hundred. "There's the court house," Dieter pointed out. They gazed at Trinity Lutheran and First German churches with their graceful spires, the State House, and the huge Continental warehouses so important in supplying the Continental Army. "Somewhere here is where we'll live," he said softly.

They reached Finney's ford on the east bank and got help crossing the river.

Dieter had been in Tulpehocken often in the last year visiting farmers for his job, but this trip was different—they were home to stay! As they passed farms on the north and on the south, he delighted in recalling the families—Klopp, Schaeffer, Zerbe, Schade. "Most of my visits were congenial," he told Lucy, "but Lauk over there was angry, ready to change brokers." He chuckled. "He's still not happy, but at least he hasn't switched."

"Oh here's the little creek" Lucy said. "I forget the name but it starts with a C."

"Cacusi. The Little Cacusi. When we cross it again we'll be home."

"Look, there's that cute little Welsh stone house you told me about."

They arrived at the Staudt homestead. Everyone was outside waiting. Even Sarah and Tillie were there. *Die Mudder* hurried to Lucy's side of the carriage and held out her arms. "I must be first to hold little Andrew," she said. "Hand him down."

Der Grossmudder and the girls surrounded Catherine and the baby, moving around for the best peek, oohing and aahing over him. *Der Daadi* greeted Dieter as he stepped off the carriage. *"Wie gayt's, Sohn?"* Adam greeted him.

"Ganz guud, Daadi. Wie bischt du?"

"Mir sin allrecht, danke."

The farm was aglow with joy, Andrew and his mother the center of never-ending attention. Claiming seniority, *die Grossmudder* took charge, determining whose turn it was to hold *der Bubel*.

Catherine's prayer before dinner was long and heartfelt, setting the tone for weeks of remembrance and joy, of work in the soil, and, for Dieter and Lucy, thoughts about their future. They had, had they not, hinted to his parents about wanting a business and living in Reading?

Lucy supported Dieter's dream of owning a bookstore. Several times a week they rode into the town looking for empty lots or houses for sale. "There's heavy foot traffic near the court house," he said to Lucy, "so that would be a good location. You recall we talked about living on the second floor and having the store on the first."

"I hope we'll have room for my parents to visit," she said.

Walking the streets of Reading Town, they narrowed down the possibilities to three—a lot in the first block of north Callowhill, a lot in the first block of north Prince, and a house at the northwest corner of Prince and Thomas. "This one has good possibilities," Dieter said. They inquired at the court house and learned the house was rented out by a Philadelphia proprietor.

They'd need a loan. Recalling overheated lectures about owning one's own land, Dieter knew better than asking *der Daadi's* opinion. Adam was relieved when Dieter told him he paid back George Ege for his generosity in sending him to college.

After weeks of indecision, Dieter and Lucy decided the house at Prince and Thomas could be altered for their purpose. Through lawyer Edward Biddle, Dieter learned the Philadelphia owner would sell the property at the right price. Dieter rode to Charming Forge and came away with a low-interest twenty-year loan from George Ege.

"I trust you like my own son," Ege said. "Your plan is sound and Reading is one of the most important and fastest growing inland towns in Pennsylvania. I wish you success."

Dieter engaged a carpenter to make the alterations. Meanwhile, he rode to Philadelphia several times to visit the book stores of John Conrad, Patrick Byrne, and others. The proprietors, some publisher/booksellers, were congenial and generous with suggestions—books to stock, wholesalers, prices, and what to avoid. He picked up ideas for the design and décor of his store in artist Charles Wilson Peale's bookstore on Walnut Street.

On one of his trips home, Dieter had their furniture from Philadelphia loaded on a rented wagon. He stored things in the hay loft of the big barn.

Excitement grew as everyone kept up with progress on the house in Reading. *Die Mudder* and Rachael went shopping with them for household items, the White Store at Penn and Callowhill the best source.

Every third day Dieter left his farm duties to ride into town to check the construction. The only disappointment was that the kitchen would have to remain in the rear of the ground floor. To compensate, the carpenter built a second staircase. The main downstairs room was enlarged by removing a wall, and in another couple weeks, the carpenter told Dieter, he'd get to the final job, installing shelves.

Three weeks later Dieter, Lucy, *die Mudder un der Daddi* awoke to a special day. The men loaded the stored furniture onto the wagon, Dieter and Lucy rode the wagon, and Adam and Catherine rode the carriage into the city. As they turned onto Prince Street, Lucy spotted a colorful sign. "Look, dear. This is what we've been waiting for." There it was, proudly announcing to the world—DIETER STAUDT BOOKSELLER and STATIONER.

The four had a happy time, the women arranging furniture upstairs and later preparing a meal downstairs, the men unpacking boxes of books from Philadelphia. The ultimate joy of stacking the shelves fell solely to the store's proud owner. Late in the afternoon Adam and Catherine left in the wagon, and Dieter took the carriage to the livery stable on Duke. He bustled home for their first night in their new home.

In the afternoon of the next day Adam and Catherine rode up Prince Street, Catherine holding Andrew tightly in her arms. In the bookstore Lucy and Dieter were chatting cheerfully as they browsed through the books and arranged them on the shelves. When they saw a carriage approach, they rushed out. Lucy reached up to take her son. "Andy, my Andy, I'm so happy to see you." She smothered him with kisses. "Come see your new home."

Three days later shoppers and lookers were waiting outside the store when Dieter opened the door. "*Kumm rei, alliebber,*" he greeted them.
"*Ei, ei, ei. Des iss schay,*" people said as they entered.
In a mixture of English and Palatinate German, Dieter invited them to look through the books. "When you're finished, put them on the table here. All the books in German are on this side," he said, motioning.

He and Lucy played a guessing game about the first day. How many people would come into the store? How many books would they sell? Which book will sell first? Dieter won that game when a well-dressed German plopped down ten dollars for a German Bible translated and printed by Christopher Sauer in Germantown. After the last customer left, Dieter said, "That's a good omen." Checking the price he paid for the book in Philadelphia, he said, "We made three dollars on our first sale."

Lucy pulled him back into the stockroom and gave him a kiss. "Congratulations, Dieter dear. After we close for the day, we'll open the bottle of Madeira we've been saving."

TWENTY-FOUR

AFTER SIX MONTHS THE STAUDT BOOKSELLING business broke even. *Der Daadi*, Dieter reflected, would be shocked to know his son was dipping into his loan to buy food. Copies of the newspaper the *Gazette* were selling out the day they were delivered. He doubled the order and added the *Aurora*. He was surprised too at how well stationery and pens were selling. "We should ask *die Grossmudder un die Mudder*," Lucy said, "if they have fancy needlework pieces they want to sell."

"Let me think about that," Dieter said.

The store was fast becoming the town library. Visitors sat at the library table and paged through books of their choice. Dieter needed to become a salesman-psychologist when he judged which frequent visitors had no intention of buying and how to handle them.

He was wary of his store becoming a gossip center. The town had had a population of about two thousand, but that number doubled when prisoners and refugees arrived — Tories from the Carolinas, French prisoners taken at St. Johns, English prisoners from Brandywine, Hessians from Trenton. How should he receive them? Dieter wondered. But lawyers, officers of the court, and courthouse workers — Dieter welcomed them with open arms. From them he learned what was going on in politics not only in Reading and Berks County, but in Philadelphia and throughout the colonies.

Prothonotary James Read was an early customer. "Do you have any of Samuel Johnson's books?" he asked.

"I'm going to Philadelphia next week and can get what you want."

"I'm interested in his *Lives of the Poets*."

"I'll get it. Incidentally, do you know Edmund Burke, our defender in Parliament, is a member of Dr. Johnson's famous Literary Club?"

"Good. Right here in Reading Town," Read said, "we had a little intrigue of our own. Have you heard of the Irishman Thomas Conway? He was the Brigadier General who plotted to have General Gates replace Washington as commander-in-chief."

"Why would that take place here?" Dieter asked.

"Because General Mifflin liked the countryside so much when he was here recruiting he bought a thousand acres in Angelica just to the south and built a mansion. They say he especially liked the hordes of birds that flew in and out of the hills. He wasn't directly involved in the cabal, but he was piqued at Washington over a minor matter, so Conway and a few others came to Angelica to meet him."

"I assume the scheme failed."

"Congress got wind of it and of course favored Washington." Read started for the door. "Mr. Staudt, I'm very glad you took a chance on opening Reading's first bookstore. Good luck."

In the middle of October a post rider from Philadelphia brought startling news to the Court House. Read rushed over to Dieter's bookstore. "We just got word that Cornwallis surrendered at Yorktown, Virginia. This calls for a celebration." He handed Dieter a couple bottles of Madeira.

The store soon overflowed with court house people, bookstore regulars, and excited citizens who saw the commotion. Dieter rushed to the kitchen and returned with all the glasses he could scrounge.

Read made the toast. "A miracle! The end of the war is in sight. Here's to America!"

The town buzzed with excitement. How did it happen? What about British forces in New York, Charlestown, and the South? Was Parliament ready to make peace? From the Philadelphia newspapers, Dieter knew Congress had already appointed Franklin, Adams, and Jay as a peace commission.

At home that night Dieter shared his reflections with Lucy. How could thirteen separate colonies defeat one of the most powerful armies and navies in the world? In his nearly four years in the service he had seen more American losses than victories, more failures in strategy than successes. But he also observed major failings of the British, especially the inexplicable reluctance of their generals to follow up promptly on victories. He recalled Gen. Green's observation that the British wasted great resources protecting their Tory supporters.

"What happens now?" Lucy asked.

It was a question he'd pondered often. The war may be ending but the Revolution will continue, and there will be more struggles ahead for the young nation. Tomorrow is Thursday. The Kurtz gang could hardly wait.

———

The years that followed were happy ones for Dieter and Lucy. She gave birth to a girl they named Abigail. The business growing, they moved into a larger house on the first block of North Prince Street and expanded the store in the house they vacated.

Then sorrow suddenly struck the Staudt family — *die Grossmudder* died suddenly of a heart attack. Catherine set the tone for the family, grieving, praying, but praising God for a Christian life well lived. Their lives came to a halt. All but essential farm and house work stopped as they stayed inside in their Sunday clothes receiving neighbors and friends, the Eges among the first. Dieter and Sarah brought their families. Pastor Waldschmidt visited to console them and talk about arrangements for the funeral service. Clara would be the first of the *Friendschaft* to be buried in a lovely tree-lined cemetery plot Adam had purchased earlier.

Rachael was the most disconsolate. "Next to Hans, I believe I was *Grossmudder's* favorite," she said, tears in her eyes. "I feel so bad he will not know and will not be here."

"After the funeral, I will find him," Dieter said.

Early in the morning on the day after the funeral, Dieter saddled up and left for Germantown before dawn. He arrived before noon and entered Sauer's print shop.

"You still have problems with your brother, *gell*?" Herr Sauer said.

"Do you know where he lives?"

"I don't get in your family squabble." After Dieter told him of the death, he said, "You have my sympathy. I am not sure, but I hear he lives in the city, on Front Street near Market."

Dieter left immediately. When he got to the wharf he approached a gang of vagrants. "Do any of you know Hans Staudt?"

"I know the bastard. What's it worth to you?" one said.

Dieter handed him a dollar, rode to the address, and knocked.

Hans opened the door cautiously. When he saw his brother he tried to slam the door shut. Dieter was ready. He blocked it with his foot and forced his way in. Hans attacked him. They fought. Dieter threw him to the floor and held him face down, twisting his arm.

"I've had enough of you," Dieter shouted. "This time you are going to hear what I have to tell you." He twisted his arm hard.

Hans cried out in pain. "All right, all right."

"I warn you, if you try to escape I'll give you the worst beating you'll ever have." He released him and they stood up.

"I came to tell you *die Grossmudder* died."

Hans slumped to the floor. For the first time, Dieter saw feeling in his brother. Dieter said softly, "We buried her yesterday in Hain's cemetery."

Tears came to Hans' eyes. He wiped them away with his hand.

"Hans, I want you to ride home tomorrow and say a prayer at *die Grossmudder's* grave. She loved you more than any of us. No one will be at the house except *die Mudder, der Daadi*, and Rachael. I know you have it in for *der Daadi*, but go home and make up with them. They love you and need you—and you need them."

Hans remained seated, motionless, his head down.

"It's time to do what is right," Dieter said. "Forget the past and go home." He turned and left.

A few months earlier Dieter and Lucy had joined the German Reformed Church near their home in Reading. Dieter had been uneasy when he told his mother about leaving Hain's.

"*Ich verschteh,*" she said. "It gives too long a ride every Sunday. *Ennichau*, it's *Reformiert*. Maybe we ride to Reading some Sunday and go with to church."

The German Reformed's and Trinity Lutheran's spires were beacons of strength and beauty towering over the Staudt's new home. Dieter and Lucy liked the German Reformed's Parson Bernard Willy immediately. He was sensitive to Lucy's problem with his German sermons, and he had a fatherly manner with Andrew and Abbie.

They were happy with their decision to live in the city. Lucy confessed she missed the theaters and the social scene in Philadelphia, but if there wasn't as much to see or do, familiarity with Reading's houses and buildings became a joy.

With their children in tow, they took walks in a clockwise circle—east on Thomas to Duke, south on Duke to Richard, west on Richard to Queen, north on Queen to Penn Square, then home. They passed the apothecary's Sign of the Golden Mortar, the quaint Liberty Alley, the jail with its donjon, the new red brick court house, Widow Finney's log house, and houses belonging to the Potts, the Biddles, the Muhlenbergs, the Birds, and the Hiesters. More than a dozen taverns dotted their route. For eating out, their favorites were the American Eagle Tavern and the Bald Eagle Inn.

Stories about the taverns fascinated them, especially one about the visit of Major James Monroe of Virginia. In Reading in 1777 to inspect the huge Continental Army storehouse, he took a room at the Fountain Inn on Penn Street between Tenth and Eleventh. Another major staying in the inn, James Wilkinson, was in Reading en route to the Congress in York with a report from Gates on the Saratoga surrender. Together Monroe and Wilkinson enjoyed dinner and perhaps too many glasses of claret. Wilkinson let slip details of the treasonable Conway Cabal. Major Monroe immediately dispatched word to Washington.

On their walk the Staudts came to the Green Tree Tavern on the north side of East Penn. People said it was here that Ben Franklin stayed on New Year's Day 1756.

Lucy and Dieter's best friends were Michael and Martha Ege. The Staudts rode out to Charming Forge to visit in the beautiful mansion once a month or so, reveling in the beauty of the Tulpehocken Valley and the "Tully" creek. On other Sundays they ventured north to Maidencreek, east to Oley, south into Lancaster County, impressed with the scenic beauty and the variety of farms and barns, inns, taverns and ordinaries everywhere.

They became friends of several customers, particularly lawyers John Mather and James Biddle and their families. Dieter remained active in the militia, mostly so the family could enjoy the fairs, dances, and picnics.

The only other diversions they took their children to were horse races on north Duke Street and animal attractions advertised in the *Reading Impartial Gazette*. Little Andy was especially impressed with the traveling camel "from the wild wastes of Arabia" exhibited at the tavern of Jacob Graul.

Next to Christmas, July 4 was the most eagerly awaited day of the year, always celebrated enthusiastically by the whole Staudt *Freindschaft*. As *der Daaddi, die Mudder*, and Rachael rode to Reading on the Tulpehocken Road, they saw Liberty Poles of all sizes and designs. Along the road, farmers and their families were out, smiling, waving, huzzahing, shouting. Gunshots, most too meek for the occasion, filled the sky.

The town was crowded. *Der Daadi's* carriage was first to arrive. "Happy Fourth," Lucy said as she handed Abbie to *die Mudder.*

"Sarah, Rebecca, Tillie, and Ruth and their broods will be here soon," Rachael said. "We have games for them."

Three more Staudt carriages turned onto to Prince Street at the same time. "We met on the road by chance," Sarah said.

"I hear drums," Dieter said. "You came just in time to see the militia drill. After that there'll be field games and horse races."

Between the four Staudt families there were four huge picnic baskets bulging with salt meat, salad, fruit, pies, and jugs of lemonade. They picked out a place in the grove at Hampden Spring, close enough to the platform where politicians and dignitaries would later regale the crowd with long-winded speeches and convoluted toasts.

After a long day of celebrating another Glorious Fourth, at dusk people began packing up to leave.

———

On some of Dieter's businss trips to Philadelphia, Lucy bundled up the children and visited her mother on Chestnut Street. Mrs. Smithton had plenty for them to do. The Smithtons returned the visit only once in the first year, staying in the Federal Inn. Emily Smithton made several trips a year on her own after that, each time staying a week in the inn.

Business brisk, Dieter made weekly trips to Philadelphia to pick up books at bookseller Henry Miller's place. He returned with a dozen, including three he was especially eager to read — the novels *Tom Jones* and *Tristram Shandy* and the German philosopher Immanuel Kant's *Critique of Pure Reason.*

Late that evening Dieter sat down with the *Gazette.* A three-line filler on the back page caught his eye. "*It is* reported that New York Attorney General Aaron Burr is under consideration by Governor Clinton as next U.S. Senator from that state."

Dieter immediately wrote to Aaron. Since last they were together in Valley Forge, Dieter mused, his own life was dull and unimpressive by comparison to Aaron's. He kept the letter short, an outline of his work with farmers, his move to Reading, the bookstore, and his happiness with Lucy and their children. He closed: *"I am eager to hear about your political life in New York, especially the likelihood you will be a U.S. senator! Congratulations."*

Burr's reply arrived in nine days.

September 5, 1789

Dear Friend Dieter,

What a wonderful surprise to hear from you! I can't count the number of times I thought of you and your friend Michael Ege. You were the only ones at Princeton who treated me with kindness in the beginning when I needed it. If you are still in touch with Michael, please give him my thanks and my warm regards.

Many times through these years I have thought of the times we crossed paths in the army. I don't know where I heard it, but I seem to know you resigned your commission after three years. Perhaps you know I resigned after Monmouth, ostensibly because of illness, but the real reason was — I was fed up with military life, especially the machinations of general officers maneuvering for promotion.

Enough of this dreary war business. Before the war I read law with a brother-in-law. After the war I was apprenticed to three lawyers, finally getting serious with Thomas Smith in Haverstick. I practiced law in Albany for a year then moved to New York City. I was elected to the New York General Assembly in '84 and became Attorney General early this year.

I envy you having such happiness in your family and in your business. Selling books sounds more interesting than practicing law. I won't bore you with details of my marriage except to say I first met Theodosia when she was the wife of a British officer. After his death we married at her family's estate in New Jersey. Incidentally, she made the Hermitage available to Washington for his headquarters after the battle of Monmouth.

Enough about me. It occurs to me you would be a superb political leader. I clearly remember how interested you were in Dr. Eaton's government classes, and how excellent a debater you were in the Whig Club. I urge you to run for office. I envy you people in Pennsylvania for having so liberal a constitution. You could be of service in government and enjoy doing it.

If it happens that I become a senator, I'll spend a good bit of time in Philadelphia. We must arrange to meet.

Best wishes to you and your family,
                                            Aaron

Dieter put down the letter. What a rational thinker Aaron Burr is, he mused. Maybe he should take Aaron's advice and think seriously about running for office. It was true; Attorneys Biddle, Read, and others in the court house broached the subject with him. It was also true that he enjoyed Princeton classes in politics and government. And since political office is part-time, he would not have to give up his his bookstore. He'd discuss it with Lucy.

"Oh yes, Dieter dear. You'd be good in politics," she said. "What about the bookstore?"

"We won't give it up. When I'd be in Philadelphia, we'd hire a man to handle the store."

"Philadelphia! You know what I'm thinking, dear, don't you? We could all pack up and spend time with Mother."

Mother, he thought. Has her father left her? "Before I decide, I want to talk with *der Daadi*. Why don't we go to church at Hain's on Sunday and visit with the family in the afternoon."

The Tulpehocken Staudts were surprised to see them drive up early on Sunday morning, surprised and pleased. Friends and parishioners were especially happy to see Andy and Abbie in church, well dressed and well behaved.

After dinner *die Mudder*, Rachael, and Lucy had a wonderful time with the "two little bees," as Rachael called them. Andy ran to the barn to see the animals.

Dieter and *der Daadi* sat on the bench out front. "*Ya Sohn*, it pleases me if you are in politics. With your education, you must do your part. What have you in mind?"

"The courthouse people tell me there may be a convention for a new state constitution. I'd like to be a delegate."

"*Ya, ya, guud.* You get your feet wet on that." He paused. "You haven't been to the tavern lately. The men like to see you."

"*Guud*, I'll ride out on Thursday."

Der Daadi, George Riegel, Rolf Ludwig, and a man Dieter didn't know were at the bar. "*Kumm rei*," Rolf said. "This is a friend of mine, John Bollman."

"*Guud*," Dieter said, extending his hand. "Do you know Bully Lenhardt?"

Bollman shook his head.

"You're in for a treat," Dieter added.

The regulars straggled in, Bully last. "I'm *daschdich* tonight, Shorty. Give me a double." He noticed Dieter. "Well here's Reading's bookman. That's what we need—someone who knows what's going on."

The farm talk and joshing behind them, quiet and serious John Lamm said, "I read in the *Gazette* a new constitution is planned for Pennsylvania. What do you hear from the courthouse people, Dieter?"

"I guess it's a spillover from the new Federal Constitution. The word I get is the Pennsylvania Federalists are fed up with the constitution of 1776. It's too liberal for them."

Sam Fidler said he remembered talking about that here in the tavern. "I remember something about only one house of lawmakers, no one representing the upper class."

"*Ya*," Michael Kintzer said, "and too many executives, I believe a board of twelve. Maybe they wanted to be *too* democratic."

"I never understood this," Paul Stiely said. "Wasn't there a council of censors too? Dieter, can you explain this?"

"Mike had it right," Dieter said. "But that was about fifteen years ago. Things change. The conservatives are gaining now."

"What changes do they want?" Riegel asked.

"They want two houses in the Assembly, a house of representatives and a senate, a governor elected for three-year terms, the bill of rights revised, and a change in the religious test for office holders."

"Dieter, do you believe changes are needed?" John Lamm asked.

"Some changes, yes. The two sides must compromise," Dieter said.

Bully spoke up. "Men, the best delegate we could have is right here. Let's raise our glasses to Dieter Staudt."

Shouts of "Huzzah for Staudt! Hazzah for Staudt!" rang out.

Bully cupped his hands and yelled, "Shorty, another round for everyone. I pay."

"*Ai, ai, ai,*" George Riegel said. "I never thought I'd see this day. Are you sick, Bully?"

The ruckus died down and the gang savored their drinks. Dieter rose to leave. "I have a one-hour ride home" He said goodbye to *der Daddi* and waved to the gang as he left.

———

Dieter Staudt made it known around the courthouse he'd be willing to serve as a delegate to the Pennsylvania Constitutional Convention of 1790, and in late October he and his family left for Philadelphia. It was a long, restless ride for Andy and Abbie. Finally the carriage pulled up to the Chestnut Street house their mother grew up in. Emily Smithton and Chloe rushed out to greet them. The servants unloaded the carriage. Dieter didn't hear a word about Mr. Smithton.

On Monday morning Dieter walked to the revered State House for the first session of the convention. He took his seat, fell back and closed his eyes a brief moment. He was in the room where the great men had met to declare

America free! The Federalists in the majority, Thomas Mifflin was elected president of the Convention.

For the first couple weeks, Dieter kept his mouth closed. When the Constitutionalist Party learned he was a college graduate, he was assigned to the committee on drafts and motions. He noted that the convention was about equally divided between easterners and back county men. There's no correlation, he mused, between dress and speech on one hand and thought and reason on the other.

Packing a supply of books, he rode home every Friday afternoon. He was pleased that with Silas Etchberger as manager, the store was doing well. Dieter rode out to Tulpehocken to spend Sundays with his parents and returned to Philadelphia on Monday afternoons.

The convention went into recess for the Christmas-New Year Holiday. For Andy and Abbie, for Lucy and Dieter, Christmas in the big city would be the liveliest ever. Then they'd pack up and spend second Christmas with the Tulpehocken family. Andy could hardly wait to check on the animals.

After a happy week on the farm, Dieter and his family returned to Philadelphia. In three months the convention reached what Dieter considered a fair revision of the state's 1776 constitution. Early in February the convention adjourned and the Staudts left for Reading. Dieter judged he and Andy were happier to be headed home than the rest of the family was.

Back in Reading, Lucy and Dieter and their children settled into their routine. Dieter walked to the bookstore and went about stacking the books he'd brought back from Philadelphia.

That evening at home he picked up the latest *Gazette*. In the list of new senators to be seated in the next session of Congress he spotted the name of a new senator from New York — Aaron Burr! Dieter immediately took out his pen. He congratulated Burr on his election then wrote about his own experience as delegate to the Constitutional Convention and his hope of election to the Pennsylvania General Assembly.

He ended, *"I'd very much like to see you again soon. I'm in Philadelphia most Fridays on business. Please set a date and place at your convenience."*

TWENTY-FIVE

IN THE TWILIGHT OF THEIR YEARS, ADAM AND Catherine Staudt were astounded when it came to them they'd soon be living in a new century. In 1800 Adam would be eighty, Catherine one year shy. Even so, they worked as hard as ever, secure in their faith, proud of their children and grandchildren. "It was hard to leave Frankenthal, but it was the right thing to do," Catherine said.

"*Ya, ya,*" he said softly, looking down, staring.

They worried about Rachael. Forty, not well, what will become of her? Dieter and the girls—Sarah, Tille, Rebecca, and Ruth—they will look out for her, Catherine felt certain.

Adam and Catherine kept their greatest sorrow to themselves. It wasn't just that Hans deserted them; Dieter suspected he was working for the enemy. Adam gave up hope, but for Catherine, not a day went by without prayers of love and hope and forgiveness.

It was Dieter who brought the brightest light into their lives—Continental Army officer, owner of a thriving bookseller business, delegate to the Constitutional Convention, member of the General Assembly. For the Staudt *Familye*, the nineties were productive and happy. For the young nation itself, Dieter reflected, the decade may be a decisive one.

In Philadelphia, representing heavily Democratic-Republican Berks County in the Legislature, Dieter was upset by the harshness of party politics. By revising the state constitution in 1790, the Pennsylvania Federalists weakened local authority and put in place a strong governor with veto power. On the national level, Federalists were wary of the "peasant Republicans" and the nearly one hundred Democratic-Republican Societies that had sprung up, fearing takeover by a "mobocracy." Ironically, both Republicans and Federalists espoused liberty as their primary goal.

Dieter concurred in the Republican idea that the Revolution was more than a war for independence—it was a continuous march to greater freedom for all individuals, a goal best achieved by local and state control. To the Federalists, liberty required submission of individual freedom and local and state authority to a strong central government. Their ideology motivated them to replace the weak Articles of Confederation with a constitution.

In the election of 1789, the Germans of Berks and other southeastern Pennsylvania counties gave little thought to presidential politics, for the only viable candidate, everyone knew, was his Excellency George Washington. Throughout his first term Washington had the full support of the country. But in his second term, even while decrying political partisanship, he proved capable of playing the game.

Dieter took his family to Philadelphia to meet his old friend Aaron Burr. They met at the City Tavern. Nine-year-old-Andy was thrilled.

"What a good-looking family you have, Dieter," Aaron said. "I remember," he said to Lucy, "I met you first at the Princeton graduation ceremony." He kissed her hand, his style exuding the feminine image she'd heard about. Abbie giggled when he turned and kissed her hand.

"I'm so happy to see you again," Lucy said. "Congratulations on your election. What it's like to be a senator?"

"Like any job. You use your common sense, you try to be fair. Sometimes things don't go your way."

After they'd eaten, Lucy and the children walked up Chestnut Street for a surprise visit to her mother.

The two men moved to a comfortable nook in the tavern and ordered Madeira. "I'm eager to hear how things are really going, Aaron, especially the politics. When I first went to the General Assembly I was shocked to learn how much power the parties have—and use!"

"Yes, and there's dirt on both sides. I've had a problem swallowing the Federalists' stuff. Washington himself puzzles me. He's changed since we served on his staff."

"How well I remember those days in Valley Forge," Dieter said, then pausing. "I try to keep up with you men through the *Gazette*, but I'm never sure I'm getting the facts. How has Washington changed?"

"You recall," Aaron said, "how he sought the opinion of his generals before he acted. Well, he's not as open to the ideas of others anymore. He has a good cabinet—Jefferson, Hamilton, Randolph, and Knox—but it's mainly Hamilton who has his ear." He paused. "By the way, do you know that both Hamilton and Knox were also booksellers?

"Anyway, New Yorkers built a handsome building at Broad and Wall Street for the Congress during Washington's first term. They were outraged when they learned the capital was going to be moved to Philadelphia then permanently to a site to be chosen on the Potomac by Washington. Some in the Senate blamed Washington for negotiating this deal in the bill Hamilton pushed forcing the states to assume the federal debt. The *New York Advertiser* roundly upbraided Washington for his ingratitude in leaving New York City."

"What's your opinion of Hamilton?" Dieter asked.

"Abigail Adams doesn't trust the little squirt and neither do I. Do you know he too was a bookseller at one time? About Washington—I hate to think he was directly involved in this, but the great one forced something even worse on the Senate."

"That doesn't sound like him. What about Madison? I hear mixed opinions on him."

"Good old Jemmy." Aaron chuckled. "The best thing

I did for him was introduce him to Dolly. But he's a leader in the House. "You remember him from Princeton. He's still unimpressive, even shorter than Hamilton and so shy he's afraid of his own shadow. But the *Federalist Papers* he and Hamilton put out are well written. I think of the two as the little Federalist twins."

"About Washington, you were saying . . . ."

"He completely cut the Senate out of debate on the Jay Treaty. Are you familiar with that?"

"Yes, but I suspect there was some behind-the-scene intrigue."

"Washington sent Chief Justice Jay to London to settle a rift between England and France over the seizure of American ships. I didn't consider that an appropriate role for a justice. Monroe and I led the opposition against the appointment, but we lost. Jay returned from England with the proposed treaty and Washington kept it from the Senate for seven months. When we Republicans finally saw it, we were shocked at the concessions it made to England. I wrote to Washington requesting a conference. He didn't respond. I made a speech in the Senate requesting a postponement, but the Federalists prevailed 20-to-10, and the bill was ultimately approved. But that's in the past. Now we have Adams to put up with."

"What's your next step, Aaron, for you personally, I mean? You have a next step, don't you?"

He chuckled. "You know me well. After I lost my bid for governor of New York, I looked ahead to the election of '96. I went out campaigning, you might say, in New England, and three months in Virginia to feel the pulse on overriding the Jay Treaty. I spent a day with Jefferson at Monticello."

"How did that go?"

"I'm not sure. In the High Federalist paper *American Minerva*, Noah Webster ridiculed me as that certain little senator running around whispering things in peoples' ears." He paused. "Keep this to yourself for now, Dieter, but I may decide to run for President. I think Adams is vulnerable."

"President? That is big news! Keep me posted."

Buoyed by Aaron's enthusiasm and courage, in

the Legislature Dieter pushed the actions of his heavily Republican Berks County constituents. They petitioned to have legal documents and bills translated into German, and they called for elected, not appointed, justices of the peace. Dieter thought of *der Daddi* and the strong opinions of the men at Kurtz Tavern. Dieter supported the Republican party but he crossed to the other side on some issues, steadfastly voting his conscience. Parties were a necessity, he supposed, but down deep he agreed with Washington they might ultimately lead to harm.

A new century was looming. Dieter and Lucy the years since they moved to Reading had treated them well. In a tradition begun by his grandfather Dietrich in the old country and continued by his parents in America, they gave their children lessons in English and mathematics. Abigail was sixteen and doing well at the Linden Hall Girls School in Lancaster. Andrew was bright; he'd enroll in Princeton in the fall. Only two dark clouds hung over the family — the estrangement of Dieter's brother from his family, and the estrangement of Mr. Alan Smithton from his.

Then from Philadelphia came shocking news. The Fifth Congress passed an act outlawing "false, scandalous, and malicious writings against the government, Congress, or the President to stir up hatred or sedition." In already politically charged times, why would the Adam's Administration act so provocatively? Dieter wondered. Jefferson left for Monticello. Adams' Vice President wanted nothing to do with an act he considered shameful.

Tulpehocken farmers flocked to the Kurtz Tavern to vent their anger. Bully Lenhardt set the tone. "*Des iss schtupid!* What are they afraid of? Who decides what is false, scandalous, or malicious anyway? The courts will overflow. *Dummkopp* Federalists! We get rid of Adams and put in Jefferson."

In churches, taverns, inns, on street corners in Reading and crossroads in the Tulpehocken and all settlements, people talked about nothing but the vile Sedition Act.

Just as the tumult began to fade, the Federalist wise

men in Philadelphia caused even more havoc. They passed, and President Adams signed, a direct tax on lands, houses, and slaves!

"This is the last straw" was on everyone's lips. People understood a direct tax was the sole right of local and state governments. A national tax was imposed now, the Administration said, to cover the extraordinary costs of military preparedness for an imminent war with France. The *Universal Gazette* reported that the government's debt was alreay $3.2 million and growing by the day. Dieter felt strongly that the tax was antithetical to the ideology that drove the country into a war of independence fought to secure the rights of individuals.

Bully jumped on his horse and rode from farm to farm. "We can't wait till Thursday for this," Bully cried out. "We meet Monday at seven o'clock at Shorty Kurtz's Tavern."

"Yes sir, Paul Revere," Sam Fidler said, smiling. He gave Bully a snappy salute.

The Monday night session at the tavern was raucous. Jacob Noecker lit the match. "Those sons-a-bitch Federalists aren't getting away with this. The tax is *schlecht* enough, but then they go and appoint their high-handed party hacks as assessors."

"*Ya*, I guess this ain't funny," Rolf Ludwig said, "but I hear *Hausfraas* over in Bucks County throw hot water on the assessors."

"It wonders me how they make their assessments," George Riegel said.

"It goes by windows," Michael Kintzer said. "This ain't fair, but if you and I have the same size house and you have one window more than me, you get *bschisse*."

John Lamm spoke up. Slow-talking, reasonable, he said, "What is really unfair is our farms are assessed higher than the empty forest land owned by speculators."

"*Ya gewiss*," Bully ranted. "Our shady Congressman Joseph Heister found out what we think of speculators."

"*Was meenescht?*" Kintzer asked.

"We voted for him every two years until we found out he bought land from veterans for pennies on the dollar. Didn't you see the article in the *Weekly Advertiser*?"

"Nay," Kintzer said, "but I read in the *Readinger Adler* he's a turncoat. He voted for the Sedition Act and the Direct Tax. I'm finished with him."

The men kept Shorty and Minnie Kurtz busy at the bar. Overheated about the tax issue, enjoying the extra night out, the men stayed on until midnight.

The Staudt *Freindschaft* could hardly wait for the last Saturday of August. It was Rachael who'd come up with the idea years earlier—celebrate the coming of the harvest by getting together for fun and games, food and gabbing. The annual celebration grew as more children came along. Again this year there'd be the same grand total of twenty-two, one new baby to add to the cousins but *die Grossmudder* no longer with them. She would be deeply missed, especially by the youngest children who flocked to her. By tradition, the only guests were Michael Ege and his family.

City dwellers Abbie and Andy loved their trips to the farm and counted the days till the big harvest day.

The program of races and games for the young children would be the same as always—leapfrog, marbles, blindman's buff, prisoner and base, kites, hoops. But activities for teenagers, Sarah and her sisters determined, would be curtailed this year. Wood-chopping, the husking bee, and rifle shooting contests would be cut in half and the fish-catch in the Little Cacusi would be eliminated. The new activity and new fun this year—making a giant, elaborate liberty pole and signs protesting the tax!

Did Dieter hear this right, he wondered—a liberty pole, potent symbol of opposition to the British, this time demonstrating against our own government? The idea intrigued him. There may be a handful of his constituents who'd object, he assumed, but the First Amendment guaranteed even a representative of the Assembly the right to protest actions of the Congress and the President.

The day was cloudless. Three carriages of Sarah's

large family were first to arrive. By one o'clock, the whole *Friendschaft* was there. Rachael took care of the squealing little children, assigning babies to whichever *Weibsmensch* wasn't busy, starting the races and tag games for the rest. Dieter and *der Daddi* set up wood-chopping and shooting matches for the young men. Teenage girls and *Weibsleit* sat around giggling and gossiping.

Sarah's husband, Jacob, took charge of the liberty pole project. "*Allrecht*, I need two or three *Buwe* to cut down and trim the tree. I pick out a nice straight tulip tree. Then I need a few more *Buwe* to dig a four-foot hole to plant it in. *Schlag nei*."

Jacob ordered Sarah to bring out needle and thread and red, white, and blue ribbon for a liberty cap with flowing streamers. He nailed it to the top of the pole. "Who can print nice? We need signs for the middle of the pole reading *No Gag Laws, Liberty or Death, The Constitution Sacred.* And more signs to tie between trees."

When the pole was finally finished, Jacob said, "This is one beautiful tree. Everyone, raise your glasses and join me as loud as you can 'Huzzah for Liberty! Huzzah for Liberty.' "

The last but most anticipated event of the day was the picnic spread — for twice as many mouths as were there! After more than an hour of *fressing* and drinking, no one was surprised when the *Weibsmensch* in charge announced, "We go home. The food is all."

Just after sunset Sarah's large family jumped on their carriages and waved goodbye, the first to leave. "It was a *wunnerbaar Daag*," Sarah said, peering lovingly at *die Mudder*.

TWENTY-SIX

DIETER STAUDT WAS SURPRISED TO SEE BULLY Lenhardt in the bookstore. "What brings you here, Bully?"

"I had some business in Reading," he fibbed. "As long as I'm here, I figured I might as well come see your place. *Des iss arig schay.*"

"*Gross Dank.* Can I help you find something? We have more than books."

"Not today. The old lady expects me home by three." He paused. "I set a minute and tell you something I hear. Mind, this is only a rumor." Pausing for effect, he said, "*Die Leit* over in Bucks and Montgomery — they are even madder than us about this tax business. They talk about — mind, this is only a rumor — maybe marching to Bethlehem to free some Northampton men jailed over a fight with tax assessors."

"When will this take place? Do they have a leader?"

"*Ich wayss net wann, awwer* their leader is something like 'Frees' or 'Frys'."

Dieter put a hand to his jaw. "This is big news." He waited. "Assemblyman Cyrus Donmoyer lives in Hatfield. I'd ride over to talk to him about this but a bookman from Philadelphia is coming to see me today. I wonder if John Lamm can go in my place."

"I ask him."

"*Danke*, Bully. If this takes place, we must join them. If they take the Tulpehocken Road to Reading we meet them here. But if they take a different route, we march out on our own."

"*Gunz guud.* I go now," Bully said. "Next time I maybe buy a book . . . a German book."

Lamm was astonished to hear from Bully about a march taking place. "I leave right now to visit Mr. Donmoyer. Tomorrow I ride to Reading and tell Dieter."

The discontent Lamm found was fanned by the *Readinger Adler*, popular in Berks County and also read widely in Bucks and Montgomery counties. Jacob Schneider, the paper's publisher, castigated the Federalists for pushing the Sedition Act and the Direct Tax through the Fifth Congress. He started a local Republican political club they called the "German Society."

Not educated but intelligent and ambitious, Lamm was a self-made man. What he heard from Donmoyer was vague. "*Ya*, people here are worked up, but there's more commotion over in Montgomery County."

"We hear the name 'Frys' or 'Frees'. Do you know him?"

"*Ya*, his name is John Fries. I spell it for you—F-r-i-e-s. He's an auctioneer. Everyone knows him and likes him. He likes to tell jokes." He waited. "You should ride up to Quakertown and talk with Assemblyman Jonas Schneider. He knows more. The Assembly is not in session so he should be home."

"*Ich bedank mich.* If this happens," Lamm said, "Berks County joins. Dieter asks you to send a rider up to Reading when they start out."

Lamm got more news from Schneider. "Most of my constituents are German farmers. They believe the Federalists are getting us into a useless war with France. And they will not put up with a direct tax."

"Why do they take it out on the assessors?" Lamm asked.

"Because they are Federalist hacks. We are in touch

with people in Northampton. They chased off the assessors and held meetings where the people get worked up. Nineteen men are prisoners in the Sun Tavern in Bethlehem and will be taken to Philadelphia for trial." Schneider's voice became louder. "This violates the Sixth Amendment which requires trials where crimes are committed or alleged."

"*Ya wohl. Dank vielmole,*" Lamm said. "We join you. When you start out, send a rider up to Dieter Staudt at his bookstore at Prince and Thomas Streets in Reading."

Lucy Staudt had little interest in politics, but she was alert to the growing division between Republicans and Federalists. And she knew her father was a die-hard Loyalist and a Federalist. "Do you think it's wise," she asked Dieter, "for a Representative of the General Assembly to get involved in this?"

"Fair question. But I've thought it over and decided there's no conflict, so long as the protest is peaceful."

Excitement showing in his voice, Andy said. "I'm going along. I can't wait."

"And me," Abbie said.

"No Abbie, not you," Lucy said more firmly than they were used to.

"Why not? It's mainly walking," Abbie said.

"You stay in school in Lancaster. Girls don't do this kind of thing."

"Maybe this girl does. Father, tell Mother I may go."

"I'll decide later."

That night in bed Lucy confessed she was deathly frightened about Abbie's going. "Andy can take care of himself, but I don't want her to get involved. Please dear."

Dieter was about to say something about women's rights. Lucy's body language inviting snuggling, he changed his mind.

On March 7 the rider sent ahead by John Fries galloped up to the Staudt Book and Stationery Store. Panting heavily, he said, "Sir, Captain Fries and the militia marched out at 8 o'clock. He expects to meet the Northampton troops at Ritter's Tavern near Emmaus."

"Militia? Are the men armed?"

The rider laughed. "It doesn't look much like a military formation. Some brought out their old uniforms and a few have muskets. I doubt they scare anybody."

"How many are there?"

"Maybe fifty militia and another thirty tagging behind. They will pick up more as they go."

"Inform him the Berks group will leave at noon. We will take the Reading-Allentown Road, maybe stopping in Kutz Town."

Dieter locked the store and hurried home. "Son, ride out fast to the Tulpehocken and alert the sentinels. Then hurry back and we'll say goodbye to your mother and Abbie."

Andy put his horse to the test, returning home in a half-hour, his record time. "Good news, *Daddi*. The people west of Womelsdorf hear about this and are also on the march, maybe seventy-five from Lebanon, Myerstown, Stouchsburg, and along the route."

"Good. We'll watch for them. Do they have guns?"

"Maybe five or six do. People are having a good time—men, some women, even a few *Buwe un Maed*—laughing, singing, huzzahing when they see liberty poles and big 'Constitution Sacred' and 'No Gag' signs."

Dieter became the leader of what seemed more to him like a Republican rally than a rebellion. As they marched out, he and Andy walked at the head of the growing mob, more than two hundred now, Dieter estimated. They reached Kutz Town at dusk, the residents out in force to greet them, huzzahing loudly.

The trek to Kutz Town took six hours; Dieter and his son held their longest father-son conversation ever. Andy pushed him to talk about how *der Grossdaddi un die Grossmudder* survived in the Tulpehocken wilderness, his early years on the farm, the war years, and how he got into politics.

Dieter concentrated on the next job—feeding and

housing his contingent. The region heavily German, heavily Republican, he knew the townspeople would be hospitable. He was right: the elders of the village were ready. Except for some assigned to two ordinaries, a tavern and an inn just outside the village, the group was parceled out to host families. After a hearty supper, the marchers were ready to lie on the floor and get some sleep.

"We start out for Emmaus at 7 o'clock tomorrow morning," Dieter told them before they split up. "Get a good rest."

A few sleepy heads fell out late, delaying the start by twenty minutes. Hosts handed their guests *Dutts voll Eppel un Bretzels* and sent them on their way. A dozen or so townspeople joined them.

At 3:30 they spotted Jacob Ritter's Tavern. Captain Stahler's hundred Northampton volunteers, some in uniform, had just left, headed for a certain confrontation in Bethlehem. John Fries, Peter Gable, and a handful of Fries' other lieutenants were at the bar.

Dieter approached Fries and shook his hand. "I am happy to meet you, Captain. I may be putting myself at risk in politics, but I am adamant about our first amendment rights. We are at your command."

"I believe you represent Berks County in the General Assembly, *gell?*" Fries said.

"*Ah, mir kenne au deitsch schwetze. Guud.*"

Fries smiled. "*Glay bissel.* I want to free the men, but I want to do it peacefully. I see more guns than I like. My name is Fries, not Shay from Massachusetts. I don't want to see 10,000 federal troops facing us." Looking around, he chuckled. "I bragged about having five hundred protestors. I guess I was nearly right."

Dieter saw in Fries a brawny, loquacious man with a folksy, humorous manner. "My first problem," Dieter said, "is to house my gang. Maybe the people of Emmaus will do like the people of Kutz Town. They took everyone in."

"Sir," Fries said, smiling. "We are ahead of you. Lodging is arranged. Early tomorrow morning we go to Bethlehem. We have word that the Northampton County men are already there. *Hock dich* and have a drink."

Dieter wondered whether Fries had second thoughts about wearing his uniform. At least he carried no pistol. The talk in the Assembly was that until recently Fries had been a Federalist and had served in the army in the Whiskey Rebellion in western Pennsylvania. But, Dieter thought, the Germans seem strongly behind him now.

The protestors, 130 militia and 240 unarmed protestors, left early the next morning. In the middle of the afternoon they came to the toll bridge over the Lehigh River, Stahler's troops waiting on the other side. Dieter had his wallet but not enough bills to pay everyone's toll. Fries smiled and paid the toll for all.

They entered Bethlehem, the militia wearing their regimentals, liberty caps on their head, marching smartly in loose close order to discordant fifes and irregular drums. The motley crowd of more than two hundred unarmed protestors, loud but orderly, filled the court in front of the Sun Tavern.

Fries shouted to the jailers, "No one will be hurt if the prisoners are freed on bail to stand trial right here." Motioning for Dieter to join them, Fries, Gabel, and another aide entered the tavern to negotiate with U.S. Marshall William Nichols.

Not enough federal troops yet in place, Fries' men could readily have subdued the marshal, taken over the tavern, and freed the nineteen prisoners. But more was at stake here than that—they let it be known they were putting their rights under the Constitution to the test. The Sedition Act, they stated and reiterated, was unconstitutional.

Marshal Nicholas' retort was military, not ideological: he was doing his duty. Negotiations went on for hours. The crowd outside grew unruly. Inside, an opera buffa played out as the tavern owner did a lively business at the bar, with some liquor going out the door steadily to drunken and disorderly *Versoffneren*. Fries and Dieter agreed to make one last attempt at negotiation. It failed.

Fearing a riot if his men didn't get what they wanted, Fries demanded the release of the prisoners, backing it up with threat of force. Fries shouted to his men, "Please, for

God's sake, don't fire except we are fired on." His men entered and led the prisoners out one by one without incident.

Dieter left before all the prisoners were released. He walked toward Andy in the back of the crowd. Looking beyond his father to the far end of the court, Andy suddenly spotted a rifle being raised. He shouted, "*Daadi!* Get down! Get down" He shoved him to the ground. A shot rang out.

A stunned crowd instantly formed around Dieter. "A doctor! Quick, quick! Someone get a doctor!"

TWENTY-SEVEN

HOME ON PRINCE STREET RECUPERATING, DIETER Staudt was well cared for, waited on like royalty by Lucy and Abbie. He was surprised when Lucy told him that during his three weeks in Bethlehem he'd been drifting in and out of consciousness. "You lost a couple quarts of blood, Dieter dear. Thank God you came through."

"Did *die Mudder un der Daadi* come to see me?"

"A few times, in Mr. Ege's best coach," Lucy said. "We always went with them."

Dieter smiled. "It's vague, but I picture *die Mudder* down on her knees beside the bed." He paused suddenly. "I seem to remember seeing . . . is this possible? . . . do I remember Doctor Otto there too?"

"Yes dear," Lucy said, "but a different Doctor Otto. Governor Mifflin interceded for you as a member of the Legislature and a veteran to get you the best care. The elder Doctor Otto died ten years ago, but his son John answered the call. He and the Bethlehem surgeon pulled you through."

"Yes, right there in the Sun Tavern where we released the prisoners. Ironic!" Dieter said. He paused. "But it seemed like a good place to recuperate. I heard Lafayette spent two months in Bethlehem after he was wounded at Brandywine."

One concern Dieter did not have in his recuperation

was his book business. Lucy and Andy tended the store and enjoyed it, alternating days. "Get a good start on some classical readings for college, son," Dieter said. "When you get to Princeton you'll love the library's open stacks as much as I did."

Every other day Andy happily worked the farm with his *Grossdaadi*. "A chip off the old block," Rachael teased.

Nor was the wound on Dieter's mind, his leg splinted and bandaged. He no longer felt pain. Equipped with crutches, he moved around the house with ease. He spent most of his time reading. At least once every day, Lucy and Abbie noticed, their patient put down the book he was reading, looked up, and stared into space.

One evening on the farm Catherine said to Adam, "It's time we tell Dieter. I do it."

"I go with," he said. "It will be hard."

"*Verleicht* it makes best if the others stay away. I tell them."

"*Kumm rei*," Dieter called to them when he saw them at the door two days later. "*Hock dich hie.*"

"Where is everybody?" she asked, fibbing.

"Lucy will be back soon."

Used to his mother's frequent prayers, Dieter was not taken back when she knelt before him. He noticed his parents' nervousness; he knew they were going to broach the subject.

"*Sohn*," she said, "this is hard but we talk now about Hans."

"*Mamm, Daadi*, sit back. Relax. *Ich wayss. Ich wayss.* Hans was the one who shot me."

Their heads fell back. "*Du wayscht? Du wayscht?*" Adam blurted out. "Who told you? *Des iss unbehofft.*"

"It had nothing to do with the rebellion and I have no other enemies, so it had to be Hans." Dieter waited. "Was he arrested?"

"*Meenest kennt net sei*," Adam said, looking down, shaking his head slowly.

Catherine waited in awkward silence. "*Nay Sohn*, I

tell you . . . I tell you . . . ." She broke down in a torrent of tears and ran to the kitchen.

Only once before had Dieter seen tears in his father's eyes. "What is it, *Daddi*? Is Hans in prison?"

Die Mudder returned, sobbing hard. "I . . . I tell him," she said to Adam. "I tell him."

Kneeling, she took Dieter's hand. "*Sohn*, Hans is dead. *Er iss dod! Er iss dod!*" She rose and ran again to the kitchen, her cries pitiful.

Dieter fell back in his chair. He covered his eyes and waited.

Clearing his throat, wiping his eyes, Adam spoke at last. "You know how he always ran to *die Grossmudder*. He was her favorite." Adam paused and took a deep breath. "Well *Sohn*, he came home to her in the cemetery." He paused a long moment. "He shot himself and fell on her grave."

Dieter closed his eyes, put his head down, and slowly crossed his arms. He shook his head slowly, recalling his plea to Hans to go to *die Grossmudder's* grave.

Lucy, Abbie, and Andy returned and saw Dieter completely still. Abbie moved toward him. Lucy raised her hands and shook her head. The three left quietly.

For three days Lucy allowed no one to visit. Then, every other day or so she allowed a visitor or two, the first Peter Gable, close friend of Fries. "You remember me, *gell*? I come to see *wie du bischt*."

Dieter extended his hand. "*Ach, du kannscht aa Deitsch schwetza?* I'm so glad you came. I read in the *Gazette* that Fries and two others are sentenced to be hanged for treason. Treason! I can't believe it."

"*Ya, ya, awwer* it gives a new trial in Norristown because a juror showed bias."

Dieter rose and walked to a window. He turned to Gable. "Why in Norristown?"

"I guess because they moved the prisoners there. *Ennichau*, I'm glad you're healing. When I saw all that blood I thought you was gone."

"*Yuscht glicklish*," Dieter said, smiling. "I left

Sun Tavern before all the prisoners were released. What happened after that?"

"*Ya well*, Fries and I knew the fight was not over. The next day 200 protestors met at Gerysville Tavern. Using his auctioneer skills, Fries got them to give in to the assessors for the time being. But the sons-a-bitches Federalists wanted blood. Adams made a proclamation saying what we did was an act of war."

"An act of war? An act of war?" Dieter shook his head. "I can't believe this. But I did read in the *Adler* that the Secretary of War called out Continental troops and ordered Governor Mifflin to activate the Pennsylvania militia."

"*Ya*, 500 regulars marched to Newtown and Bristol. Then early in April the militia marched on the Bethlehem Road to Spring House, where they arrested Fries and sent him and two others to prison in Philadelphia. The troops then marched to Quakertown, Macungie, Allentown, and Reading and arrested more, fifteen for treason and fourteen for misdemeanors."

Lucy entered. "Dieter dear, I think you should rest now. Thank you for coming, Mr. Gable, and bringing the news. Good luck."

"*Gaern gschehne*." He started to leave then turned and said, "You are married to a good man."

Andy went to the tavern on Thursday night to ask the Kurtz men to visit his father. Dieter was delighted to have visits from every one of the gang, Bully Lenhardt's visit, of course, the liveliest.

Politicians came to see him, the most prominent the Republican Speaker of the State House. "You lost one contest for Congress," Cyrus Balthaser said, "but your chances will be better next time. Berks County could use a well-known Reading man in the Sixth Congress."

"I'd be pleased to serve. But I must wait to see about my leg."

"By the way, are you aware that your friend Aaron Burr is running for President?"

"Yes, I read that in the *Gazette*." Dieter chuckled. "At

five feet six he's a bit short for the job when you consider how tall His Excellency George Washington is. Aaron is a brilliant thinker. He would be a good president."

A few weeks later the town of Reading was abuzz with news that Aaron Burr was coming to visit his friend Dieter Staudt. Nearly fully recovered, Dieter was eager to see him.

Crowds gathered on North Prince Street when Burr's carriage was seen coming down Penn Street. Loud huzzahs and applause greeted him as he pulled up to the Staudt house. A candidate for president here in Reading? *Wunnerbaar!*

The Staudts all rushed out to greet him. The old Princeton friends shook hands and hugged. Aaron kissed Lucy's hand. "What a pleasure to see you again. And your beautiful children! They've grown up."

"Aaron," Lucy said, "May I reintroduce grown-up Andy and Abbie."

He shook Andy's hand then turned to Abbie. "You are even more beautiful than the last time I saw you in Philadelphia, and the image of your mother."

They entered the house and Lucy and Abbie served tea and cookies. "What a charming house," Aaron said. "That pianoforte looks brand new."

"It is," Lucy said. "It was a wonderful Christmas present from Dieter."

"I'd love to hear a little Mozart."

"And I'd love to play for you right now," she said.

After a pleasant half-hour, Aaron said, "I'm eager to see your bookstore. Is it close-by?"

"Just around the corner." He turned to Lucy. "We'll be back soon."

"Walk carefully, dear."

As they strolled to Thomas Street, Aaron said, "This is a well-planned town. I had no idea. It's like a miniature Philadelphia."

Dieter laughed, "Except that we have a mountain," he said, pointing east. "Yes, Thomas Penn learned from his father how to lay out a town."

They entered the store, greeted by even more *Wunnernaases* than Dieter had predicted. He knew most of them. "Everybody," he said, "this is Senator Aaron Burr."

They applauded loudly.

"I'm happy to be here in your lovely city," he said. Turning to Dieter, he said, "This is a great book collection. I had no idea there were so many readers in your town."

"Well," he said with a wry smile, "I do sell many German books."

After a short time Dieter and his guest returned to Prince Street. "How is Michael Ege?"

"He is well. He regrets he has to be in Philadelphia on business this week. If you have time we could ride over there. The mansion is beautiful."

"I'd like to but I arranged to meet several of your politicians at the Federal Inn for dinner." He laughed. "Everywhere I go I'm always politicking, you know."

"Would you do me a favor, Aaron? My parents would be thrilled to meet you. We could stop first for lunch at our own town hall, the Kurtz Tavern."

"Certainly. Do they still live on the land they settled?"

"Yes, on the land where I was born." He paused. "I wonder how many lively debates our farmers have had in our tavern. You might be surprised at how much they know about the Dickinson letters, the Stamp Act, taxes, the Sedition Act, even Parliament. I'm proud of them."

"Let's go," Aaron said. "We can take my carriage."

En route to the tavern, Aaron talked about a young German physician he met recently in Philadelphia. "His name is Justus Erich Bollman, an idealist and an adventurer, to say the least. He and an American learned where Lafayette was imprisoned in Vienna and helped him escape. Then Bollman himself was detained for a year and released only after he agreed to leave Austria. He may be useful to me."

They pulled up to the three-story Kurtz Tavern. "You're going to hear the Palatinate tongue here." Dieter chuckled. "I'll be your translator."

Shorty Kurtz served them rum at the bar and they

walked to a small table. Burr smiled. "You're right about the dialect. It doesn't altogether sound like the German I know."

"The big men Franklin and Adams at first ridiculed us," Dieter said, "but they soon looked beyond our broad vowels and mixed-up v's and w's and saw we produce the best wheat in the colonies."

After they had eaten, they drove the short distance to the Staudt farm. "This is the heart of the Tulpehocken Settlement." Dieter added softly, "The soil is rich."

Rachael heard horse hoofs. "It wonders me who this is," she said to *die Mudder*. She rushed out.

Dieter jumped off the carriage and gave his sister a big hug. "*Mudder, Mudder,*" she called, "it's Dieter. Dieter's here!"

They entered the house and saw *die Mudder* awakening from a nap in her chair. She stood and shook herself. "*Was gayt an?*" she said.

"Ah ha, this time I caught you napping, *Mamma*. I brought a guest," Dieter said. He gave her a long hug. Tears came to her eyes. "Where is *der Daddi*?" he asked.

"Out on the back field," Rachael said. She laughed. "Where else would he be?"

"*Mamma*, Rachael, this is my friend Senator Aaron Burr."

"Senator Aaron Burr," Rachael said. "You are the one running for president, *gell*? My oh my!"

"Have a seat, Aaron. I want to go out back and surprise *der Daddi*," Dieter said.

Adam saw him and hurried to him. "I'm surprised to see you. I didn't know you were moving on your own yet. *Was doost do?*"

"We'll go to the house," Dieter said. "I brought a friend."

They stayed an hour, Aaron taking in everything inside the house and outside.

"Thank you for bringing me here," he said to Dieter after he'd said goodbye to the family. "It was wonderful— the first time I visited a settler's house. Your parents are so

... so sincere, so real. How different from the Congress. No wonder you're the man you are."

They began the half-hour ride to Reading. "Speaking about Congress, Dieter," Aaron said, "I know the Federalists called out troops and marched to Bethlehem, but that's all I know about that rebellion. You were involved, weren't you?"

Dieter described the politics that led up to the rebellion. "If Adams loses the election, you can thank Fries and his gang."

"Yes, and you were in the gang. Was there much bloodshed?"

"This is embarrassing, Aaron. I was the only one injured." Vacillating a moment, he told him Hans' full story.

"I'm glad I asked," Aaron said. "You needed to get this off your mind."

They crossed the Schuylkill, rode up Penn Street and tuned onto Prince Street. "I hope you'll be able to stay a little while longer."

Lucy served them hot rum.

"I hope you don't mind my asking, Aaron, but how did you lose your Senate seat?"

"I got support for my election when I became Grand Sachem of Tammany Hall. But then Hamilton worked up so much fervor in the Assembly over possible war with France, the Federalists gained the majority and I was out." He paused. "But I'm shooting higher now."

"I'll say you are. Even if the Republicans get more electoral votes than the Federalists, and it looks as so they will, isn't Jefferson the likely candidate?"

"Probably. But I have time. I can look ahead four years."

"You have a deal with Jefferson?"

"In a sense. I promised to deliver all New York votes for him as president if he delivers Virginia's votes for me as vice president. With the support of Tammany, I can hold up my end of the bargain. I've been actively campaigning, especially in the city's Seventh Ward." He paused. "Incidentally, Dieter, you'll be interested to know the Seventh Ward is heavily German."

"So you expect Jefferson will get the most votes and you will come in second." Dieter paused. "State electors are fickle. He may come in second and be *your* vice president."

Aaron smiled broadly. "What would be even more interesting is Jefferson and I both getting the seventy-three Republican electors' votes."

"A tie! How would that be handled?"

"The House of Representatives would vote, but each of the sixteen states would have only one vote."

"This is fascinating stuff. You're sure Adams couldn't sneak in?"

"We figure the Federalists have sixty-five electoral votes, so he'd be eight short. No matter, the election will be close—close and dirty. In their religious views, Adams and Jefferson both lean toward Deism." Aaron paused and snickered. "You'll hear cries of "infidel" from the Jefferson camp and "hypocrite" from Adams' supporters."

"At least they won't hit *you* with that?"

"No, but I do expect to have mud thrown at me over some personal stuff." Aaron rose. "It's been a pleasure visiting with you, old friend. I must leave now for my meeting at the Federal Inn."

Dieter left the room quickly and brought the children in. "Say goodbye to Mr. Burr. The next time you see him he may be President or maybe Vice President of the United States." Turning to Aaron he said, "I'll walk with you and show you the way. Lucy and I are early risers. Please stop by a last time after you pick up your carriage tomorrow."

Early the next morning Lucy and Dieter heard horse hoofs and rushed downstairs. Aaron jumped down and embraced Lucy.

"I hope you'll visit me in the new President's House," Aaron said. "On second thought, meeting in Philadelphia might be better. Washington's Potomac city will be a muddy mess."

Dieter extended his hand. "Goodbye, old friend," he said. "You'll be in our thoughts and prayers."

As they watched the carriage turn onto Penn Street, a warm, profound moment struck Dieter. For nearly fifty years the Staudts of Frankenthal had made it in this wonderful new land. Images of *Grossdaddi* Dietrich, *der Daddi, die Mudder,* and *die Grossmudder* flashed by. Remarkably, he reflected, he is now a friend of a man who may become President of the United States!"

His reflective mood grew. In bed he said, "Lucy dear, with Christmas and the New Year coming, I can't get my mind off the future. What does it hold for us?"

"This has been a difficult year," Lucy said, stroking his arm. "Next year will be better."

"A new year and a new century. Lately, dear, I think more and more about how unselfish you've been. You had a wonderful life in Philadelphia but you gave it up so we could build a life together here in the back country."

"*Liebschdi*, I'm happy here. My life is perfect."

"But your estrangement from your father must wear on you. It's the one thing we never talk about."

She kept silent.

"Don't you want to talk about it? Maybe I can help."

He heard soft sniffles. He embraced her.

"Lucy dear, even if your parents aren't living together, there's no reason we can't be in touch with your father. I'm sure the children would like that. His politics may be different from ours, but the war's over. We are all Americans. Besides, I like him. When I worked for him he was always fair."

They lay quiet for a long time.

At last he said, "Dear, no matter what else we do on New Year's Eve, let's resolve to face this problem in the bright new century."

He felt her stir. "*Liebschdi*, you are wonderful. Did I ever tell you I love you? Please snuff out the candle."

Acknowledgments

My thanks to the many persons who helped me. When I first considered a novel on this subject, I had the immediate support of Dr. David L. Valuska, president of the Pennsylvania German Society, and Veronica Backenstoe and other Board members. Early on, Professor Valuska put me on the track of the Fighting Parson, General Peter Muhlenberg.

Dr. Michael Werner, linguist from Ober-Olm, Germany, advised me frequently on dialect words and phrases and on the culture of Palatinate Germans. Dr. Werner is publisher of *Hiwe wie Driwe*, a newspaper that bridges the gap between the Palatine and Pennsylvania German dialects and culture.

I consulted local friends who know much about the Tulpehocken Settlement, including Grace Bare, former owner of the farmland on which I live, and sisters Catharine and Frances Sheidy, whose knowledge of local history and Hain's Church is remarkable. Skip Henderson, owner of the nearby 18th century Charming Forge, graciously invited me to visit the magnificent mansion.

The courteous and efficient librarians of the Wernersville Public Library were indispensable in obtaining through interlibrary loan more than a hundred books and dissertations on early-American history. My thanks to Virginia Diehl, Pamela McGettigan, Janet Moore, Jennifer Reinsel, and Lara Thomas, and to the Reading Public Library and Kathy Hess, Pennsylvania Room librarian.

The Reverend Peter Goguts critiqued my draft pages concerning Hain's United Church of Christ. Jim Wren and Meghan Wren-Briggs helped me with Eighteenth Century seafaring. Randy Forry came to my aid on computer use. Many friends shared their German ancestry and knowledge of local history and the Pennsylvania dialect and culture. Robert F. Grim, a former student of mine, designed and illustrated the handsome front cover.

As they have been for my seven prior books, my daughter, Anne Constein, and my companion, Millie Sawers, have been unstintingly generous with their time as proof readers and perceptive editors. Love and great thanks to both.

Glossary of Pennsylvania German Words

aa – also
abaddich – especially
alliebber – everyone
allrecht – all right
an – on
alt – old
Appel – apple
arig – very
awwer – but
ball – soon
Bauer – farmer
Bauersleit – farm people
Bauerei – farm
Bedanke – thanks
bedauerlich – sorrowful
Belsnickel – Santa Claus
besser – better
bischt – are
bissel – little
Bobbel – baby
Braucher – powow doctor
Bretzel – pretzel
Brezis – exactly
Briwwi – toilet
Brot – bread
bschisse – cheat
Bull's Geig – violin
Buwe – boys
da – there
Daadi – father
Daag – day
dale – some
dank, danke – thanks
Dankeshay – thanks much
dappich – careless, sloppy

daschdich – thirsty
deier – expensive
deitsch – German
Deitscher – a German
Deitschlenner – Germans
Demogratt – Democrat
denk – think
denkscht – do you think?
des – this
dir – you
Disch – table
do – here
dod – dead
Dorf – village
du – you
Du bischt recht – You're right
Dummkopp – blockhead
Dunnerwedder – cuss word
Dutt – bag
Ebbel – apples
ebbes – something
eier – your
Eisehammer – forge
Ennichau – anyhow
emol – once
Er iss dot. – He is dead.
esse – eat
Familye – family
faricht – afraid
Fierblatz – fireplace
Fraa – housewife
frehlich – happy
Freindschaft – family
fresse – eat like animals
gaar nix – nothing at all

Gaern schayni – You're welcome
ganz – entirely
ganz recht – entirely right
Gar net – not at all
gayt's – goes
gebaddent – disturbed
Geld – money
gell? – not so?
Gemische – mixture
genau – exactly
gewiss – certainly
Gezwwel – commotion
glay – little
glay bissel – a little bit
Gut – God
Grischtdaag – Christmas
Grischtdaagsbaam – tree
gross – big, large
Grosssdaadi – grandfather
Grossmudder – grandmother
Grumbeere – potatoes
Gsoffner – drunkard
gucke – look
gut – good (Ger)
Guten Tag – Good day (Ger)
guud – good
Guder Owed – Good evening
Haus – house
Hausfraa – housewife
hayss – am named
heese – be called
heilich – holy
heit – today
Herr – mister
Himmel – heaven
himmlisch – heavenly

Hinkelfleesch – chicken meat
Hinnerdale – buttocks
hocke – sit
Hock dich hie – Sit down
ich – I
Ich hab dich gaern. – I love you.
Ich wayss net. – I don't know.
ihr – her
iwwerfalle – surprised
Kaes – cheese
Kannbrot – rye bread
kannscht – can
Karich – church
Kartoffel – potato (Ger)
Keenich – king
Keenichin – queen bee
kenne – can
Kich – kitchen
Kind – child
Kinner – children
Kloster – cloister
Komm herein – Come in (Ger)
kumm – come
Lattwarrick – apple butter
Lebkuchen – unseasoned cookies
leedmielich – sad
Leit – people
Lieb – love
Liebhawwer – lover
Liebschdi – darling, dear
liegschdt – to lie (unruth)
Liewer – darling, dear
Luderisch – Lutheran
Lutteraaner – Lutheran person
Mach's guud – goodbye
Maedel – girl

Mamm – mamma
Mann – man, husband
Mannsleit – men
Mannsleitnarrish – man-crazy
Mariye – morning
meenscht? – do you mean …?
mei – my, mine
mich – me
mied – tired
mir – we
Mischt – manure
mit – with
Mol – time
Mudder – mother
Naame – name
naasich – nosey
Nacht – night (Ger)
nau – now
nay – no
nei – new
nein – no (Ger)
Nei Yaahr – New Year
net – not
net zu guud – not so good
nix – nothing
nix kummt raus – nothing doing
nochemol – once more
Pei – pie
Pennsilfaani – Pennsylvania
Platz – place
recht – right
Reformiert – Reformed
rei – in
Republikaaner – Republican
Rinskopp – stubborn person
Rot – advice, counsel

rumrutsche – slide around
rutsch – to slide
saage – say
Sauergraut – sauerkraut
Schatz – apron
schay – nice
Schdadt – town
Scheier – barn
schlag nei – dig in
schlappich – sloppy
schlecht – bad
schloof – sleep
Schmierkaes – cottage cheese
schmackt's guud – tastes good
schmutzich – filthy
Schnitz – dried fruit
Schnitz un Gnepp – apple & dough
Schpritzer – sprinkle, shower
Schteddel – town
schtill – still
schtolsich – stylish
schtupid – stupid
Schtubb – room
Schuhmacher – shoemaker
Schussel – a scatter-brain
schwach – weak
scshwetz – talk
sehr gut – very good (Ger)
sei – be
Seifleesch – pork
sell – that
sin – are
sitzen sich – sit (Ger)
Sohn – son
Supp – soup
Tutt – bag

uffgschafft – excited
umgerennt – upset
un – and
unbehofft – unexpected
unglaawich – unbelievable
verdammt sei – cuss word
verdolltsei – absolutely
verleicht – perhaps
verrickt – crazy
Versammling – get-together
verschtaunt – surprised
verschteh – understand
Versoffner – drunkard
viel – many
vielmols – many times
wann - when
Warscht – sausage
was – what
was iss letz – what's wrong?
wayss – know
Weibsleit – women
Weibsmensch – men
wichdich – important
widder – again
wie – how
Wie bischt? – How are you?
Wie gayt's? – How's it going?
Weiwer – housewives
Wilkumm – Welcome
wieviel? – How much?
wohl – of course
wu – where
Wu gehschdt – Where are you going?
wuhne – dwell
wunnerbaar – wonderful
Wunnernaas – busybody

wunnerlich – strange
ya – yes
ya wohl – yes indeed
Yuni – June
yuscht – just
zimmlich – pretty good

Sources

A bibliography is not standard in fiction, but for readers who may wish to do further reading on the subject of this book, here is a select topical list of sources I found particularly useful.

Palatinate German immigration to America. Stanford H. Cobb, *The Story of the Palatines*; Aaron Spencer Fogleman, *Hopeful Journeys*; Marcus Lee Hansen, *The Atlantic Migration*; Walter A. Knittle, *Early 18th Century Palatine Emigration*; Pennsylvania German Society, *German Immigrant Accounts*; George Rude, *Europe in the Eighteenth Century*.

The ocean voyage. Nathaniel Philbrick, *In the Heart of the Sea*; Pennsylvania German Society, *Proceedings and Addresses, 1911*; Simon Schama, *Rough Crossings*.

Early struggles of the settlers. Stevenson W. Fletcher, *Pennsylvania Agriculture and Country Life, 1640-1840*; James T. Lemon, *The Best Poor Man's Country*; Elsie Singmaster, *I Heard of a River*; Conrad Richter, *Light in the Forest*.

Colonial life. Arthur Cecil Bining, *Pennsylvania Iron Manufacture in the Eighteenth Century*; Wayland F. Dunaway, *A History of Pennsylvania*; Allen Keller, *Colonial America*; Joseph J. Kelley, Jr., *Life and Times in Colonial Philadelphia*; James L. Purvis, *Colonial America to 1763*; Jerome R. Reich, *Colonial America*; Edwin Tunis, *Colonial Living*; Michael Zuckerman, *Friends and Neighbors*.

Lead-up to war Robert A. Becker, *Revolution, Reform, and the Politics of American Taxation*; John Dickinson, *Letters from a Farmer in Pennsylvania*; Richard Holmes, *Rebels and Redcoats* (DVD); Charles H. Lincoln, *The Revolutionary Movement in Pennsylvania, 1760-1766*; Peter C. Mancell, *Origins and Ideologies of the American Revolution* (DVDs and text); T. Harry Williams, *History of American Wars*.

Congress and historic figures in Philadelphia. Joseph E. Ellis, *Founding Brothers*; Tom Huntington, *Ben Franklin's Philadelphia*; Nancy Isenberg, *Fallen Father*; David McCullough, *John Adams*; David McCullough, *1776*; Martin P. Martin, *City of Independence*.

War and Revolution. Mark M. Boatner, *Encyclopedia of the American Revolution*; Charles Knowles Bolton, *The Private Soldier under Washington*; Carl Bridenbaugh, *The Spirit of '76*; John Ferling, *Almost a Miracle*; James Thomas Flexner, *The Traitor and the* Spy; Edward W. Hocker, *The Fighting Parson of the American Revolution*; Joseph Plumb Martin, *A Narrative of a Revolutionary Soldier*; Robert Middlekauff, *The Glorious Cause*; Gary B. Nash, *The Unknown American Revolution*;

Samuel J. Newland, *The Pennsylvania Militia*; Charles Royster, *A Revolutionary People at War*; James L. Stokesbury, *A Short History of the American Revolution*; James B.B.Trussell, *Birthplace of an Army*; James L. Stokesbury, *The Pennsylvania Line*; David L. Valuska, *Von Heer's Provost Corps*; *Marechausee, the Army's Military Police, an All-Pennsylvania German Unit* (paper); Claude Halstead Van Tyne, *The Loyalists in the American* Revolution; Garry Wills, *A Necessary Evil*.

Pennsylvania German culture. C. Richard Beam, *Revised Pennsylvania German Dictionary*; Arthur D. Graeff, *The Pennsylvania Germans*; Frederick Klees, *The Pennsylvania Dutch*; Marcus Bachman Lambert, *Pennsylvania-German Dictionary*; Edwin B. Mitchell, *It's an old Pennsylvania Custom*; Howard Snader, *Glossary of 6167 English Words and Phrases and their Berks County Pennsylvania Dutch Equivalents*; Eugene S. Stine, *Pennsylvania German Dictionary*.

Life in and around Reading Town. Raymond W. Albright, *Two Centuries of Reading, PA, 1748-1948*; Laura Leff Becker, *The American Revolution as a Community Experience* (dissertation); Rev. P.C. Croll, *Annals of Womelsdorf PA and Community*; Benjamin A. Fryer, *Congressional History of Berks District*; Morton L. Montgomery, *Berks County in the Revolution*; J. Bennett Nolan, (1) *Early Narratives of Berks County*, (2) *Play at Reading Town*, (3)*Southeastern Pennsylvania*, volume one, (4) *A Tale of Reading Town,* (5) *Walks in Reading* Town; Reading Eagle Company, *Reading Towne, 1748-1998*; Kathy M. Scogna, (1) *The Ford at the Schuylkill*; (2), *Lower Heidelberg Township – Then and Now*.

Political strife and tax revolt at the end of the century.
Elisha P. Douglass, *Rebels and Democrats*; Kenneth W. Keller, *Rural politics and the Collapse of Pennsylvaniasm Federalism*; Edward J. Larson, *A Magnificent Catastrophe*; Edmond S. Morgan, *The Birth of the Republic, 1763-89*; Paul Douglas Newman, *Fries's Rebellion*; J. Bennett Nolan, *Southeastern Pennsylvania, volume two*; Henry J. Young, *The Treatment of the Loyalists in Pennsylvania* (dissertation).

About the Author

Dr. Carl Frey Constein, born into what Tom Brokaw has dubbed *The Greatest Generation*, grew up in the southeastern Pennsylvania town of Fleetwood during the Depression of the 1930s. After college he enlisted in the Army Air Corps. For his ninety-six cargo missions as C-46 pilot across the Himalayan "Hump" from India to China he was awarded two Air Medals and the Distinguished Flying Cross. He recalls his year in the China-Burma-India theatre of operations in the WWII memoir *Born to Fly the Hump*.

After leaving military service in 1945, Constein pursued a doctorate at Temple University, majoring in English literature and educational administration. He was an English teacher, director of curriculum, superintendent of schools, education writer and newspaper columnist, and education director in business-industry.

He retired at the turn of the millennium to chase his favorite phantom—becoming an author. *From the Rhine to Penn's Woods* is his eighth book.

Constein lives outside Reading, Pennsylvania, in the borough of Wernersville.